D0122240

Death of a hero

When a crowd of ten thousand – all men, not a female in sight – assembled on the common land known as Monkenheath in memory of Loy Tanner's raggle-taggle 'army' of 1549, Detective Inspector Ben Jurnet and the aldermen of Angleby were apprehensive. Would the vigil of the sober crowd – no hash, no alcohol – end in the same rape and carnage as that of the bellicose throng of four and a half centuries ago? Was this contemporary phenomenon a disaster waiting to happen?

The tenuous peace of the vast gathering was shattered when Charlie Appleyard, the mob's Messiah in Levis, spiritual heir to Loy Tanner, was found dead at the house of the town's nicest nymphomaniac, Jenny Nunn. Not until the untidy rabble was pouring into Angleby, as Tanner's 'army' had done all those centuries ago, did the forces of law and order spring into action.

Death of a hero is the seventh and last of S. T. Haymon's Ben Jurnet crime novels. The author died in October 1995. It displays many of the qualities summed up by two leading critics of the genre: '*As an explorer of macabre relationships and inspired creator of scenes of tragicomedy, Haymon outdoes herself in the queasy ramifications of this spellbinder.*' John Coleman, *Sunday Times*; '*S. T. Haymon is a strong, heated writer who does not flinch from entering uneasy territory.*' Harriet Waugh, *Spectator*. (Both reviews of *Death of a warrior queen*)

DEATH OF A HERO

S. T. Haymon

Constable · London

First published in Great Britain 1996
by Constable and Company Limited
3 The Lanchesters, 162 Fulham Palace Road
London W6 9ER
Copyright © The Executors of the Estate of S. T. Haymon 1996
The right of S. T. Haymon to be identified as the author of this work has
been asserted on behalf of the Executors of the Estate of S. T. Haymon in
accordance with the Copyright, Designs and Patents Act 1988
ISBN 0 09 476270 8
Set in 10pt Palatino by Pure Tech India Ltd, Pondicherry, India
Printed and bound in Great Britain
by Hartnolls Ltd, Bodmin

A CIP catalogue record for this book
is available from The British Library

1

The bone came hurtling out of the sun and hit the woman squarely on the forehead. It was a long, large bone – a femur or tibia
perhaps – which had about it a shopsoiled look as if it had been a
long time since it had been parcelled up in flesh. The woman, who
was not young but still good to look upon in a genteel kind of
way, fell to the ground with a look of pleased surprise on her face.

For the visitors leaving the Tanner exhibition through the nail-
studded door marked Exit it was a welcome diversion. Wondering, with that mixture of optimism and suppressed boredom
common to all tourists, where to go next, what on earth to do to
fill in the interminable hours of an annual holiday, they milled
about the open space which stretched from the castle walls to the
steep sides of the motte on which the great stone building
crouched like some brooding monster. At the sight of the pros-
trate woman the air resounded with happy cries of 'Give her air!'
even as they pressed close, excluding it.

Detective Inspector Ben Jurnet, who had been standing at the
railings which fenced off the drop down to the streets of Angleby
– a prospect of pantiled roofs, church towers and toy-size traffic
crawling through streets designed for the passage of ox-carts
which never failed to delight him – heard the noise, turned and
made a way for himself through the clustering onlookers. They
fell back unwillingly but without actual demur, recognizing
about the darkly handsome figure an air of authority.

As he squatted down beside her, the coarse gravel skittering
from beneath his heels, the woman opened her eyes and, in a tone
which seemed to explain everything to her own satisfaction at
least, announced: 'The bone.'

Jurnet said: 'Don't move,' and took off his jacket. It was too hot
anyway for anything more than shirt-sleeves and he had only
kept it on because he had just that morning collected it from the
cleaners and didn't want to risk getting it creased by carrying it

5

over his arm. Even with the heat accumulating uncomfortably across his back and under his armpits it had – sentimental fool that he was – pleased him to anticipate the Superintendent's unspoken approval when next he answered a summons to the great man's presence at Police Headquarters and entered the room at least in some measure approximating to the bastard's impossible idea of what members of Angleby CID ought to look like.

Ah well.

Having first removed his mobile phone from an inside pocket and laid it carefully on the ground beside him, Jurnet folded the jacket up small and insinuated it gently under the woman's head. Then he picked up the instrument, prior to summoning help.

'If you're thinking of calling for an ambulance,' the woman said, sitting up and rendering the sacrifice of the jacket all in vain, 'don't. All I need is a hand up.'

'If you're quite sure . . .' The detective hovered uncertainly until, convinced by the woman's air of completely restored health, he put the phone away. He said nevertheless: 'It would still be wise to check up – '

'A touch of the sun,' the woman interrupted briskly. 'I should have known better than to stand there staring up into it directly.' To the spectators still hovering and hoping for drama she observed pleasantly: 'So sorry it wasn't something more interesting,' and, as they turned away, scrunching the gravel in their disappointment, held out a manicured hand to Jurnet with some impatience. 'If you please! These boulders are doing my behind no good whatsoever.'

'Are you sure you're all right?' The woman, Jurnet thought, helping her to her feet, certainly looked OK. More than OK: exhilarated. All the same he persisted: 'What was that about a bone?'

The woman twisted about, reaching behind her to dislodge some grit which adhered to the back of her navy dress, a garment whose exquisite simplicity of line bespoke expense louder than any price tag. Vertical, her body, shapely and no longer an object of pity, seemed at odds with her lived-in face and her iron-grey hair. At the sight of it Jurnet who, since Miriam's death and the consequent absence of a woman in his bed, tended to be over-mistrustful of his own responses, restrained an impulse to help along the good work. Instead, he picked up the white handbag which had fallen at the woman's side, then repeated: 'The bone?'

'Oh, that.' The woman took back her bag and returned unconcernedly: 'Don't worry about that. Not one of mine. Except in the most quintessential sense it doesn't even exist. Simply that I had a vision.'

'I owe you an explanation.'

In the castle cafeteria, over the iced coffee she had insisted on treating him to as a small token of gratitude for his chivalry, the woman said: 'You've seen the exhibition, I take it, slipshod and ill-researched as it is.' Jurnet nodded. 'You know something about Loy Tanner.'

'Can't be born and brought up in Angleby and not know.'

'Ah!' Her face, of delicate construction, its somewhat offputting gentility modified by the stigmata of experience, creased into a smile. 'Then you won't think me completely daft. That's what's so comforting about being back on one's native heath. One shares the same terms of reference with the other locals. Every time I come back I wonder how I could ever have left.' She sucked on her straw and made a wry little grimace. 'Though after a few weeks I wonder how I could ever have stood it as long as I did.' Then: 'As you know, I'm sure, the actual anniversary isn't for months yet. How ridiculous, then, to be sitting here, sweating over iced coffee when actually it all took place just before Christmas, a typical Norfolk day of winter, sleet driving in the wind.'

'Not all that many tourists about that time of year,' Jurnet pointed out matter-of-factly.

'Of course!' This time the woman laughed outright, a well-mannered sound, full-throated and mettlesome. 'Merely another example of that Norfolk pragmatism on which we natives pride ourselves, eh? Well, I'll forgive the city fathers. I suppose they have to balance their books somehow.' The laughter submerging in a contemptuous severity: 'Still no excuse for putting on that caricature of an exhibition. That little worm, the curator – Alistair something or other – deserves to be hung from the ramparts himself for presuming to turn a sublime tragedy into a not very interesting comic strip.' She raised her face from her glass. Jurnet, to his surprise, saw that her eyes were bright with tears.

'I wonder', she said, 'if you know how one of the crowd described it, one of the people who were actually standing there outside the castle, on that winter's day in 1549? What he said, with typical Norfolk directness, was that they had strung Loy Tanner up like a ham hung up for winter store. A ham hung up for winter

7

store!' The woman repeated the phrase with a kind of horrified wonder. 'Can you imagine how it must have felt to have been a spectator that day?'

'He was a great man,' Jurnet agreed soberly, not because he chose to let his imagination wander down those paths – coppers dealt with the here and now, their job description didn't allow them the luxury of tears over something that had happened four and a half centuries ago – but because it seemed expected of him. All of a sudden he realized where he had seen that face before. He said: 'You're the lady they made a doctor yesterday at the university. Dr Addison, was it?'

'Adamson, actually. Adeline Adamson.'

'I saw the procession on the telly. I didn't recognize you without all that get-up.'

The woman laughed again, abandoning Loy Tanner to his century.

'Wasn't it dreadful? Making believe that, redbrick though we were, we were every bit as medieval as Oxford or Cambridge. It was all I could do to keep a straight face. Whenever I moved my head that frightful hat, or whatever it was, slipped over one eye. To say nothing of tripping over my gown, which was yards too long! Served me right. They tempted me and I fell. Me an Hon. Doc! Ridiculous!'

'That book you wrote about Tanner – it sounded to me like you deserved it.'

Honesty forbade Jurnet to claim to have read the book in question.

'Irrelevant,' the other returned crisply. She sat back in her seat having with childish greed explored her glass with her straw to get at the last of the whipped cream sticking to its sides. 'I'm just part of the junketings. I let myself be used as I myself have used Loy Tanner to get some cheap publicity and boost my sales.' She finished with a simplicity Jurnet found endearing: 'I really am ashamed.'

The woman hesitated, looked at the detective as if wondering whether he could be trusted; then, having come to a decision, went on with a shyness that made her appear younger and more vulnerable.

'When I was a child living here in Angleby there were times, don't you know, coming along the Bailey when the light was right, that I could look up at the castle and there he was, silhouetted against the setting sun and still, after all those years, hanging in chains just the way they left him. Sometimes, seeing him hanging there like that, it was as if it had just that moment happened. If I strained my ears I could actually hear the chains creaking; if it hadn't been for the sun shining in my eyes I could have seen his face, told you what he had on, the colour of his doublet and hose, and the kind of fur on his winter robe. Except no – ' she corrected herself – 'not the robe. They would have made him take that off, which was a barbaric thing to do, in that weather. He was fifty-seven, an old man in terms of those days, and I feel certain he was upset about the robe. Without it he couldn't have helped shivering in the cold and giving the impression that he was afraid.

'Because', she declared firmly, daring denial, 'he was not afraid. Of that I am quite sure.'

After a moment she resumed. 'At other times I would see him hanging there as it was later, much later. No burial, a warning to Angleby of what happened to anyone who dared to buck the Establishment. At those times it was a skeleton I saw, jangling in the wind and picked clean by the crows. Every now and again another bit would fall to earth, to be carried off triumphantly by one or other of the scavenging dogs who had learned that the foot of the castle wall was a good place to wait for a tasty bone. Do you know that they say the last one fell in the first year of James I – that is, fifty-four years after the execution!' Wide grey eyes turned on Jurnet, she finished: 'They were wrong. It fell this morning, hitting me on the head and knocking me over.'

Dr Adeline Adamson pushed back the grey fringe covering her forehead to reveal an area of purple bruising on the pale skin; allowed the other a moment of open-mouthed stupefaction before, lips curved in mischief, explaining: 'I walked into a door this morning, not looking where I was going. Now do you think I'm a crazy old woman?'

'No.'

The young man was indecently good-looking. He was also in a vile temper. His golden curls tumbling over his eyes, he came into the cafeteria accepting the admiring glances turned upon him as one of the boring facts of life, his anger in no way appeased.

'Roger! Over here!'

The young man scowled: he approached the table where Jurnet and Dr Adamson were sitting, and sat down on one of the empty seats with an unnecessary amount of noise. Jurnet, who, to his own regret, recognizing in himself a failure of compassion, found it hard to like homosexuals, put the newcomer down provisionally as gay. Batterby, back at Headquarters and the only one of Jurnet's associates with the right antennae to know one when he saw one, would have been able to settle the question at once.

'For Christ's sake, Addie! I've been looking for you all over. You said you'd be outside.'

'The sun was too much for me,' Adeline Adamson responded mildly, 'and I was getting tired of waiting anyway. You're terribly late getting here.'

'Not my fault! I had to park miles away. The streets were absolutely jammed.' The beautiful young man surveyed as much of the detective as was visible above the table top. It was, apparently, enough to tell him all he needed to know. 'Fuzz,' he pronounced, at the end of his examination, and, to the woman: 'What are you doing, consorting with the fuzz? Bodyguard or something?'

Dr Adamson shook her head good-humouredly. 'Not at all. At least I don't think so. Not, so far as I know, one of the perks of an Hon. Doc. And not that this gentleman hasn't been wonderfully kind and helpful.' Turning her attention to Jurnet she requested: 'Do tell me your name so that I can introduce you to my nephew, Roger Adamson.' With no appearance of alarm at the possibility she added: '*Are* you fuzz?'

'Afraid so. DI Jurnet, Angleby CID. Your nephew is very perceptive.'

'Roger?' the other dissented fondly. 'The last adjective I'd use to describe him. It's just that he drives a Lotus much too fast and has developed a sixth sense for recognizing the forces of law and order who very properly flag him down whenever they manage to catch up with him.'

'Christ, I'm hot!' The young man peered at the used glasses on the table and plucked his white T-shirt away from his body with small, petulant gestures. The shirt and the soft beige-coloured slacks which partnered it were, Jurnet noted, on the same scale of expensiveness as what his aunt was wearing. 'What have you two been drinking? Ice-cream soda? I could do with one of those myself.'

'Iced coffee,' said the woman. 'You have to get it yourself at the counter.'

The young man made no move to do so. He fished out a handkerchief and mopped his face which, tanned, shining with sweat, looked, Jurnet thought, as if it belonged to some Ancient Greek bronze come to life – Apollo or, more likely, Adonis. Either way, the detective, whose own dark Mediterranean good looks had, carefully behind his back, earned him the nickname of Valentino over at Headquarters, felt – without vanity and against his will – a certain sympathy with Roger What's-his-name. Nobody human and breathing deserved to be burdened with so much beauty. It clouded judgement, both in the viewer and the viewed. It was equivalent to being in possession of a dangerous weapon without a licence.

Roger Adamson spoke to his aunt: 'Have a heart! I'll never make it that far.'

'You spoilt baby!' the woman said fondly, fiddling in her hand-bag for her change purse. She got up and wound her way elegantly between the tables, the young man's eyes following her progress with lazy complacency before transferring their gaze to the detective. 'This town could certainly use a few lessons in traffic management.'

'Medieval city,' Jurnet returned shortly, his lips tightening. He could not bear to hear his birthplace denigrated, even with reason. 'All those cars. We do what we can. Not easy in the holiday season.'

'Not even talking about cars.' Roger Adamson stretched out his long, impeccably clad legs. 'People. Humanity erupting from every point of the compass and sweating from every pore. You'd think they'd never watched a telly ad – not an anti-perspirant between the lot of them. One minute the streets were empty, or at least passable: the next, you couldn't move for the teeming hordes surging forward as if they were on their way to liberate the Bastille.'

Jurnet stared.

'Well, not quite the Bastille,' the other conceded. 'Too good-natured for bloody revolution. They seemed in quite a jolly mood, actually, laughing and larking about. It could have been a YMCA outing. They made a space for me to park without argument – one of them even kept the others back out of the way so I could get to the kerb.' The young man frowned however. 'I hate crowds, don't you? Especially on a hot day. So animal. They oughtn't to be allowed.'

Resisting – even though he was still on holiday leave – a desire to call in to Headquarters to ask what, if anything, was going on, Jurnet asked: 'A demonstration, was it? Any of them carrying banners or posters?'

'Nothing like that, thank God.' The other leaned back in his chair and shook his golden curls. 'Nobody marching in step shouting that gibberish which always finishes up sounding like *Sieg Heil*.' Jurnet was suddenly aware of a hard core to Roger Adamson. Perhaps he had been too fast jumping in with convenient labels. 'A traffic jam, that's all it was, only chaps, not cars, all going the same way.' Dr Adamson returning with the iced coffee, he took it from her and, ignoring the straw, partook long and deep. Surfacing, he exclaimed, laying on the charm: 'You're an angel!'

It wasn't the young whippersnapper's fault, Jurnet instructed himself sternly, that, his lips rimmed with whipped cream, he looked like a mischievous cherub.

'I'll take it out of your wages,' the woman said, reseating herself. She found a tissue in her bag, handed it over. 'For heaven's sake!' she chided humorously. 'You aren't fit to be allowed out in civilized company.'

The young man wiped his face obediently prior to taking another great gulp which smeared it afresh. He grinned, showing teeth of an exemplary whiteness.

Jurnet stood up and spoke to Dr Adamson. 'Thanks for the coffee. And keep out of the sun.'

'I'll do that,' she said. 'And thank *you*.'

He shook the proffered hand, its skin still young, its grasp pleasantly cool, thinking he would have liked the woman better if she had looked less indulgently on the young man called Roger.

The young man called Roger finished his iced coffee and wiped his mouth on the back of his hand.

'I could do with another one like that, dearie.'

'Don't call me dearie and you can get it yourself.'

'In that case,' the young man said brightly, well aware that the detective had turned back to hear what he had to say, 'I won't go running after the fuzz to tell him that I asked the guy who helped me park what it was all in aid of, where was the fire.'

Jurnet intervened without making any bones about it.

'What did he answer?'

'Oh,' responded the other, overdoing the innocence, 'I thought you'd gone. Monkenheath. Just the one word. Make any sense to you?'

'Monkenheath,' Jurney repeated slowly. Then: 'I don't know.'

2

The Superintendent was not best pleased.

That, thought Jurnet in the back seat, from time to time catching a glimpse of patrician profile frozen into a complete nullity of expression, was the understatement of the year. Even the back of the bugger's head, its expensive haircut, the custom-made shirt collar showing above the hand-tailored suit, signalled anger – an anger, however, not to be expressed in any vulgarity of noise: a frozen malice which depressed the temperature inside the Rover better than any air conditioning. Jurnet was glad he hadn't, after all, left his jacket behind at Headquarters. He needed it.

What a welcome back from leave, especially when you turned up a day early!

Going the long way round, at least they were making progress, that was something. Jurnet looked out of the car window. The tattered fringe of the city through which they were passing did nothing to raise his spirits. The road wound past ill-kempt allotments and collections of sheds erected for some industrial purpose marked out by their very architecture – or, rather, lack of it – for failure. From an intensive poultry farm rose the melancholy titter of hens immured in concrete and galvanized iron.

Not the Angleby the tourists came to see, that was for sure. Not even those others, it seemed, whoever they might be, who were currently clogging up the river road to Monkenheath.

Once, Jurnet reflected, this impoverished landscape, in all probability, had itself, before greedy men got their hands on it, been part of the great common of Monkenheath, the steep slope rising from the river, massed with trees which had provided Tanner's followers, encamped along the ridge, with fuel for their fires and for the beacons with which they had sought in vain to set England alight to the wrongs which were being done in the name of profit and progress. The deer in those vanished woodlands were what had kept the ragged army from starvation during the weeks of their long vigil.

Other times, other menus. Ought he, Jurnet, to suggest to the Superintendent that they mount a guard on the poultry farm?

'What I fail to understand', announced the Superintendent, in a

13

tone which proclaimed that he did not intend to rest until – whether by God or man was immaterial – understanding had been vouchsafed him, 'is why, on our own patch, we have to be enlightened by the local radio disc jockey, God help us, as to what is going on.'

Don't blame me, Jurnet thought but did not actually say, knowing from bitter experience that nothing was to be gained by so doing: 'I was on holiday.'

Sergeant Jack Ellers, who was driving, hazarded pacifically: 'They've been clever, sir, very clever, whoever they are. Filtered into the city in dribs and drabs, by public transport or on foot. Only reason the BBC bloke knew something we didn't was he got a phone call. No cars to foul up the traffic even more than usual, nothing to suggest a common purpose. Simply individual citizens exercising their immemorial right to use the public highways without let or hindrance, so long as they don't drop litter or relieve themselves in the gutters.'

'A disc jockey!' The words fell from the Superintendent's lips like fragmented ice.

The Sergeant slowed down to allow a rabbit safely across the road. Watching the flash of white scut disappear into a clump of heather, Jurnet thought: That's one they'll have for the pot, and immediately after: Loy Tanner had twenty thousand men camped on Monkenheath. How far will one bloody rabbit go among twenty thousand?

Taking a calculated risk he leaned forward to ask: 'It's common land, sir. In practical terms, what can we do?'

The Superintendent swivelled in his seat to the extent the safety belt would permit and favoured his subordinate with a baring of teeth that, if not a snarl, was definitely not a smile.

'That remains to be seen. We'll have to wait, won't we, until the city solicitor has duly digested the reams of by-laws relating to Monkenheath, and communicated their essence to us. More to the point – ' the ice beginning to thaw, that other man, the one Jurnet held in surprised love and admiration beginning to emerge – 'what, in the meantime, are *they* likely to do? The Chief insists that we keep a low profile. The Lord Mayor has begged us to do nothing whilst our two MPs, both the Labour and the Tory, have begged us to do nothing without first getting their say-so, which comes to the same thing.'

Jack Ellers observed philosophically: 'Only to be expected, with council elections coming up.'

14

'That's all very well,' declared the Superintendent, with an emphasis which made clear it was nothing of the sort. 'If this is what we think it is, we cannot simply ignore the presence of hundreds – if not thousands – of possibly disaffected men camped on our doorstep, however benign they may declare their intentions to be. You don't need to be told how easily demonstrations which start out to be all sweetness and light can turn into their opposite at the drop of a hat. Didn't Loy Tanner's rebellion, for that matter, start out as a peaceful protest – and look how that ended up! Fortunately for us, our local authority possesses one weapon denied to the Mayor of Angleby of Loy Tanner's day – those very same by-laws!' Smiling, actually smiling, the air in the car warming up correspondingly: 'Study them, Ben – study them! Since Tanner's time we may well, in the cause of the common good, have lost the right to dump crisp packets and drink cans where we will on Monkenheath – to light fires and, particularly, to defecate anywhere the need takes us. Who knows what other fundamental liberties we may have surrendered in the name of political correctness?'

Warned by a distant hubbub that they were nearing their objective, they parked the Rover where the road finally petered out and made their way, between gorse bushes that gave them no welcome, to the open area known as Tanner's Moot, a wide stretch of coarse grassland in the centre of which stood a solitary oak tree called Tanner's Oak. The tree, though nowhere near four hundred and fifty years old, looked ancient enough to satisfy any but a professional arboriculturist that this was the very one beneath whose spreading branches the great man had set up his open-air Parliament and introduced the realm of England to its first doomed taste of democracy.

Jurnet had still been at his secondary modern when the council had surrounded this vegetable artefact with a railing to which was affixed a fine plaque proclaiming that this was indeed Loy Tanner's Oak of Reformation. Those being days when the public appetite for violence was still in its infancy, it had omitted to add – what would have been the case had this been the genuine article – that after the rout of Tanner's army by the Duke of Warwick and his German *lanzknechte*, the good Duke had hung its branches with captured rebels as if they had been some ghastly Christmas decorations.

Moving along behind the others, careful of the prickly branches which reached out to make closer acquaintance, Jurnet sighed.

15

History, who needed it?

The detective found himself thinking back to the day he had first come to take a look at the tree in its new, official apotheosis. He had not gone alone; had asked Sabrina Starkey, a girl in his class he had been pursuing unavailingly through two long terms, to accompany him and, amazingly, she had agreed to go with him. Not until later had he found out that she had only accepted his invitation to put a certain Duggie Brown's nose out of joint, though by that time, toiling uphill to Monkenheath with the bosomy girl heavy beyond belief on the crossbar of his bicycle, his ardour had already begun to wilt more than somewhat.

Not surprisingly, as he should have known in advance, she had found the tree 'nothing much': had plumped herself down on the ground, evidently expecting Jurnet to join her there for the real business of the day to begin.

'You're lying on some harebells,' he had pointed out, overcome by the thought of those delicate little flowers crushed beneath the girl's spreading buttocks, her splayed thighs.

'So what?' Sabrina Starkey had returned coarsely, and somehow – he couldn't remember the exact chronology – that had been the end of a fine romance. The young Ben Jurnet had even shamefully cycled off home leaving the girl to find her own way back to town.

Some Romeo!

Miriam, he now thought foolishly, would never have squashed any harebells. To consummate the act of love she would, without even thinking, have found a patch of ground where there weren't any. Wrenching his mind away from a subject he still found difficult to contemplate with equanimity, he quickened his pace to catch up with his companions; hurried towards a noise which, whatever else it portended, could only mean that the harebells, if any remained after all this time, which was doubtful, had had it, in spades.

The noise was not in the least threatening, that was something to be thankful for: a wave of chatter, rising and falling, laughter, a good-natured calling to and fro. The Superintendent looked almost happy until a guitar struck up, played with an inexpertness that was almost endearing. Then his face darkened. Too often, in such a context, guitars meant hash, or even hard drugs.

So that it was even more of a relief, as the three detectives edged their way on to the crowded Moot, to find themselves confronted by none of the accompaniments they had learned to expect in a popular invasion of an open space – no ancient buses converted into a travesty of living quarters, no rusted vans with mattresses strapped to the roof, dogs and children spilling out on to the grass. No women in ethnic tat, no women of any kind, for that matter.

The solitary guitar confirmed the atypical nature of the gathering by breaking out in a jolly if approximate rendition of 'Onward Christian Soldiers'.

'No tents,' the Superintendent observed, uncheered either by the hymn or by the absence of canvas, a ban on the erection of tents being one by-law of whose existence he was certain. 'One solitary tent pole in evidence and we could have got the lot on the move before they had a chance to settle in.'

'Probably banking on the drought holding,' Sergeant Ellers offered cheerfully. 'Old-fashioned types, putting their trust in God. Or maybe they aren't planning on a long stay. Set up a photo-opportunity, hold a press conference to let us know what it's all in aid of, and then melt away as quietly as they came.'

If Jurnet doubted this interpretation of events he knew better, with the Superintendent looking the way he did, than to advance an alternative hypothesis. The newcomers still arriving, like the men already seated on the ground next to their bulging knapsacks and eating apples and bananas, drinking Cokes, were, with few exceptions, young. On every face was imprinted an expression of cheerful excitement. Most of them were dressed in jeans and T-shirts of a surprising conservatism, unadorned by logos, chains or similar extravagances, boots on their feet rather than snazzy trainers, the flat caps they wore against the unrelenting sun of old-fashioned cut. A few of the older ones in the crowd had marked the uniqueness of the occasion by turning up in their Sunday best – dark suits, white shirts, even ties. At the sight of this parade of respectability the Superintendent relaxed a little, not much.

'Somebody has to be in charge.' He stood, shading his eyes against the light. 'Something's going on at the Tree.'

The Oak of Reformation Mark II was looking splendid, if a little dehydrated after the long hot summer, some leaves yellowing early, others already fallen. Even so, it spread its shade in a wide circle over the men hauling on ropes attached to some kind of prefabricated rostrum designed to clear the surrounding rails and be high enough up the trunk to overtop the heads of the gathering

17

and be visible to all. As the three detectives came up, a sandy-haired man who had been directing the setting in place of a narrow wooden stair leading up to the platform turned with an expression which mingled relief with exasperation.

'For Christ's sake,' he greeted them. 'You took your time! Where the hell are the bloody loos?'

The man was in his late twenties or early thirties, squarely built and of medium height, dressed in conservative denim, only the somewhat lopsided Maltese cross hanging from a chain round his neck arousing misgivings. The man's face on the other hand was so open and honest as to arouse instant suspicion in the mind of any police officer worth his salt. Fortunately for the man's credit, Jurnet was relieved to perceive, in the grey-green eyes screwed up against the sun, a certain calculation, a knowingness which suggested that the ring-leader of the demonstration, or whatever was the proper name for it or for him, was not, after all, too good to be true.

'In case it didn't register first time,' the man said, speaking with the accent of one determinedly living down a public school education, 'Charlie Appleyard's the name, and if it's any satisfaction to you our corporate bladders are on the point of bursting. And not only our bladders. Unless you want an epidemic of cholera or hepatitis in your fine city, I suggest you get those WCs moving before our bowels set 'em an example they won't forget in a hurry.'

Charlie Appleyard thrust his face close to the Superintendent's in a way that suggested a certain short-sightedness, following which his features creased in a smile spiced with a boyish mischief.

'Oops! Pardon me! Not the Sanitation! The Superintendent, isn't it, and Detective Inspector Jurnet and Detective Sergeant Ellers? You see, we've done our homework.'

'Not done it all that well.' The Superintendent made no secret of being unamused at being mistaken for an apparatchik specializing in the disposal of bodily wastes. 'Otherwise you would have been in touch with us long before laying on this jamboree, or whatever it is.'

At that the man's eyes opened wide despite the brightness of the day. Cat's eyes, they now appeared, flecked with amber.

'In touch, Superintendent? What about? What possible reason could we have had to do any such thing when all our planning has been based on a determination to do nothing which might present problems for your already overstretched resources?' Looking about him in a kind of happy wonder that what was happening had actually come to pass: 'What you see here, Superintendent, is purely and simply a gathering of friends, of brothers come together on common land for a common purpose which, so far from infringing the law of the realm, can only enhance its majesty. Having made a close study of the by-laws relating to Monkenheath, I can give you my word that not one sub-sub-sub clause will be wittingly contravened by our presence here. We shall neither be erecting tents nor making fires, nor putting on lewd displays. As to how we propose to survive, we have – providing only that it doesn't go bad on us in this heat – each brought with us two days' supply of food, and thereafter, exactly as Loy Tanner did in his time, we shall throw ourselves on the goodwill of the citizens of this fair city. Note, please, that we are neither demanding with menaces nor asking for your institutionalized charity, of which we're sick up to there, but in the purest brotherly love. If you're thinking of setting up a temporary post office where we can cash our giros, forget it.' The man's smile was wonderfully attractive. 'I trust that covers everything.'

Impervious to the charm, the Superintendent demanded: 'How long are you planning to stay?'

Charlie Appleyard spread out stubby-fingered hands which scarcely matched his upper-crust voice.

'Not for us to say. For as little as it takes. For as long as it takes.'

'As long as *what* takes? What exactly are you after?'

'Ah!' rejoined the other, looking as pleased as if a valuable contribution had been made to the dialogue. 'At last we're moving beyond vulgar logistics. Anglian News will be interviewing us for their evening bulletin and I can only suggest you make a point of tuning in. I'm sure you'll understand that I don't want to deprive them of their little scoop. Contain your soul in patience until 6 p.m. when all will be revealed.'

The man held out his hand, seemingly untroubled when it was not taken.

'You'll forgive me if I have to leave you now. Those stairs could do with a bit more padding – you see how careful we are not to damage the Oak in any way? Buck!' His voice merged with the surrounding chatter as he moved towards the tree, towards a bare-chested man who wore his pectorals like a dish of Norfolk dumplings *en croute* and was engaged in wrapping a roll of foam rubber round the Oak's ample girth.

19

'Fasten it to the steps, man, not the trunk! You're using up my bed!'

3

'Turn it off, if you please, Walter.'

Walter Walters padded the length of the Grand Chamber and gingerly, as if afraid it might bite back, turned off the video recorder which had been brought into the room for the occasion. Relieved when the television image reduced itself to nothing without protest, he returned hurriedly to the side table he shared with Mrs Castle, Norfolk Shorthand Champion 1983, seconded from the City Surveyor's department to take minutes of the meeting. Naturally, in deference to his position as Lord Mayor's secretary, he too – if more slowly and in the looped handwriting he had been taught at school – was taking his own notes for the exclusive use of his lord and master and didn't want to risk falling even further behind.

As he resumed his seat, casting a distrustful glance at the notebook across from him splattered with symbols standing for God only knew what, Mrs Castle, a woman whose outsize breasts concealed a heart large in proportion, whispered a comically ironic 'Well done!' of which, even so, she felt immediately ashamed. Walter Walters, however, blushed with pleasure, even whilst, at some deep level, aware that the universal guilt he inspired in his colleagues at City Hall was the one thing that saved him from the sack.

To make up, Mrs Castle added softly: 'You haven't missed anything.'

The silence in the handsome chamber was indeed surprisingly prolonged, making the sounds from the Market Place, usually deadened by the yakety-yak of council business and by the double glazing in the tall windows, astonishingly intrusive. The great and the good of the city, seated at the magnificeant table, either looked down at their reflections or else, chins uplifted, directed their gaze up to the lofty ceiling as if checking up on the armorial bearings there displayed in an extravagance of colour and gold leaf.

George Dunton, the Lord Mayor, fingered the mayoral chain he had deemed it proper to assume for a conclave of such import-ance, reached for the glass of water in front of him and thought better of it. Even the Superintendent – Jurnet, his subordinate, sitting next to him, noted with surprise – sat silent, absorbed, one manicured hand motionless on the gold fountain pen he had placed carefully in front of him before the Lord Mayor, in a few words notably lacking in self-confidence, had opened the meeting.

Jurnet understood how he, they all, felt. He felt it himself.

Yet what had been so special about what they had just seen – what, you could depend on it, they had already seen the night before at its first showing? Anglian News had done its usual workmanlike job, nothing flashy, no arty angles or mucking about with shadows for the sake of drama. Just a crowd – the police last night had logged it at ten thousand, goodness knew what the estimate was today – a crowd of ten thousand blokes sitting on the grass drinking Cokes in the evening sunshine, munching on sand-wiches, exchanging pleasantries that seemed to be met with more laughter than the jests strictly deserved. No hash, so far as one could tell, no alcohol, not so much as a ciggy. The two or three men invited to say a few words to the mike had mumbled only that they thought it important to be where they where, and hoped some good would come of it – halting words that in no way cancelled out the elation written on their faces, their excitement, the joy that possessed their beings like an elixir of the gods. After all the months, in some cases the years, of being unemployed, un-persons, they had rediscovered a future for themselves as fully paid-up members of the human race.

'You think something will come of it?' the interviewer had persisted, professionally sceptical: only to receive the all-purpose Norfolk reply: 'I reckon.'

And what, for that matter, had been so special about Charlie Appleyard high on his platform addressing his comrades below even as Loy Tanner must have addressed his rude mechanicals four hundred and fifty years ago? Well, not exactly the same: Jurnet, suddenly startled by the thought, wondered how in the world Tanner, even up there above the crowd, had made himself heard by the twenty thousand no-hopers who had followed him to Monkenheath. He would have had to bellow like a bull to be heard by all that many, in the open air. 'What's he saying? What's he on about?' Jurnet could imagine them demanding of one an-other as they strained their ears to hear.

Charlie Appleyard, by contrast, had had all the benefit of modern technology at his disposal, electronic know-how of whose existence Tanner could never have dreamed festooning the rostrum and the lower branches of the Oak, to say nothing of the media men thrusting their long-handled broom mikes at him like a bunch of manic cleaning ladies, sweeping the air clean of competing voices. Without raising his voice and with a simplicity that hurt, it was so surprising, he had spoken, not just to his co-conspirators, not just to Angleby, but, like the Pope, to the world.

It had begun like a fairy story, once upon a time. Once upon a time, in the little town of Windham, nine miles south of the city, a man in his fifties, settled and prosperous, had lived with his family; a pillar of the community and, whatever names his enemies later used to discredit him, a gentleman of an ancient Norfolk line, entitled to a coat of arms and connected by marriage to some of the most prominent families in the county.

'I'm speaking about the first week of July, in 1549,' said Charlie Appleyard as if he were talking about the day before yesterday. 'Not, you would have said, the kind of bloke only three weeks later to be branded a traitor, commander of an army of twenty thousand desperate men.'

'How could it possibly have happened?' The cameras had zoomed in, recording for posterity the astonishment shining in Charlie Appleyard's short-sighted eyes. 'You guys sitting here, I don't have to tell *you*. But you – you out there – ' arms spread wide as if physically to embrace his hearers gathered in front of the box for their customary evening fix – 'you're the ones I'm talking to. Listen. Restrain yourselves for once. Don't go to get a beer out of the fridge or to put the kettle on. This is important. Don't switch over to *EastEnders* or that bloody panel game. This isn't about some clot back in the Dark Ages who hadn't the sense to know which side his bread was buttered. This is about *you*.'

So it had gone on, the fairy story that had ended not happily ever after. And all on account of some hedges.

'That was a laugh,' said Charlie Appleyard, not laughing, 'when you think how soft we all go today at the mere mention of hedge-rows, how worked up we get whenever somebody comes along with a bulldozer and *oops*! another bit of conservation bites the dust. If bulldozers had been invented in Tanner's time the villagers, the peasants – in those days we still had peasants, would you believe? – would have greeted their appearance with cries of delight, garlanded them with flowers. Because the hedges,

22

those ecological mini-jungles we now fall over ourselves to preserve at all costs, were going up round the common land where, from time immemorial, the villagers had had the right to pasture their sheep.

'All that fuss over a few lamb chops! Was it worth it?' Charlie Appleyard looked humorously about him, a humour that modulated without showmanship to a bitter-sweet melancholy. 'Times change – don't we know it? If anybody knows it, we do, the kids that grew up in the brave new world after the war. A farming revolution was taking place with no EU subsidies to take up the slack, more's the pity. Sheep-farming, that was where the money was, provided you went in for it on a sufficiently large scale, which meant getting rid of the peasants' common land standing between a smart operator and his profit.

'Progress, they called it, as, one after another of them, the big boys hedged the commons, as they turned the countryside into great sheep-walks, driving tenants off the smallholdings they had farmed for centuries, their cottages allowed to fall into ruin, condemning them and their families to a life of beggary, a crime punishable by branding and even slavery.

'But what am I sounding such a misery for?' The man had changed tone, all merry and bright. 'I'm talking about the fifth of July, 1549, which was a holiday, for Christ's sake, a day to celebrate the life and martyrdom of St Thomas à Becket, a saint the good folk of Windham held in particular esteem. All the fun of the fair was on tap – except that, in 1549, hard cheese, not everyone was in holiday mood. Every year, on his day, the town put on a play about the saint who had died championing the Church against an unjust king and his nobles. This time round, they were asking themselves something different – they were asking who, on that particular July the fifth, would champion the people?'

Despite the lengthening shadows it was still hot in Tanner's Moot. Sweat glistened on the faces of the men who sat facing the Oak, but nobody drew a hand across a brow. One and all, with pained attention, listened to the calm and committed voice of Charlie Appleyard telling England how it was.

'Maybe I've gone wrong,' he admitted, nothing pushy about him. 'Maybe it didn't happen that way. Maybe the locals were feeling on top of the world – there weren't, after all, all that many holidays for the poor in 1549. Maybe they had tossed back a few cups of ale and were feeling what the hell. Either way, what did they do? *That* I do know. They went and paid a visit to the local

23

capo, a guy called Flowerdew, and cut down some of his hedges, whereupon the bugger, who had a full-blown feud of his own going on with Loy Tanner, offered them money to go and do the same to some land Tanner himself had enclosed for his sheep.

'Have you got it?' Absorbed in getting over the message, Charlie Appleyard looked squarely into the Anglian cameras. On the video his face had filled the screen, childlike in its astonishment. 'Enter Loy Tanner literally on the wrong side of the fence, himself one of the bastards who were grinding the faces of the poor.

'So what are we doing here?'

Into the silence that followed only the Oak of Reformation inserted a small sound. Moved by the first of the evening breeze, the leaves in its upper branches crackled thirstily, sounding ready to fall. One or two, giving up the fight against the inevitable, actually let go, one of them landing on Charlie Appleyard's shoulder, green against the bleached shirt.

Appleyard reached up, picked it off.

'A sign!' he exclaimed, holding the leaf aloft for all to see. 'A symbol of why we are here. We are here because when – shouting and, it may be, the worse for drink – the mob took the money and came clamouring to Tanner's land, Loy Tanner came out to meet them. Took the wind out of their sails by promising to do their job for them: throw the hedges down himself.

'And that wasn't all!' The man's voice had become hushed. The leaves had stopped jangling. 'Moved by the condition of these losers, these dregs, this man of wealth, position and authority, in one mad moment of decision, threw away all three – and indeed, as it proved later, life itself.

' "*You shall have me, if you will, not only as your companion but as your general, your standard-bearer and your chief.*"

'That's what the man said.' Charlie Appleyard, eyes half closed against the lowering sun, surveyed his audience, turning his head slowly from side to side. 'Saint or bloody fool? Maybe both. Maybe you can't be one without the other. Maybe Tanner himself had been to the fair, drunk too much ale and suddenly found himself possessed of an irresistible urge to throw his cap over the windmill, break out of the shell of his ordered life, no matter what the cost. Did he do what he did on behalf of the dispossessed peasantry of England or for his own personal salvation? Had he had a row with his missis and wanted to get even? We shall never know and it bloody doesn't matter. What matters is that here was a man in whose honour it is proper for us to come here to Tanner's

24

Moot, to the Oak of Reformation where he brought his army in search of justice and where we, following in his footsteps, come seeking the same and determined to stay until we get it.

'This time round, though, it's jobs we want, not land. Today you can keep your bloody hedges and good luck to you – *and* your bloody state charities while you're about it. We're fed up with hanging on to the fringes of society like crumbs waiting to be brushed off the table-cloth once the meal is over. We want it.'

Mood softening: 'You people of Angleby, sitting back home, watching us on the box, you don't have to worry. Nobody is going to descend from the heights of Monkenheath to rape you in your beds. Like Tanner before us, we've set up this platform under the Oak so that anyone who disagrees with what we're doing can come along and say so. We've no plans to raid your larders or loot your shops even though we've only brought another twenty-four hours' food with us. Thereafter we'll go hungry unless in brother-hood, not out of charity, you decide to feed us. It's up to you, that's all, not the government. It's up to England.'

4

The Lord Mayor thrust out the square chin which was his greatest, if not his only, electoral asset, lending him as it did a totally illusory impression of strength and determination. Unconvinced, the others round the table, who knew him of old, waited for him to open the discussion.

The Lord Mayor did not disappoint them.

'Well?' he said.

A small sound from the Superintendent made Jurnet, just for a moment, expect his superior officer to be the first to set the ball rolling. A swift glance sidewards quickly disabused him of that idea. Even viewed in profile, the patrician features simmered with an irrepressible irony which his subordinate, having all too often been on the receiving end of it, knew only too well.

The Superintendent was doing his best not to laugh.

Feeling much the same himself, Jurnet nevertheless sensed the old familiar irritation rising in his bosom. The self-important so-and-so, certain he knew better than anybody else! The only reason he was present at all was that the Chief Constable had had to be rushed to hospital to have his appendix out and had named the man as his deputy; just as he himself, Ben Jurnet, was only there because, without asking, the Superintendent had brought him along.

Actually, there had been a little kerfuffle over that as well, the Lord Mayor clucking disapproval and that wimp, Walter Walters, fussing to fit in an extra chair at the table, which had meant shuffling those already seated to left and right to make room: all of which the Superintendent had obviously enjoyed. Obvious to his underling, that was. To the Lord Mayor and the already assembled guests his manners were, as always, impeccable.

Yet who did the guy think he was? The fact that he regarded the Lord Mayor and the civil servants present, as well as the Bishop and the two local MPs bidden to the conclave, with equal and impartial contempt did not mean that there was not a problem, nor that the city was not the proper entity to deal with it.

Philip Goodenough, Member of Parliament for Angleby North, had, as ever, something to say. With his short back and sides, his tailored black worsted with a discreet stripe, red rose in button-hole and a tie that could almost have come from a minor public school, he presented an impeccable image of New Labour, just as Fred Bindle, his opposite number in Angleby South, in his open-necked shirt, his light sport's jacket and cords the casual side of smart, his tan brogues matching his shock of ginger hair, looked what he was, the very model of an up-and-coming Tory.

What Mr Goodenough had to say was to the point, if not precisely the point awaiting discussion. True, it had to do with the unemployed, but not the unemployed currently squatting on Tanner's Moot. Unemployment in general was his theme, and in particular Tory responsibility therefor. What was the government going to do about it, Mr Goodenough demanded, thumping the beautiful mahogany table with a vigour which made the Mayor's secretary, who was a sensitive soul, wince and look to Mrs Castle for comfort. Without interrupting her note-taking, that kind lady reached across the space between them, patted his hand with her free one and whispered: 'A little beeswax will soon put that right, don't worry.'

To all of this, Mr Fred Bindle, brushing back his forelock and calling the Lord Mayor 'bor' in a Norfolk dialect only slightly modified by his years at Eton, replied that as everyone but a Labour git didn't have to be told, unemployment was a world-

26

wide problem, as little to be laid at the door of the government as the state of the weather.

Running true to form, neither politician had any suggestion to make as to how the city was to extricate itself with honour from its present predicament. Seasoned operators, they did not need to be warned of the dangerous consequences of action, any action. Having made their contribution, they sat back, looking modestly pleased with themselves, awaiting what others, lesser mortals who could actually be saddled with the responsibility for making decisions, had to say.

To the Lord Mayor's evident gratification what, with only one or two dissenting voices, emerged was a general consensus as to what needed urgently to be done: to wit, nothing. As Cyril Cran, the Director of Administration, a tall, thin man with a full comple- ment of predatory teeth honed by years of feasting on the car- casses of one-time colleagues who had fallen by the civic wayside, put it: 'One man can stage a hunger strike, not ten thousand. Not physically possible. Give 'em a day or two, ten thousand tummies rumbling, and they'll be heading for the nearest chippy like the Pied Piper of Hamelin.'

To this, however, Alistair Tring, the Curator of the Castle Museum, had something to say. Invited along as the fount and origin of the Tanner Exhibition currently packing them in, he made a typically bad-tempered intervention, his little puffin beak of a nose purpling with its usual generalized malice towards the human race, especially to anyone who thought he knew better.

'I must say,' he snapped, 'I'm surprised this meeting needs to be reminded of what happened in 1549 in precisely similar circum- stances. When the city denied Tanner's request for provisions for his men it left the rebels no alternative. They came rushing down the slopes of Monkenheath, across the river and into the city, overwhelming its defences and holding it at their mercy for a matter of weeks. Is that the kind of history you're inviting to repeat itself?'

'I hardly think, Mr Tring, that what happened all that long ago should trouble us today,' said the Lord Mayor, albeit a little uncertainly, history, like most other subjects, not being his strong point. 'After all, in the present case, unlike the earlier occasion, there is no question of their being armed.'

'How do we know that?' the other demanded, looking round the table and defying anyone to come up with an answer. 'If a bunch of disaffected peasantry in the sixteenth century could produce arms from goodness knows where sufficient to take over what was then one of the most important cities in the kingdom, who can say what this lot may have up their sleeve?'

'I still don't think we should let them go hungry . . . ' This from Mrs Cording, in charge of Social Services and therefore professionally caring. Whereat the Borough Treasurer pursed his lips and doubted to what extent the city had a mandate to release funds for such a purpose.

'Oh, I didn't mean us!' explained Mrs Cording, fussed at being so misunderstood. 'I meant the Red Cross, or Oxfam, or somebody . . .'

'Or the Department of Unemployment,' added the Member for Angleby North smiling at the Member for Angleby South.

The prospect of getting somebody else to foot the bill for civic compassion put everybody in a more optimistic mood. Only the recently appointed Chairman of the Parks Committee, present because Monkenheath was included in his bailiwick, objected to anything being done which might prolong the invasion of alien bums pressing down the vegetation of Tanner's Moot.

'The pasque flower,' he pointed out, his voice vibrant with the earnestness of a recent convert to the cause of conservation. 'One of the few places in East Anglia where it still survives. Proceedings are in train to designate the area a Site of Special Scientific Interest. Ought to have been done years ago,' he finished with unction, happy to bring into the limelight the criminal indolence of his predecessor.

Martin Bown, Leader of the Liberal Democrats on the council, deputy headmaster by profession, dedicated bird-watcher and amateur naturalist, fingered his bow tie, something he invariably did when about to take the floor. 'The pasque flower', he eagerly concurred, 'is, as its name suggests, and as the Bishop, I am sure, will bear me out, one that flowers at Eastertide, not midsummer. We can be thankful that by now the foliage will already have died down and no harm will have been done.'

'Eastertide,' murmured the silver-haired Bishop, steepling his fingertips and wrapping his tongue lovingly round the sacred syllables. It was his first contribution to the discussion, one that made everyone feel better.

'That's one thing settled, anyhow,' announced the Lord Mayor, thankfully. 'The pasque flower's one thing at least we don't have to take into consideration.'

'Balls!' objected the City Chief Environmental Health Officer, a

28

wiry little Scot who, by virtue of his calling, was by general consent, even in committee, allowed to call a testicle a testicle. 'Bugger the botany! If it's natural history on Tanner's Moot you're concerned about, spare a thought for ten thousand men and more up there pissing and defecating in the way of nature. That's a lot of effluent, laddie, and a whole load of cack. Believe me, in the circumstances the best we can hope for is that they go on with their hunger strike as promised. Cutting down the intake will at least reduce the tonnage somewhat, and therefore the risk of epidemics.'

The City Chief Environmental Health Officer surveyed the assembly with a stern Presbyterian eye brightened with a sparkle of humour to which only a few of those present instantly responded. Recognizing it, the Superintendent and Jurnet sat up expectantly, the Bishop was seized with a sudden cough, and Mrs Castle, shorthanding away furiously, broke into an appreciative chuckle which didn't count, coming as it did from a mere amanuensis.

'Let me tell you', the Chief EHO went on, looking about him with the air of not thinking much of what he saw, 'what, whilst you gentlemen have been sitting on your arses debating what not to do, my department has actually been doing – and God help any organization putting on a garden party this weekend because we've already requisitioned and put in place every portable loo in the city, and we've sent out an SOS for more to every local authority in the county. We've also called the Water Company out to tap into that main which, you may remember, they extended to include Monkenheath after the drought of 1976 and to activate every stopcock in the vicinity. We've been in touch with the St John's Ambulance Brigade and they'll be setting up first-aid posts just as soon as they can get their volunteers buttoned into the uniforms. The Red Cross, the WRVS, Women's Institute, Townswomen's Guild – you name it, either we've been in touch with them or they've been in touch with us. So far we can't compete with Bosnia, of course, but now that we're on screen, give us time. There's nothing like pictures on the telly to set the charitable juices flowing.'

The jocularity fading: 'One particular flow of charitable juices, however – ' a turn in the direction of the Superintendent – 'I am bound to say in the interest of the general health of the city I am not anxious to see encouraged, and in this respect I would be interested to hear what the police have in mind. They're a fine, manly bunch up there on the Moot by the looks of them, not a

29

woman among the lot, and our ladies of Bergate, I have no doubt, are as soft-hearted as any females in Angleby – '

'No problem!' the Member for Angleby South interrupted, and instantly regretted it. 'They won't be able to afford the prices.'

'But that's just it. The danger is the girls will be offering for free, making their contribution in their own way, and, I tell you frankly, I don't like the thought of it. Foreign bodies, literally, coming into the city, bringing in the Lord knows what along with their willies.'

'Dear me!' exclaimed the Lord Mayor, alarmed. 'That is indeed a serious point, one on which I think we should hear from the Superintendent.'

The Superintendent took his time. He took his hand off his gold pen slowly, almost regretfully. At last: 'I have to say, to you, my Lord Mayor, and to you all, the city elders gathered here, that I can no more react profitably to what your Chief Environmental Health Officer has just said than I can to anything else which may be proposed round this table.' With an air of humorous regret that had Jurnet killing himself internally: 'You would be quite right to condemn me out of hand if I did. Leaving out the fact that I am only here to hold a watching brief for the Chief Constable who is unfortunately indisposed, I am quite sure that I don't need to remind you of the absolute necessity of the police keeping strictly to their own province, which is to keep the Queen's peace. To uphold, but never to encroach upon, the prerogatives of the duly elected civic authority.'

'That's all very well!' cried the Lord Mayor, his voice full of a peevish disappointment. 'But it does nothing to answer the question of what we are going to do.'

'Not that we haven't already been in communication with the Home Office and the crowd control experts at Scotland Yard,' the Superintendent continued silkily as if there had been no interruption, 'and taken on board their corporate wisdom, which amounts to covering all eventualities whilst keeping as low a profile as possible. As of this moment, thankfully, everybody connected with this extraordinary expedition appears to be unaggressive and in amazingly good humour, everybody behaving himself even to the extent, so I am told, that they are collecting their litter carefully in plastic bags which, when full, have been placed in the road outside the Moot for collection.'

'Wait till they get round to the booze!' This from Fred Bindle MP.

'I understand from the Cleansing Department that a random examination of the bags so far collected has shown up nothing stronger than Coke and 7-Up.' The Superintendent surveyed his audience in the friendliest way. 'Whilst – human nature being what it is – I can well understand Mr Bindle's scepticism, I have to say that I myself have never before had to do with such an unaggressive crowd.'

'Trespassers!' snapped the Parks Committee, getting his own back for the pasque flower. 'If they're so docile, why don't the police clear them off Monkenheath before any more of them turn up? Before they have time to get bedded down and turn the whole Moot into a ruddy wilderness?'

'Trespassers?' The Superintendent tossed the word into the air, examined it with head slightly to one side. 'Let me remind you that we're talking about common land where certain citizens who, so far as we can tell, pose no threat to anyone have chosen to sit down. You will no doubt, if you have not already done so, be taking legal advice, including an elucidation of what, if any, are our visitors' rights under the Treaty of Rome. But I have to say, gentlemen, that, pending a directive from a higher quarter, there is nothing the police can do other than keep a close watch on the situation whilst holding in reserve a pool of uniformed officers sufficient to deal with all eventualities.'

'In other words,' summed up the Lord Mayor, relief written large all over his large, flattish face, 'we should do nothing.'

'That', said the Superintendent austerely, retiring into a detachment inside which, Jurnet suspected, he was laughing his aristocratic head off, 'is not a matter on which the police can properly advise you.'

'What about this fellow Appleyard?' the Director of Administration demanded. 'Who is he? Where did he pop up from? How's he managed to get a show like this on the road without anybody – not the police, not anybody – having an inkling?'

'It's a good Norfolk name.' Alistair Tring, as ever, took the opportunity to show off his local knowledge. 'More than that. In case you didn't know, Loy Tanner's wife was born an Appleyard. Could be a descendant on the distaff side . . .'

The Superintendent said: 'We are making inquiries about the gentleman.'

'Making inquiries!' This time it was the Environmental Health Officer, a man by nature on a short fuse, who thumped the table. Walter Walters, fortified this time by Mrs Castle's sympathy,

31

smiled bravely. 'Can I not get it into your thick heads – this isn't a matter of history we're discussing, ancient or modern. Angleby is no longer the walled city it was four hundred years ago, with cannon mounted on the walls to keep out the enemy at the gate. Not that it would be any help today if it was. That rabble up there on the Moot constitutes a potential seedbed of infection, a health hazard the city can't afford to ignore.' The Scotsman looked round the table in exasperation, his gaze finally coming to rest on the Bishop.

In a voice heavy with sarcasm he demanded: 'What does His Grace have to say?'

Benign, fingertips together, the Bishop nodded acknowledgement, looking gratified to be asked. His eyes of faded blue went to the blue brashness of sky on view through the lofty windows of the Grand Chamber.

'If I were you,' he suggested mildly, 'I should pray for rain.'

5

The house was small, at the end of a terrace which, at the beginning of the century, had been artisans' cottages, honest in their lack of pretension. Now, the door at which Jurnet, finding no other means of making his presence known, rapped on the peeling brown paint was the only one which did not boast a brass knocker in the shape of a fish or a lion's head, nor a fanlight fathered by Regency out of Do-It-Yourself. The paint – or lack of it – the front garden, a mini-wilderness of withered stalks among which a pair of plaster gnomes, faded but indefatigably cheerful, dipped their rods in a non-existent pool, puzzled Jurnet. He himself had nothing against polyurethane; thought the shining reds and blues and natural wood finishes of the rest of the row a distinct improvement on what he saw before him. Dr Adamson was not short of a penny. In the context, her home's neglected appearance could only be either a tease or an arrogance, a deliberate challenge to the gentrification on either side.

Somewhat sourly, Jurnet decided that the lady had the kind of humour peculiar to the well-heeled. All right for some.

He rapped on the door again, dislodging a few more of the brown flakes; unnecessarily, for the woman was on her way,

32

flinging the door wide with a generosity which pleased him even as his brow creased in a professional frown at her lack of caution. He had not phoned to make an appointment, there was no security peephole, and it could have been anyone, a burglar, a rapist, one of her neighbours maddened by the way her whims were debasing the value of his property.

'Detective Inspector Jurnet!' she exclaimed. 'This *is* pleasant!'

Absurdly gratified that she had remembered his name, he followed her down a slit of a hall into a living-room that seemed reasonably spacious only because it contained hardly any furniture, and what there was of it – undistinguished stuff, patently unloved – small in proportion. Only the rug on the rough-boarded floor – Persian by the look of it, glowing and sensuous – was what one might have expected to find in a home owned by Dr Adamson.

Dr Adamson said: 'I won't ask how you found me. I suppose the police can always find anybody, if they have a mind to, even if they're ex-directory or whatever.'

'Actually, I phoned the Vice-Chancellor. I spoke to his wife.'

'Eleanor! She should have known better. She knows this is the one place where I'm absolutely incommunicado.'

'I said I was the police.'

'Ah! That explains it. She must have hoped you were going to arrest me.' She smiled, looking suddenly young and mischievous, despite the grey hair. 'The Vice-Chancellor fancies me rotten, and my nephew – the one you met – is engaged to marry her beautiful daughter, who, she is convinced, probably with reason, is much too good for him.'

'If you're incommunicado, why did you answer the door?'

The smile blossomed into a laugh.

'Because I was so bored with my own company. I thought, oh goody, maybe it's Prince Charming come to whisk me away on his gallant steed. Maybe it's Jehovah's Witnesses come to offer me eternal salvation. And I opened the door and there you were!'

'A copper come to ask questions.' Jurnet, made uncomfortable by her levity, managed something of a laugh himself. 'What a let-down!'

'That's life!' Dr Adamson responded cheerfully. 'Have I embarrassed you? I do hope so. If one's about to be put through the third degree I'm sure it's good tactics to get one's inquisitor at a disadvantage. Would you care for a cup of coffee whilst you recover your composure and tell me why you're here?'

33

*

Coming back from the kitchen with loaded tray, she said, without prompting: 'Not difficult to put two and two together. The Tanner connection!' She handed the detective a mug which he took with a further small surge of annoyance. Bright orange with splashes of black, it was the kind of crockery teenagers could be expected to go in for, not sober-sided Hon. Docs of universities. Her mugs and her general air of caprice put him increasingly off balance, made him feel the way he felt with gays and schizos – as if it were he, not they, who refused to fit into the scheme of things. 'You're here to ask about Charlie.'

Jurnet took a sip of the coffee and was surprised by its excellence – the real thing, full of Eastern promise. Overwhelmed by a sudden searing recollection of the ghastly brew on which Miriam, his dead love, had slanderously bestowed the name, he took a gulp, too much, too hot, and nearly choked, the woman watching with sympathetic but uninvolved interest as he fought to get back his breath.

Satisfied at last that she had regained his attention, she repeated her inquiry.

'It *is* about Charlie, isn't it?'

'As you say, the Tanner connection. We need to know about him. I remembered our meeting at the castle, and I thought you might be able to help.'

Ignoring the implied question, she demanded: 'Why do you need to know? Has he done something wrong?'

'No. We just want to keep it that way.'

'I've always understood that Monkenheath is common land. When I was a child the Moot was our favourite place for picnics. I thought anybody and everybody who wanted to was free to go there.'

'So it is and so they are, in normal circumstances. But I'm sure you see that moving in at the head of an army of ten thousand followers raises problems a bit more complicated than those raised by picnics.' Jurnet took a chance and drank some more of the coffee. It slid down his throat, superb, untroubled by any ghost of the past. 'You do know Charlie Appleyard, then?'

'I know him. He was one of my students.' Dr Adamson's own mug of coffee was untouched. She had become serious, academic. 'You understand – one feels a certain loyalty. I shouldn't want to get him into trouble . . .'

34

'Of course not. All I'm hoping is to pick up a few pointers. It helps to know who one's dealing with.'

'Does it?' The other frowned, concentrating. 'I suppose so. Though I hardly, with the best will in the world, see how I can be of assistance. Please don't quote me, but the relationship between a student and his Supervisor of Studies is, generally speaking, a quite superficial one – a purely academic coming together conditioned by the syllabus, by the necessity, on the one side, of earning one's living and, on the other, of absorbing as much of the current in-jargon as will get you through your exams. As for Appleyard in particular, he did his BA here in Angleby, not London. In London I only knew him as a postgraduate, which means I missed entirely the really revealing phase in his development – the first-year rookie, dewy-fresh from school, taking his first tentative steps in the adult world.'

'Was he good at his work?'

'Bright. So far as I had time to form a judgement.' The woman's grey eyes narrowed, her generously shaped lips compressed themselves into a line of severity. 'He never came back after the summer vacation.'

'Did he say why he dropped out?'

'He never even paid me the courtesy of a letter of explanation – wrote to the college office to say he wasn't returning; wouldn't be needing his grant any more.'

'But you must have had your own idea . . .'

'I assure you I had nothing of the kind. I did know he played the guitar – he and a couple of other students had formed a group which played at Student Union dances and so on – and, so far as I gave my mind to it at all, I wondered desultorily if he hadn't thrown up his studies to go into show business professionally, for which I could hardly blame him. There seems to be so much more money these days in pop than in history.' Dr Adamson smiled with renewed animation. 'Though today, doesn't it, it looks as though they've found a way to combine the two. Not surprisingly, with all the publicity and seeing him on TV, we were speaking about him only last night, at dinner at the Grants' – the Vice-Chancellor's. In fact, the person you ought to be talking to is Julian – Julian Grant, my nephew's fiancée. She and Appleyard were at Angleby at the same time, they graduated in the same year and, from what she was saying yesterday, I got the impression they knew each other quite well. To be thoroughly indiscreet, I got the impression they could well have known each other in the

Biblical as well as the literal meaning of the word. Nowadays,' she commented indulgently, 'it's the done thing, isn't it? Though of course, with Mummy sitting with ears pricked, to say nothing of Roger there too, she would hardly have come out with it outright.' Laughingly: 'Eleanor! She thinks her daughter purer than the Virgin Mary waiting for a visit from the archangel Gabriel.' Dr Adamson broke off, then said brightly: 'Hang around a little and you'll be able to ask Julian yourself. She's calling to pick me up, to drive me out to Monkenheath. We thought it would be interesting to see the fun of the fair in 3-D.'

'Monkenheath! I have to warn you, you may have trouble getting through. The approach road is closed to unauthorized traffic.'

'Humanitarian aid,' the other explained, brushing aside the objection with the certainty of one who was never refused admittance where she wished to go. 'We're delivering three gross of doughnuts, courtesy of the local bakers' benevolent society. It was Julian's idea. She's picking them up first and then coming on here. She said last night that Appleyard's crazy about them, used to eat them by the dozen, got the sugar all over the sheets.'

'That must have made Mrs Grant sit up.'

'Probably why she said it.' Dr Adamson's eyes shone with pleasure. 'She's a girl of spirit. I'm terribly glad about her and Roger.' After the briefest of pauses: 'Perhaps, since, for your own good reasons, you've obviously decided to slot us into one of your policely pigeon-holes, this might be a good moment to say that Roger is something more than just a nephew. My brother and his wife were killed in an air crash when he was four years old, and I've more or less made myself responsible for him ever since.' Lips twisted in humorous self-derision: 'Not that he's needed all that much looking after, bless him. I don't think I've ever met anyone more certain of where he was going in life and more determined to get there.'

'And where was that, if I might ask?'

'Why, nowhere! Or rather, where, by the grace of God, he is already, the lucky boy. It's the most difficult thing in the world, don't you agree, to have absolutely no ambition? Try as we will, for most of us it's always there, lurking in the background, putting in an appearance when we least expect it. Even a monk, one you'd say at first thinking has rejected everything the world has to offer, is ambitious to attain God, or salvation, or whatever it is he spends his time praying for. Roger, now, has perfected the art of going nowhere better than anyone I know.' Dr Adamson inclined her head to one side as she examined the detective with smiling approval. 'He may even be able to give you a few pointers, Inspector. If I may say so, you don't look all that happy and fulfilled yourself.'

Damn the nosy cow! Jurnet thought. He'd be buggered if he let on about Miriam. Aloud he found himself saying, stammering slightly: 'I – I've had a bereavement recently . . .'

'How crass I am!' Instantly aglow with sympathy Dr Adamson took his hand. 'Roger is always telling me off for barging ahead regardless, on top of which – being who, what, I am – I naturally thought it must be about money. When you have as much of it as Roger and I have you do tend, in spite of yourself, to think it's the only mover of consequence.' She took back her hand and gave it some attention, turning the palm upward and then down again, watching the way the pearl and amethyst ring on her third finger advertised its presence with exquisite discretion before withdrawing into shadow. 'You know about us, don't you? That we're Adam and Eve shoes?'

'The name – Adamson. I wondered if there was some connection.'

'Nathaniel Adamson, my grandfather. Roger's great-grandfather. Founder of Angleby's most famous industry. And now Roger and I are the two left with the pickings.'

'Nice for Roger. Nice for you both.'

'Is it?' The other examined the statement seriously. 'I don't know. Nice is such a nice ambiguous word, isn't it? Great wealth can either be a great challenge or else it paralyses the will. I'm not sure yet which way Roger will go.'

'Was he at the college with his fiancée?'

'Roger at university!' Dr Adamson's laugh was warm now with a tender mockery. 'Roger would have been a drop-out at nursery school if he'd known how to find his own way home. Not that he doesn't possess an exceptionally good business brain when it amuses him to make use of it. From time to time he deigns to put in an appearance at a board meeting and dazzles us all with his commercial insight. If, however, what you're really asking is did my nephew know Charlie Appleyard whilst he was doing his BA at Angleby, the answer, I gather – a little to my surprise because Appleyard never mentioned the connection to me – from what was said yesterday, is yes. It appears that Roger and Julian and Appleyard and some girl or other – I didn't get her name – used to hang about together.'

37

'So Roger lived here in Angleby?'

'He did, he does, in this house until – quite recently – he had a splendid penthouse built on top of the factory. He says Angleby's the only place where he feels at home. As a matter of fact, it was Roger who bought this delectable *pied-à-terre*.' The woman looked about her, smiling. 'I gather it's meant to be a statement, but what about I'm not sure – only that the geyser threatens to blow up every time you take a bath, there's no freezer, black beetles in the larder and bats in the attic. Old world charm with a vengeance.' An old-fashioned bell jangled in the kitchen. 'See what I mean? That'll be Julian now.'

The Superintendent was in his usual bad temper. No, not usual: unusual in that his ill will was directed, not, as was generally the case, towards one or other of his underlings waiting about uncomfortably for orders, but at the television set which had been brought into his room and now squatted on its chromium stand, a brash invader blinking its pictures, mouthing its clichéd captions, generating in that hallowed space dedicated to the exercise of pure reason a phoney excitement which commanded attention regardless.

'Turn the bloody thing off!' roared the Superintendent, the employment of an expletive not known hitherto to exist in his patrician vocabulary having the effect of rooting Detective Sergeant Ellers, who stood nearest to the infernal machine, to the spot, so that the picture of the clerical gentleman and the sound of his unctuous implorings continued unabated. 'I said, turn it off!'

'Sir . . .'

The little Welshman recalled himself to realities, leaned over; the screen went blank. The hatred and contempt which infused the air almost palpably slowly diminished. The Superintendent, who had opened a window where he stood taking deep breaths as if to replace the TV-tainted mish-mash infecting his lungs with the healthful vegetable odours of the Market Place, turned back to the room.

'I don't know what I'm angry about,' he announced, astonishing as always. 'Yes, I do.' Reseating himself at his desk, his fingers momentarily touching the gold pen that lay in front of him like a mini-mace, a symbol of authority: 'Vanity. The fear of being outmanœuvred by a clever manipulator and not a thing we can do about it. I hope you know me well enough – some of you at least – to believe me when I say I am not without sympathy for fellow creatures desperate for work and mounting a peaceful demonstration to draw attention to their plight. But – ' his gaze sweeping the room as if daring his subordinates to come up with an answer – 'the question is, is it what it seems to be or are these amateur theatricals up on the Moot an elaborate charade disguising something altogether more sinister?' With the deep sigh of one imparting even worse news: 'I've already had the Home Office in touch, the Met, MI5, to say nothing of every MP who sees the chance to make political capital out of the situation. I've seen the Chief in hospital and the same answer goes out from one and all: do nothing.'

'It's the heat, sir.' Sid Hale, a detective inspector forever saddened by the world's follies but never surprised by them, spoke gently, reinforcing his words by producing a crumpled handkerchief with which he mopped his long, melancholy countenance. 'It's getting everyone down. Still, got to start raining sooner or later. One good soaking and all the manipulators in the world won't stop them, they'll be on the move.'

'Be on the move where?' the Superintendent demanded, rejecting the unsought sympathy. 'Ten thousand men, a disaster waiting to happen, and we haven't a clue as to their intentions – only to remind ourselves that when their hero, Loy Tanner, chose to commit mass suicide, move his twenty thousand down from Monkenheath into the valley, it ended up with three thousand dead and heaven knows how many more killed on the run or executed, including the great man himself. Anyone with eyes in his head, looking downhill, seeing the German mercenaries gathered there waiting, professional soldiers professionally armed for battle, must have known they hadn't a dog's chance, yet down they went, every last Tom, Dick and Harry, with their makeshift weapons, no body armour, because Loy Tanner asked them to.

'What I ask myself, four hundred and fifty years later, is what will they do if and when Mr Charlie Appleyard gives the word?'

Jurnet had not been listening. He had been thinking of Julian Grant.

Not about all of her, he silently corrected himself. The girl herself had been pretty enough, he supposed, and desirable enough, if a doll's face sporting cupid's-bow lips stamped with a peevish discontent was your cup of tea, or a body just this side of anorexia was what turned you on. Haunted by the memory of Miriam's generous mouth, the lovely curves of her body, Jurnet ordinarily would not have favoured Roger Adamson's bride-to-be with more than the professional curiosity he directed towards every member of the human race with whom his work brought him into contact.

But her hair! Standing, eyes on the Superintendent, a picture of alert attention, the perfect copper, bright but not dangerously bright, Jurnet imagined how it would be to bury his face in Julian Grant's hair as he had loved to bury his face in Miriam's. Would it smell the same? Would it spring from beneath his fingers as Miriam's had sprung, rounding itself into waves of silken bronze in which he could happily have drowned?

Until today he had never seen anyone else with hair of the same colour and texture – until today when the girl had come through the door of Dr Adamson's poky little house and transformed it into magnificence.

She had not been pleased to be questioned, even by one only too obviously bowled over by her charms. He supposed she was used to that anyway; probably – having already awarded Roger Adamson the gold medal – bored by the homage of lovelorn swains surplus to requirements. Jurnet noted the amused mischief in Dr Adamson's eyes as she introduced the two of them, and wished he could say aloud what, so far as he was concerned, the bint could do with her Barbie-doll face, her trendy body, everything but the hair. A flush of anger and embarrassment had briefly succeeded his wonder at the sight of it. That anyone else should have hair like Miriam's was at worst a blasphemy, at best an infringement of copyright. The feelings of guilt did not last, however, submerged in a beauty he had thought lost to him for ever.

Frowning, the girl had demanded: 'What kind of questions? Can't they wait for another time?' To Dr Adamson: 'Are you ready? I've got the doughnuts in the back, oozing jam all over the place . . .'

Jurnet managed: 'I understand you were at the university with Charles Appleyard?'

'So? So were hundreds of others. And everyone calls him Charlie.' The girl turned to the older woman. On either side of the cupid's-bow the shallow lines of discontent had deepened. 'What have you been telling him?'

Dr Adamson raised her hands in smiling disclaimer. 'What is there to tell?'

'Exactly! Nothing at all. Are you ready to go?' Julian Grant wheeled round towards Jurnet, apparently unimpressed by the Mediterranean good looks which, generally speaking, stood him in good stead in his encounters with young women. But then Roger Adamson was a raving blond, wasn't he? No accounting for tastes.

'If you must know, Charlie was part of the crowd, that's all. We all went around together.'

'Were you – if I may ask – by any chance his special girlfriend?'

'Me? You must be joking. He went about with Jenny Nunn, so far as he went about with anybody specially. Or she did, for that matter.' Her voice, high-pitched to match her face, slid without effort into a giggle spiked with a childish malice. 'Nunn,' she finished. 'That was a name if you like. Addie, are you ready or aren't you?'

Outside the front door, waiting for Dr Adamson to lock up, Julian Grant had bent down and plucked a poppy which had somehow managed to survive among the withered grasses. She broke off the length of stalk and tucked the flower absent-mindedly into her hair.

At the sight, Jurnet's heart turned over, so reminiscent was the gesture of his lost love. He clenched his hands in his pockets, restraining an overwhelming impulse to attack the girl's vapid prettiness, claw off the foolish mask in the certainty of finding the never-to-be-forgotten beauty revealed beneath.

Fortunately for his self-control the girl thought better of the conceit; almost immediately pulled out the poppy and tossed it away, already wilting.

'They don't last,' she complained, setting her foot on the frail petals. 'Nothing lasts in this heat.'

In the brightness of day her hair blazed, bronze and gold. The woman clothed with the sun. Jurnet forced himself to confront the vision, play the role, speak the lines fate had allotted him. 'What about this Miss Nunn and her name? What was so special about it?'

'Only that by rights she should have been the last one to be called that. Anyone in trousers, she'd have had them off before you could say Jack Robinson.' There was more amusement than spite in the girl's voice.

'Is she still living in Angleby, then?'

'No idea. I haven't run into her in years. Doubt it, though. She's probably exhausted the local talent long ago, and moved to pastures new.'

Dr Adamson came towards them, dropping a large, old-fashioned key into her handbag as she came.

Julian Grant said: 'Thank goodness! Those doughnuts'll be cooking all over again.' As the three of them made their way out to the street, she turned back to Jurnet, last in line. 'If you want to know about Charlie, why don't you ask his father? He used to be deputy head at Angleby School and he's still around. He can tell you all about Charlie Appleyard.'

6

'Waste of time,' asserted the Superintendent, as Detective Sergeant Ellers drove the three of them swiftly towards Monken-heath, along the River Road this time deserted save for a scattering of pensioners absorbed in the superintendence of their pets' evacuations on the strip of depleted lawn leading down to the river. The park benches, where, at that time of the day, you could often be pushed to find a place to sit, were deserted, Jurnet noted, animals and owners alike moving about nervously, as if in a hurry to get the business over and done with, and then back to the blessed safety of home. No one seemed to have brought a ball, no one threw sticks for retrieval: every dog was on a lead for once, no pooper-scoopers in prideful evidence of good citizenship – in sum a scene that could only fuel resentment in one who saw it as his remit to ensure that life in Angleby continued on the same even keel as it had yesterday and the day before that, even into the mists of time.

'Waste of time,' repeated the Superintendent, not bothering even to incline his head towards the rear of the car. 'When did you ever run into a father who had the slightest conception of what made his offspring tick?' The tone in which this last was uttered, exasperation underpinned by a savagely repressed pain, reminded Jurnet of something he had heard around Headquarters – that the Superintendent's son had recently left the firm of solicitors to which he had been articled and taken off for Nepal or somewhere similar where life could be lived in flip-flops and a haze of hash.

'Or a son who didn't regard his father as an endangered species not worth the saving?' Staring ahead with eyes screwed up against the glare, the Superintendent finished: 'Unless he had money, of course. That has to make a difference. Does Appleyard's father have money, do you know?'

'Don't know, sir. Shouldn't think so. A retired deputy head, living off the ring road, Magpie Street way. Not exactly a district overflowing with millionaires.'

A lorry labelled Red Cross passed them, coming down from the Moot.

'What does our Charlie need money for?' Ellers put in. 'Free grub, no rent to pay, picture in all the papers. Even without a penny in his pocket he and his mates are sitting pretty.'

'Ten thousand men don't come together like that, at a toot on a whistle. You overlook the fact that it had to take money – a lot of money – to put this so-called demonstration together in the first place. Just as it's going to take money to keep it going. Before long, in the way of things, and once they've milked the story for all the so-called human interest they can squeeze out of it, the tabloids are going to have second thoughts about the propriety of encouraging a pack of layabouts to indulge their flights of fancy at the expense of the taxpayers who buy their papers. The media generally will be looking around for some new sensation to latch on to. As for charity, that's invariably a two-edged weapon. It has a sell-by date. Sooner or later charity fatigue is bound to set in. Now, Appleyard's saying that they're going to stay sitting on the Moot until December the fifth, the anniversary of Tanner's execution, but long before then even the most altruistic of do-gooders will be wanting to see some return for all the hours spent stirring those cauldrons of soup, or making those mountains of sandwiches, and who can blame them?'

'In that case, sir,' objected Ellers, the little Welshman perhaps foolishly confident in his role of court jester, 'what have we got to worry about? All we need is patience.'

'Patience!'

The word, the tone, was sufficient to kill dead conversation.

The road, ascending in lazy bends towards the heath, had left the river and was no longer deserted. Police cars were parked along the verges, their doors ajar to cool the raging infernos within. Police officers stood about, red-faced and bored. At a makeshift road block a police ribbon stretched between a Norway spruce and a may tree on which the haws were already reddening; the Rover was waved through with barely a glance. Too hot. Too bloody hot.

43

A sudden thought struck Jurnet, one that made his forehead break out in a sweat heavier than any the heat had already engendered. What if Julian Grant's hair was dyed, conjured out of a bottle by some poncy genie down at the hairdressing salon? He felt the sweat, cooling, dripping down the sides of his nose, odious, unclean, a punishment. What difference did it make, for heaven's sake, what colour the girl's hair was, how attained? Miriam being dead and buried, it could have been sky-blue-pink for all it mattered to him. Thank God he wasn't one of those weirdos with a thing about hair.

Just the same, the hateful thought persisted. Did Julian Grant – as Miriam had often done – pile her hair on top of her head for coolness, the short hairs at the nape of the neck curling free and innocent, baby's hair? Those were the hairs that gave the game away. Somehow he would have to find out the truth of the matter.

Something was going on at the Moot. It was too quiet. Ten thousand bodies, even at rest and unspeaking, normally made a measurable sound, and there was no sound. Behind the trestle tables which had been placed in position along one side of the grassed area, the Red Cross and the other volunteers had paused in their labours and stood still. The police, puzzlement on their faces, had moved in a little closer.

On the Oak of Reformation the leaves hung unmoving in the sun. Below, on the wooden platform which had been erected there, Charlie Appleyard, in a faded check shirt and jeans, sat on a kitchen chair in judgement, the Maltese cross round his neck his sole symbol of office.

'I just want to remind you', he began, in an easy conversational tone that yet managed to convey a deep conviction, 'that Loy Tanner, when he held his camp here four hundred and fifty years ago, also established his own court of law. Denied justice by the bastards who were running the country, condemned as rogues and vagabonds, he set out to prove that ragged, dispossessed men, the dregs of society, could yet possess a sense of honour at least as great as that of any nobleman, and that, so far from being a landless rabble, they could conduct their affairs with a proper regard for the rights and dignity of all other citizens. Whether they sided with Tanner or against him, it made no difference. Anyone with a complaint against anyone in the camp, from Tanner on down, could come to the Oak of Reformation and be sure of obtaining a fair hearing, restitution where appropriate, and punishment of any wrongdoing. Well . . .' The man stood up and, still holding a microphone, moved towards the front of the platform, where he stood, legs apart. 'Today, as in so much else, we are following in Loy Tanner's footsteps. Not making a thing about it, not out to play phoney historical games, but because, if this demonstration of ours is to mean anything, it has to be above reproach. Joe!' He called down to a little group waiting at the foot of the stairs. 'Fetch 'em up!'

'Impertinence!' muttered the Superintendent who, together with Jurnet and Ellers, had found a point of vantage near the Oak, where the lower branches offered a modicum of shade; but he did not move, did not protest that it was not for mere mortals to take the law into their own hands: waited and watched as Joe, a young man in a pair of frayed shorts and trainers and possessed of a joyous sense of his own importance, ushered three people on to the platform.

One, middle-aged and uncomfortable in a blue suit too tight for him, was obviously the complainant, the other two the accused.

Charlie Appleyard resumed his seat as a signal that the court was in session.

'This won't take long,' the young man called Joe asserted confidently. 'The accused both plead guilty and admit everything. This is Mr Bardon, the landlord of the Duke's Head down the road.'

'How do you do, Mr Bardon.' Charlie Appleyard and the perspiring complainant shook hands, causing Jurnet to repress a smile – a judge in court hobnobbing with the plaintiff! A sideways glance confirmed that the Superintendent, for all his official outrage, was also not lost to the humour of the situation. 'I'm sorry I haven't a seat to offer you, and I'm even sorrier we haven't any money to pay you for the damage done. As a matter of interest, how much was it exactly?'

'Don't reckon there'll be much change out of a couple of hundred.' Mr Bardon ran a plump finger round the inside of his shirt collar. 'But tha's all right, you don't have to worry yourselves. What I come up here to say, as a matter of fact, is, after it were all over, the chaps in the bar had a whip-round. Said it were their fault they kep' on standing the buggers drinks when they could see they weren't up to it, neither of 'em. Bit of a lark, they didn't mean no harm. If I hadn't been up to my eyes, barmaid off with

45

the Lord knows what, I'd have seen the lie of the land meself, nipped it in the bud before it came to anything.'

'That's very handsome of you, Mr Bardon, I must say, and a credit to your regulars, I'm sure. We do have some painters and carpenters among us who I know would be happy to help you get everything back to rights again.'

'No, ta very much,' the other returned hastily. 'We can manage. Only other thing I wanted to say – in the circs, you'll understand if we don't want any more of your lot coming in.'

'They're already here on the understanding that yours and every other pub is out of bounds to them for the duration. I see I shall have to drive the message home. Leave it to me, Mr Bardon, and thanks again for your co-operation.'

When the publican had gone, thankfully loosening his tie and the top button of his shirt as he went down the stairs, Charlie Appleyard turned for the first time to look at the two offenders. One was little more than a boy, butter-coloured hair above a baby face reddened by sun and crying.

'What's your name?'

'Pete Gilbert.' The boy's eyes filled with fresh tears. 'And I'm very sorry.'

'No need to ask mine,' his companion put in harshly, without waiting to be spoken to. He was several years the elder of the two, dark and scrawny. 'And like the man said, it wasn't our fault, looked at realistically. We're neither of us beer drinkers and that Angleby muck, it takes the roof off your head.'

'Nobody forced you to drink it. To say nothing of the fact that you had no business going into the pub in the first place.'

'It was the heat. Only had enough for a Coke, anyway. Only accepted the beer because it was so bloody hot and there was nothing left to drink up here and the water out of that standpipe tastes of sewage. Knew they were having their bit of fun because we're gay, but what the hell.' By now the boy called Pete Gilbert was bawling openly. The other favoured Appleyard with a glare of anger. 'Now look what you've done. If you've finished with this bloody charade . . .' The man put his arms round the boy and kissed him on the lips. 'It's OK, lovey. All over.'

'Not quite,' Charlie Appleyard contradicted mildly. 'You broke the rules, Danny, and you must take the consequences. Pick up your things and get moving. Joe'll see you down to the bus station and put you on a bus for London. Much as I hate to dip into our meagre pot of gold on your behalf it'll be worth the price of a ticket to get rid of a trouble-maker. Can't think why you decided to favour us with your presence in the first place.' To the boy, still sniffling, Appleyard spoke with an exasperated kindness. 'Put a sock in it, laddie, for Christ's sake. I don't mean you. You're young, you were influenced by someone who should have known better than lead you astray. All I want is your word that nothing like it will happen again.'

'What are you on about?' The other barged in again. 'We're an item! If I go – and personally I can't wait – we go together. Just because we're gay – or rather, just because I'm proud to admit it, unlike some I could mention – you think you can treat us like dirt, playing the great I-am, Messiah in Levis, the way you always do, always have, always know better than anyone else – ' He broke off abruptly, his voice changed to tenderness: 'Come on, Pete. We're going back to town. You'll like that, won't you? All the Coke you can drink. All the old, familiar places . . .'

The boy ran the back of his hand across his nostrils, took a deep breath: hung his head and looked through lashes long and curling as a child's, from his lover to Appleyard and back again.

'Come on, love . . .'

'He said I didn't have to go.' Pete Gilbert lifted up his head and in a voice trembling between fear and exultation declared: 'I want to stay, Danny.'

'We can't, love. You heard what His Lordship said. He's giving us the order of the boot.'

'Not me, Danny.' The boy's voice had steadied. He looked towards Appleyard, seeming to find in that unremarkable figure a source of strength. 'Only you.'

'You don't mean it!' The thin face had gone pale, the eyes wild. 'You're upset. You don't know what you're saying!'

'I do mean it. I'm sorry . . .'

7

The serving of the midday meal was proceeding smoothly, an orderly crowd filing past the trestles where the volunteer workers doled out a largesse of sandwiches, baked beans, bananas and 7-Up. The Superintendent, albeit reluctantly, was impressed.

'Can't cope with the whole shoot at one go,' explained Buck, the cheerful giant Charlie Appleyard had deputed to be their guide. 'And anyway, so far at any rate, there in't enough grub come in to go round two meals a day for everyone, so it's turn and turn about. Them with green tickets eat now, them with red have to wait till suppertime.'

'Anyone object?'

'They better not,' replied the giant, grinning ferociously to reveal a mouthful of broken teeth. 'Jes' kidding,' he added immediately.

'A band of brothers in fact, eh?'

'Christ, never that! Me and my brothers we never stop ragging. Natural in a family.'

'Mates, then?'

'Not that either. Mates are guys you run into at the Job Centre, meet over a pint in the pub. Have a natter, share a laugh, then so long, bob's yer uncle.' The man's expression changed to one of a great and contented earnestness. 'Here, even if nothing comes of this, we'll have something to take away we'll never forget as long as we live. We've learned what it is to be friends.'

'Your Mr Appleyard wasn't all that friendly to that Danny chap he's just sent packing.'

'Oh him – Danny Saunders! Just because he knew Charlie from back when, thinks he can get away with murder. Have to have discipline.' The man spat. 'That poofter!'

Jurnet was looking in vain for a glimpse of Julian Grant. The women workers all wore what looked like white shower caps into which their hair was tucked, presumably for purposes of hygiene, unless whoever was in charge of the catering had ordered the fantastically unbecoming headgear in the hope of discouraging lascivious thoughts in the ten thousand males forgathered on the Moot without women. It certainly discouraged Jurnet, who discovered that he could not even remember what the girl's face looked like except that it had held no attraction for him. He felt more discouraged than ever to find himself yearning kinkily over nothing more than a hank of hair.

Ellers came up to him munching a doughnut.

'Don't tell Rosie,' he admonished. 'She'll kill me. Only what was I to do?' He nodded towards the trestles. 'I said I was just looking, I hadn't a ticket, red or green, and she took pity on me. I couldn't say no.' Catching an ooze of jam in the nick of time: 'Somebody was saying the Secretary of Trade and Industry's due to give a pep talk from the Oak this afternoon. What you think? He's going to offer the lot a job?'

'Shouldn't think so. There's no election coming up.'

'Politicians!' The Superintendent, who had rejoined his subordinates, directed a stare of exasperation and accusation at the crowded Moot, the brassy sky. 'I'd better have another word with Appleyard. He's got enough sense to see it's in nobody's interest to get these men all worked up.' He looked resentfully towards the Oak, where Appleyard could be glimpsed munching on a sandwich and exchanging banter with his comrades nearest to hand. The sight apparently induced in the Superintendent a humility which surprised himself as much as his listeners.

'What on earth is it about the chap?' he mused aloud. 'Nothing much to look at. Not much of an orator. So *ordinary* you'd find it hard to put a name to him if you chanced upon him in the street. A mystery – ' he finished with a straightening of the beautifully tailored shoulders, a reversion to the omniscient bastard Jurnet hated and loved – 'a mystery we have to deflate before the fellow gets himself blown up into a myth, with all the dangers that implies.'

'Loy Tanner wasn't a myth, sir,' Jurnet felt impelled to object. 'He was a hero.'

'Hero! No such animal! A title we give to an irresponsible sub-species which, out of either stupidity or vanity, completely lacks that in-built self-protection which keeps the rest of us from falling flat on our faces.'

The Superintendent transferred his gaze to his underlings.

'What do we know of Loy Tanner's motivation, eh? Not a damn thing! Only that he led more than three thousand ignorant men to a totally unnecessary death.' With a gesture which encompassed the ten thousand encamped on the Moot: 'Four hundred and fifty years later, even one death would be one too many!'

Jurnet drove home. After another day of a leaden sun that, fagged out with its own heat, it seemed, slithered slowly down the sky, he was more than ready for the quiet of his flat above the delicatessen where his peace was undisturbed so long as he was careful not to look out of the window giving on to the blackened ruin across the road, the block of flats where he had lived with Miriam, the forecourt where his love and his happiness had gone up in smoke. And even in this regard, after nine months, he was getting better at schooling himself to look in that direction without being unmanned afresh by shock and sorrow.

49

Home! It was the first time, it suddenly dawned on him as he manœuvred the Rover through the narrow entrance into the yard at the side of the shop, he had given that name to Johnny Valenti's pad, proffered by his father Mario as first a temporary and then a permanent haven once Johnny had made clear his intention of settling permanently in the US. Suddenly, the heavy, Continental furniture, the swagged curtains and frilled bed-linen installed by Maria, Johnny's loving mother, had become part of a world uniquely special to him, to him alone. Even the Christ on the crucifix over the bed, with its hanging head and unseeing eyes, had ceased to be a mockery with its impertinent suggestion that there was at least one other whose suffering had surpassed his own: had become a companion in distress.

Jurnet locked up the Rover with a wry smile at the thought of what Rabbi Schnellman would have to say to that. Although, with Miriam dead, there was no longer any need to continue with his conversion to Judaism, a condition she had laid down if she were ever to marry him, he had continued his periods of study with the Rabbi – why, he could hardly have said.

Because it was something Miriam had wanted? Because the Rabbi no longer needed to remind him there was more to Judaism than a pretty face? Because a God who could wipe out Miriam just like that was a power it was only good sense to keep on the right side of? Whichever it was, the Rabbi said he was making progress.

Jurnet pulled off his tie, rolled it up and put it in his pocket; unbuttoned his shirt, passed his tongue over his dry lips. Savoured in advance the *citron pressé* Mario, downstairs in the shop, had got into the habit of having ready for him.

What a day! The Secretary of State for Trade and Industry – surprise, surprise – had turned out to be a right shit, oozing charm like perspiration as he explained with a stomach-churning sincerity how the two million plus unemployed were victims, not of the government but of the trade cycle, a soulless machine which, to hear him speak, orbited the universe on a trajectory as immutable as that of the planets. From which it followed that the ten thousand should all go home like good fellows and trust in him, he wouldn't let them down.

Someone had offered the exalted visitor another of Julian Grant's doughnuts which he had accepted gracefully and bitten into, only to have a stream of jam emerge jet-like from the further end on to his silk shirt and snazzy linen pants. How charmingly, after only a moment's hesitation, had he joined in the general laughter, the shit.

In the delicatessen there was no *citron pressé*, only Mario and Pnina Benvista making sandwiches.

True, at the sight of the detective, the delicatessen owner had exclaimed in welcome, wiped his hands, gone to the fridge and got out a Coke, apologetically, but it was not the same thing. As for Pnina Benvista, the Israeli girl, Miriam's protégée, who had taken over the running of her knitwear business, she was too busy even to acknowledge Jurnet's arrival, and that was not the same thing either. Agreed, the brightening of the dark eyes, the lighting up of the whole countenance with which the girl habitually greeted him were more a source of guilt and occasional irritation to Jurnet than a pleasure, something he could do without – except that, deprived of such an unsought advertisement of love, it too, like the *citron pressé*, had become something to be missed.

The girl's olive skin looked cool, her straight black hair uncomplicated. The memory of Julian Grant's waves of tumbling bronze came flooding back unbidden, increasing Jurnet's dissatisfaction.

'That makes two hundred and twenty,' the Israeli girl announced triumphantly, pressing down the last slice of bread on a filling of sausage and tomato, and wrapping the finished sandwich in film. 'Twenty more than you promised.'

'They will get eaten. I will tell the lady tomorrow when she comes to collect.' The delicatessen owner stacked the sandwiches in the fridge, brought out another Coke which he handed to the girl. 'Now it is time for you to sit down and have a rest.' To Jurnet: 'You have been to see the men up on the heath?'

Jurnet nodded unwillingly. He was feeling up to there with the men on the heath. As for Pnina Benvista, she could keep her looks to herself, for all he cared.

He put down the Coke, half-drunk.

'I'm going to have a shower.'

The Israeli girl looked at him. Asked: 'What is it like up there? We saw it on TV but it is not the same. What is it really like?'

'Damn hot, if you want to know. Smelly – there aren't enough bogs. A damn-fool carry-on that can have dangerous consequences if it gets out of hand. Does that answer your question?'

The girl shook her head, smiling but serious. 'It is noble,' she said. 'You are tired, you cannot take a detached view.' Her face had changed, the purple shadows under her eyes faded, the high cheekbones less prominent. It was the face of love.

51

Too late.

She said to him quietly, so that Mario could not hear: 'I have sent Mrs Levine to London to look at some new machines. She will not be back until tomorrow.' Mrs Levine, one of the workers at the Courland Connection, was Pnina Benvista's landlady. When Jurnet made no comment, she added, hesitantly: 'If you wish it, I could stay all night.'

Jurnet looked at the girl's hair, straight and black and strong, and thought of Miriam, red and gold. Thought of Julian Grant and shook his head.

'I'm all in . . .'

'That is quite all right.' Colour, strong and red, flared briefly in the olive cheeks and as quickly subsided. 'I just thought . . .'

'Sorry.'

Even as the word left his lips he wished it unsaid. The memory of Julian Grant's hair had started a familiar process in his loins. Hating himself, he glanced down at the loving face upturned to his and made a correction.

'No. Please stay.'

Until the telephone woke him up he had thought himself already awake; unable to sleep, tossing hot and guilty next to the girl sleeping peacefully beside him, steeped in the innocence of love.

For Christ's sake, what was happening to him? The girl was a cripple, he reminded himself angrily. All the more reason to use her – if use her he must – without guile or specious excuses. Her permanently dislocated hip had proved no impediment to her passion, that was something, he supposed: whilst, as to himself, even in the transports of orgasm he still had the honesty – if you could call it that – to recognize their coming together for what, so far as he was concerned, it was – a coupling strictly for therapeutic purposes, not a fantasy that it was Julian Grant who had opened her legs to him.

Above the sheet pushed aside in the airless night, Pnina Benvista's pointed breasts were beautiful, whereas Julian Grant was flat as a boy . . .

The voice at the other end of the telephone woke him up to let him know Charlie Appleyard was dead.

'Bergate?' he had mumbled, finding it hard to take in the message being relayed to him from Police Headquarters. 'What's he doing in Bergate?'

As if he didn't know. Same thing as he, Jurnet, had been doing gratis in the flat over the deli, under the incurious eyes of the suffering Christ on the wall.

How pig-stupid he had been, that Devil who had tempted Jesus in the wilderness, offering Him power and a full stomach instead of unlimited sex, something that would have settled the question of the guy's humanity once and for all.

No doubt about Charlie Appleyard's humanity.

Pulling on jeans and shirt, stuffing his feet into trainers, the detective reflected on the way that high principles never seemed to apply below the waist, a no-go area when it came to gracious living. March ten thousand men up the hill to Monkenheath – great idea, great dedication to the cause of the poor and oppressed – and all for nothing on account of that bloody itch in the balls.

Leaving the girl still sleeping, Jurnet hurried down the stairs, out to the yard and into the Rover; drove to Bergate, the nearest Angleby possessed to a red light district. Four and a half centuries ago Loy Tanner had left a wife at home in Windham; but then he had been fifty-seven, the fever in the blood cooled, not a young man like Appleyard.

Nevertheless, whilst recognizing the absurdity of this post-mortem stricture, especially in view of the way he himself had elected to pass his evening, the detective felt obscurely let down. Heroes had a duty to stay heroic, not to go fucking around like lesser mortals. What was going to happen to those ten thousand men still slumbering peacefully on the Moot who had put their trust in Charlie Appleyard? More to his particular point, how was the Angleby police force going to get them, their high hopes gone, down from the heath and out of the city without trouble?

For all that he worried over these matters as he drove, Jurnet did not worry overmuch. He was never one for generalities. What stirred him to the depths, made him angry as always in the presence of violent death, was that a man – that solitary man who, in his book, at such a time, stood for the whole human race – had been violated, put beyond help and beyond justice.

Without much hope he reminded himself that the message from Headquarters, or else his muddled understanding of it, had been maddeningly inexplicit. What exactly had happened, and how? He needed to have some answers. For all he knew to the contrary, the bugger could have had a heart attack in the middle of a bonk.

In which case, serve him right.

8

Bergate, under the street lights and the last of the night, had undergone its usual nocturnal transformation. A street of elegant Georgian houses which, by the end of the nineteenth century, had become the warrens of the Italian immigrant poor, it had been turned by later visitations courtesy of the Luftwaffe and the Planning Committee into a thoroughfare above all others where Angleby citizens went to shop for a car.

In daylight, that is. By night, goodies of a different kind were for sale.

Somehow, randomly, between the acres of plate glass housing the Mercs and the BMWs and the lesser fry, a number of the old houses of Bergate, battered by war and time, had survived against all the odds to reach that haven of civic caring, listed as historic buildings to be preserved henceforth as a precious part of the English heritage.

Not the only thing about Bergate that was listed, Jurnet thought wryly, as he turned the Rover into the street, making for the bright cluster of police vehicles he could see ahead, half-way down its length. The police had their own little list of the tenants of the old houses, most of them occupying no more than a room apiece. Had the do-gooders of the city, so nobly active in the rescue of Georgian Bergate, really been so naïvely unaware their untiring efforts had saved Angleby's very own red light district from extinction?

Perhaps they knew what they were doing, the buggers.

His colleagues, the birds of prey – as, in occasional moments of revulsion against a situation in which, all said and done, he had chosen of his own free will to put himself, Jurnet had designated them – were already there, gathered round the carrion, their faces, carefully impassive, not quite concealing an inner excitement. Only the Superintendent, who took violent death on his patch as an insult directed at him personally, was going about with a face like thunder: moving, too, with a certain stiffness of the joints as

54

if the onset of rigor mortis in the corpse was replicated in his own skeleton.

'Ah – there you are!' He greeted Jurnet with no friendliness in his voice. 'No doubt *you* can tell us what on earth we're to do about this?'

'This' was the body sprawled face up on the steps leading down to a basement flat, an entry its tenant had obviously made some effort to prettify with pots of geraniums on the treads and a couple of ornamental baskets dripping fuchsias and petunias hanging from the whitened walls. One of the pots had been broken, apparently by the man's fall, showering the dead face with soil and shards of terracotta, and decorating his upper torso with flowers of a red brighter than the red of the lines of congealed blood that led from nostrils to chin, fastidiously circumventing the engorged tongue that lolled from the gaping mouth.

There was no doubting the instrument of death, only its propriety. The heavy copper cross which Jurnet had noticed round the man's neck on the Moot was banged tight against the carotid, its chain embedded deep in the flesh. Without it, Jurnet would have found it hard to recognize Charlie Appleyard, spiritual heir to Loy Tanner, failed hero, failed everything.

'What does Dr Colton say?'

The Superintendent frowned, his world full of enemies.

'You know as much as I do. He's down in the flat. The woman who lives there has been having hysterics.'

Before he had finished speaking, Jack Ellers came out of the basement door; edged a careful way up the steps, keeping clear of the scene-of-crime team still busy taking measurements.

Acknowledging Jurnet's arrival with a discreet nod, the little Welshman took care to concentrate his attention on the Superintendent.

'He's managed to calm her down, sir. Far as I can make out, she returned to the flat from what I suppose you'd call a business appointment and found him lying on the steps. The woman who lives on the ground floor heard her screaming her head off and thought she'd landed a bloke who was doing her in. She's the one phoned the police.'

'Is she in a state to be spoken to?'

'I'd have said more or less composed. Dr Colton wanted to call an ambulance, but she wasn't having any. She wouldn't take anything, either. I'd say, not the kind normally to go off the handle.'

'Mm. What about the body? Did Dr Colton say it's all right to move it?' Without waiting for a reply, the Superintendent ordered: 'Go back and tell the doctor I need to have a word. Stay with the woman until I'm sure what the position is.' To Jurnet: 'You'd better go down there, too. There's a WPC on the way. You don't have to say anything. Just sit quietly and think about how we're going to get ten thousand bereaved men out of Angleby without all hell breaking loose.'

Any other time, the living-room of the flat could have made you laugh, or at least smile nostalgically, so exactly did it embody adolescent fantasies of what a tart's bower ought to look like: red satin drapes and swags, tumescent upholstery, dolls and cushions and gilt-framed mirrors awash in a special kind of air that, interlaced with talcum powder and the scent of violets, did not quite mask a substratum of antiseptic.

In piquant contrast to her surroundings, the girl who sat hunched on the sofa, hugging her body as if she feared for its safekeeping, looked frail and virginal, her sleeveless shift, patterned with small flowers, well down over her knees, her straight brown hair held back from her face by a velvet band of the same deep blue as the background colour of the dress material.

The face itself looked childlike and unused, made even younger by the lipstick and mascara smeared over her tearstained cheeks. Jurnet could not see her eyes, which she held tightly closed, a child escaping reality. When at last, reluctantly, she opened them, it was no surprise that, the redness of tears notwithstanding, they were of a piece with the rest of her, a sparkling brown innocence, the whites dazzling.

Ellers, who, there before him, was standing on a bearskin rug with an arm round the neck of a ceramic giraffe, three-quarters life-size, effected the introduction: 'This is Miss Jody Nesselrode.'

Jurnet said: 'Hello, Jenny.'

At that the girl gave a little start and lifted her head. Her eyes narrowed in a certain speculation.

'Just a guess,' the detective answered her unspoken question. 'We haven't met before, either in the way of business or elsewhere. It *is* Miss Jenny Nunn, isn't it?'

The girl nodded, staring up at the handsome, Italianate face. 'If we *had* met, I'm sure I would have remembered.' Fresh tears

56

began to course down her cheeks. 'Charlie must have told you about me.'

'Charlie told me nothing, and now he isn't able to tell anyone anything any more. That's why you're the one will have to do it.'

'I don't know anything!' the girl cried, her voice high. With an effort she regained control of herself. 'I came back home and there he was, on the steps.'

'Came back from where?'

'From a job. One of my regulars.'

'Where was this job, then?'

'In his car, of course, like the rest of my punters.' Jenny Nunn raised her head and looked about her, at the furnishings of her room. 'All this stuff – might just as well have saved my money, but I wasn't to know, was I? All I wanted was to provide a pleasant ambience but instead, all they want is to pick me up and drive out to the heath or somewhere, and do it there, in the back of their cars.' Finishing with what seemed to her listeners an almost maternal indulgence: 'Sometimes I think, without their Mercs or Jags or whatever it is, they couldn't do it at all. But then, the customer's always right, that's what they say, isn't it?' With a swift modulation from mother to bereaved child: 'Not like Charlie, always wanting to know if you were comfortable.'

Jurnet asked smoothly: 'And what time did he turn up tonight?'

The girl stared, the tears drying up instanter.

'I told you! He was on the steps when I came back.'

'Could your punter have seen him when he dropped you back home?'

Jenny Nunn looked at the detective with something approaching pity.

'Dropped me back home! Whatever it is you do in the police, it can't be anything to do with Bergate. Nobody drops a Bergate girl back home. We all get picked up and dropped back round the corner, you could call it a local tradition. Top end of the Cattle Market, past where the girls that haven't got a guy fixed up beforehand wait for what comes along.' With a touching pride in her professional status she finished: 'With me, of course, it's strictly by appointment, and recommendation.'

'Phone, do they?'

The girl nodded, pleased with herself. 'You wouldn't catch me standing about on spec like those other riff-raff.'

'I'm glad of that. Because that way, you'll be able to put us on to the bloke you were out with tonight.'

'I can't do that!' The brown eyes widened with shock. 'I don't even know his name and if I did I wouldn't tell you. It wouldn't be ethical. You ought to know better than to ask.'

'Look,' Jurnet said reasonably, 'I don't want to pry into your business, or his. But if a customer phones he must give you some name, even if it's a false one. And if he's one of your regulars, as you say, you must surely, in all the times you've got in and out of his car, have noticed its number, if nothing else.'

'I haven't, as a matter of fact – but if I had it'd still be strictly confidential. My punters know they can trust me one hundred per cent. It's my goodwill, the reason I do so well. Anyway, I told you, he dropped me off at the Cattle Market, as usual. I got out of the car and he drove off, back towards the castle. He never even came into Bergate.'

'I accept that. Actually, it's not him I'm thinking about, it's you. You say you came back and found Charlie lying on the steps . . .'

'Yes.' A sudden sob wracked the slight form, followed, however, by a determined straightening of the shoulders.

'So you say. But how am I to know you ever went out, if you can't produce the fellow you say you were out with? How can I be sure you're not having me on, and that you're not mixed up with Charlie's murder here all the time? You see my difficulty.'

To Jurnet's surprise, instead of the vehement denial he expected, Jenny Nunn wrung her hands, hung down her head and whispered brokenly, 'You're right. I killed him.'

'Tell me.'

'You saw – how he died. The chain and the cross?'

'I saw.'

'The cross – I made it. Charlie said I ought to take up a hobby, he used to tease me for being too intellectual. Just because I was a whore with a first class degree in art history he said was no reason. He said I ought to learn to do something else with my hands besides –' The girl stopped abruptly, her face fiery, absurdly young. 'Anyway,' resuming, 'he brought round the prospectus from the night school and I picked out the metalworking course, chiefly, I have to say, because it was on Mondays, which is my slowest day of the week. But do you know – ' the beautiful eyes brightened with pleasure – 'it was brilliant. The cross was the first thing I made. It's a bit lopsided, but was I proud of it, and when Charlie saw it he said he loved it, so I bought a chain – I hadn't learned enough to make one myself – and gave it him for a present. Not that he was religious and ordinarily he'd

58

never have worn a cross, but he wore it all the time because I made it.' With a change of mood which seemed to surprise herself, she cried out wildly: 'I never meant it to be the death of him!'

'Am I right that you and Charlie knew each other at the university?'

'We were there at the same time.' Tearstained, Jenny Nunn looked scarcely old enough to make it to the local comprehensive. 'I got a First.'

'Good for you. I bet you did better than him.'

'He had so many other interests.' The girl came quickly to the dead man's defence. 'He could have done anything he wanted to.'

'Always the way, the best ones fall by the wayside,' Jurnet murmured placatingly. Then: 'I should have thought, covered with honours the way you were, you'd have gone on to something in the academic line, rather than – ' spreading out an arm in some embarrassment – 'this.'

'Oh, I did, for a while. The Courtauld offered me a job, but after a few months, I don't know . . .' The girl stopped, straightened her back and looked at the detective with a touching seriousness. 'It didn't seem right to be wasting my special gift.'

'What gift was that, then?' Jurnet asked, his voice and face carefully devoid of expression.

'It's like playing the piano,' Jenny Nunn explained. 'You either have it or you haven't. And I had it. I didn't see why I shouldn't do it for a living, just like Brendel, or Ashkenazi.'

'Play the piano?' echoed Jurnet, deliberately obtuse. 'You've lost me there.'

'Bonking,' the other returned, losing her patience a little. She tugged at her skirt, smoothing out the creases. 'I'm what they call a nymphomaniac, if you know what that is.'

Jurnet admitted: 'I've heard of them.'

'They make it sound like a disease.' Jenny Nunn frowned. 'I can't think why. Actually it's something wonderful. It means your body is a musical instrument, like a violin, a clarinet, a messenger of joy. It means every time – the hundredth, the thousandth time, no matter how many – it's a wonderful surprise, the first time all over again.'

Her lips pursed in a blend of contempt and pity: 'Sometimes I watch them kissing and all that on the films and on the telly – they haven't an idea! So of course – ' coming down to earth – 'it had to be only a matter of time before I realized that art history wasn't really my bag, not only because it didn't pay one quarter what I could earn on the game. I owed it to myself and to the men I could make happy to be what I was, true to myself. And so I set up here.'

'With Charlie's help? I suppose he wasn't your pimp, by any chance?'

'Of course not! You sound like something out of Queen Victoria. Today girls like me are serious professionals. We handle our own affairs, we don't need anyone to do it for us. It's only those scrubbers waiting under the street lights for somebody, anybody, to turn up, who let some bully-boy take over their lives.'

At that, Jack Ellers looked up from his notes and intervened mildly with: 'Iffy Jones.'

Her voice heavy with dislike, the girl returned: 'What about him?'

'When I was out on the beat I did a stint this end of town. From what I understood then, the only way a girl could get herself a pitch here in Bergate was through Iffy Jones. One way and another, he had the whole street in his pocket, though every time we hauled him in for questioning we could never make it stick. Slippy as an eel. As it was, a girl want a pad anywhere hereabouts, she had to ruddy put her name on a waiting list.'

'Not me!' Jenny Nunn flushed with pride and remembered triumph. 'Not once I knew the ropes, that is. I did go to him first off because it seemed the only way, and he did give me a room, a poky little hole you couldn't swing a cat in, *and* ants in the lav – and for that, would you believe it, he wanted fifty per cent of everything I made! Daylight robbery!'

Jurnet observed: 'Nice little place you've got here now. How'd you persuade Mr Jones to come up with something better?'

'Charlie,' was the loving reply. 'Charlie fixed it. He wasn't going to let me be exploited, if he could help it, and as it happened the lease of this house was running out and he found out that the ground landlords were the Church Commissioners. Well! Once he went to them and put them in the picture you can imagine! More than their reputation was worth! They wouldn't grant Iffy a new lease at any price.'

'But in that case . . .' Jurnet looked puzzled. 'I mean, the house is still being used for . . .'

'For immoral purposes?' Jenny Nunn laughed delightedly, her cheeks dimpling. She clapped her hands like a child. 'They're so busy being ecclesiastical, bless them. And besides, Charlie saw to it that the person who took over the new lease was so very respectable.'

'Who was he, then?'
'Mr Appleyard, of course. Charlie's father.'

9

Impossible to find out, then or later, who, up on the Moot, first put about the word that Charlie Appleyard had been done to death. Close questioning of everyone in the know at Police Headquarters, and of the attendants who had collected the corpse and brought it to the mortuary, had got nowhere. It could, of course, have been Louella, the girl on the ground floor who had phoned the police in the first place, or one of the other girls who rented rooms on the upper floors of the house in Bergate, but Jurnet did not think so. When asked outright by Jack Ellers if they had been the ones to spread the word they had stared at the little Welshman as if he were crazy. Murders were bad for business. They scared away the punters. Of course they hadn't said anything.

Jurnet, when it was all over, half wondered if there hadn't been something in the air which had let the cat out of the bag all by itself; murder a contagion which spread itself without the need of a human agent to send it on its way.

Later it transpired that Charlie Appleyard's absence from the Moot in the early morning light was not, of itself, enough to trigger off unease. Apparently it wasn't the first time he had slipped away in the dark, returning in time for breakfast without letting on where he had spent the night – as if one couldn't guess! Buck and Joe, his closest lieutenants, had smiled at each other knowingly, and smiled at Charlie Appleyard with love and understanding when, always, eventually, he put in an appearance, pooped and needing a shave. The man was their leader, above and beyond the rules laid down for everybody else on the Moot.

Perhaps it was the unrelenting heat which set things off, jangled tempers, raised doubts that had not before existed. Perhaps it was the late arrival of the tea-urns, or the way the ladies behind the trestles, no fault of their own, were handing out rolls from which the marge was already oozing on to their fingers.

Of the journalists and press photographers who, in the first heady days of the sit-down, had taken to camping out on the heath within earshot and camera range of the Oak of Reformation, only a token few remained. Yet perhaps one of that few, scenting the air with that infallible nose for a good story common to the species, had twitched the death of Charlie Appleyard out of the dawning day and returned it, amplified, for less sensitive organs to pick up in turn.

Whichever it was, by the time the Chief Constable, awakened from his slumbers and alerted by his underlings to the perils of the situation, had summoned up reinforcements to supplement the Angleby force in the task of getting the demonstrators on the Moot to disperse peacefully, it was too late.

Drifting off at first in twos and threes, then in larger and larger formations, the ten thousand men who had come together to honour the memory of Loy Tanner left their breakfasts and their ablutions, their early morning stretchings and belchings; spilled out on to the tarmac and, faster and faster, moved by some half-understood but compelling purpose, took off down the hill towards the river and the awakening city.

In the beginning, such policemen as remained on sentry-go let them pass willingly, glad to see the back of the buggers who had gone off leaving their knapsacks and ground sheets abandoned under the Oak Tree, the untidy sods, typical. Not until the untidy sods were pouring over the Bishop's Bridge as Loy Tanner's army had done four hundred and fifty years earlier did the penny drop and the forces of law and order come to attention.

Even then, so far as one could judge, the instructions which came over the personal radios of the men stationed in the four police cars drawn up at the entrance to the bridge seemed to order nothing but masterly inactivity. It might have been a marathon in aid of charity, the way the police officers on duty watched, smiling encouragement as the runners swept past, the way they signalled any passing car on to the footpath in order to leave the roadway clear for their passage.

It took a Jurnet, flaked out and leaning against the wall of the Control Room at Police Headquarters, to wonder that nobody on the ancient bridge seemed to be aware of those others running with Charlie Appleyard's men – the ghosts of those who, unable to force a passage by land, had, all those years ago, swum for it under a hail of arrows from the city bowmen; among them, according to the chronicles, vagabond boys who had come among the thickest of the arrows, gathering them up for reuse by their own men *'when some of the arrows stuck fast in their legs and other parts'*.

The long-dead boys had passed the salvaged shafts to their own archers, desperately short of ammunition and themselves exposed to the murderous shower from over the water. '*Some, having the arrows sticking fast in their bodies (a thing fearful to tell) drawing them out of their wounds just received, gave them as they were, dripping with blood, to those who were standing around, that they might again make use of them.*'

The detective sergeant manning the monitor looked up briefly to report: 'No sign of any weapons. That's something.' Only to be rebutted by the voice of somebody higher up: 'Ten thousand is a weapon all on its own. Lethal!'

The Chief Constable might have felt better had he been down on the ground to see the runners crossing the Cathedral Close, not moderating their pace yet keeping off the grass and the bedded begonias like model citizens who intended no harm. Churchmen who lived in the precinct came out of their lodgings and stood by benignly, if a little uncertainly, in the early sun. Only the cathedral pigeons, used to more decorous processing, flew up in high dudgeon to circle the cathedral steeple, half-way to heaven.

'They're in Shire Street now,' the detective sergeant volunteered. 'That'll be the test. All those shop windows.'

Jurnet, who could not think why (according to the Superintendent) the Chief had requested his presence, made a half-hearted attempt to leave the room. He had a murderer to find.

He levered himself upright, slumped back against the window frame. He had discovered that he didn't want to hear about Shire Street, about shop windows caving in, looting, wanton damage. It wasn't a fitting way to celebrate the death of a bloke for whom, if he had his deserts, the golden gates should be opening wide this minute, the trumpets sounding.

Now that, for better or worse, it was hopefully over, the sit-in on the Moot struck the detective as a gesture ridiculously sublime, a thumbing of the nose at the compromises men choose to live by for lack of the guts to do anything else. He couldn't be sure where Charlie Appleyard's men were heading though he could guess – which, he suspected, was more than they knew themselves. Maybe all they wanted was to share their grief with the city, maybe they wanted justice, revenge. Or just somebody to say sorry.

Maybe.

No prizes for what the Superintendent would be expecting. This time – to the accompaniment of the detective sergeant relaying the welcome news that Shire Street, so far at least, appeared to have suffered no damage of any kind – Jurnet achieved the vertical, only to be diverted by what was happening outside the window, down in the Market Place.

Out of Shire Street and into the Market came the runners, into that vast open space clinging to the side of the hill where, sweating in his armour in the heat of a summer's day equally sweltering, the Marquis of Northampton, awaiting Loy Tanner's expected onslaught, had deployed his Italian mercenaries. Come to think of it, thought Jurnet, the Italians, natives of a warmer clime, had probably welcomed the unaccustomed sun, the only ones who did as the rebels had rushed in to take the city.

If the heat affected Charlie Appleyard's men, they gave little sign of it other than the perspiration glistening on their faces, the damp patches darkening their T-shirts. The pace set by the first in line did not slacken. Uphill they pressed, dividing spontaneously as they made their way up the narrow aisles between the rows of stalls where, striped with coloured shadow from the awnings overhead, the market people were busy setting out their wares for the day's trade.

'Mind out!' they shouted, reddening with anger as the foremost of the runners surged towards them. Protective of their freshly erected pyramids of oranges, onions and cabbages, their protests turned to incredulous rage. 'What the fuck you think you're doing?'

It was Jurnet's conviction that Charlie Appleyard's mourners had instinctively come to the city seeking solace for their bereavement. Now, albeit imperfectly, his view of the Market Place impaired by the striped awnings, he watched as grief turned to uncontrollable anger, a transformation with which he was only too familiar. Miriam's violent death had aroused in him exactly similar feelings, a turbulence probably never to be damped down completely.

Who exactly triggered off the inevitable outcome – the market people or the men from the Moot – was never to be determined. Perhaps it was no single person's fault. Perhaps it was all down to those piles of fruit and veg, the vibration of feet pounding the alleyways enough to set the mountains of apples and oranges sliding to an untimely death on the cobblestones, a sight enough to send their owners round the bend.

Higher up the hill the police, drawn up in serried ranks outside the City Hall and the adjoining Police Headquarters, ready if necessary to advance on a broad front, were caught off-balance; though even so, once the order was given, they moved with gusto into the fray. But by then the invaders, hitherto unarmed, had found ammunition to hand. Everything from potatoes to Cromer crabs – claws flexed for attack – flew through the air, punnets of strawberries splatting against crisp uniforms and raised truncheons. A flower stall heeled over, spilling lilies and chrysanthemums, roses and carnations to be crushed underfoot, whilst the stallholder, a sweet little old lady who ruled the Market with a rod of iron, laid about her with a metal vase and an air of demure fulfilment.

Next to go was the chip stall, and that was dangerous, for the oil, though fortunately not yet brought to chipping point, was a slippery trap and no respecter of persons, on whichever side they fought. As more and more participants pressed into the Market Place, taking no account of the jam already there, the fire brigade arrived with its hoses, directing them with delicate precision and turning the alleyways into mountain streams, cooling to inflamed tempers and damaged bodies alike.

Slowly but surely, the rain of missiles dwindled to a drizzle, the young men responsible for the ruin of the Market surveying their handiwork in a dulled daze of astonishment, as if suddenly awakened from a deep slumber and surprised to find themselves where they were, doing whatever it would appear they had been doing. The madness abated, the police had no trouble making arrests, the only problem being how many it was physically practical to take into custody. All the nicks in the county were hardly room enough to provide for Charlie Appleyard's defeated army.

Having waited within doors, as was only right and proper, for the pandemonium to die down, the Chief Constable, looking bereft of more than his appendix and accompanied by the Lord Mayor in all the glory of his civic strip, appeared resplendent on the steps of City Hall. The Chief's accoutrements, silver, the Lord Mayor's gold chain, shone in the strengthening sun.

The sweet little old lady from the flower stall, cradling in her arms a sheaf of roses scraped off the cobblestones, trotted uphill until she came to that little group of the great and the good. Smilingly, they awaited her coming.

'For you, love,' she explained, with her sweet smile, thrusting the bouquet, thorns and all, into the Chief Constable's face. 'Thanks a million.'

Jurnet breathed the hot, dusty air with something approaching relief. Still no promise of rain but, whatever the weather, it was good to get away from Police Headquarters, and not just because the Superintendent, running true to form with a fresh corpse to cosset, was behaving even more insufferably than he usually did towards his subordinates during the opening stages of a murder investigation.

How he hated the man, Jurnet thought, unbuttoning another button of his short-sleeved shirt. How he loved the bastard.

More than the Superintendent had been getting the detective's back up. Just because the uniformed branch, decked out with a positively obscene agglomeration of bandages, plasters and eye patches, were promenading the corridors with the air of defenders of the faith against the pagan hordes was no reason for the pitying contempt directed towards the guys of the local CID, mere spectators of the bloody confrontation, unwilling to dirty their whiter-than-white shirts, their lily-white hands.

For Jurnet, for whom – since those first, far-off days of pounding the beat – Police Headquarters had been a home from home, his refuge from an imperfect world, the atmosphere of rejection had been particularly painful. Since Miriam's death he had cherished more than ever his membership of that band of brothers, men and women whose delicacy of compassion during that terrible time had, more than anything else, persuaded him it was worthwhile carrying on.

But now . . .!

Only Sergeant Jack Ellers, hurrying alongside and trying to lengthen his stride so as to keep up with his superior officer, kept his usual expression of rosy good humour.

'At least the Chief isn't making a song and dance about *his* scars.'

'It could have been serious. He could have lost an eye,' Jurnet returned with due seriousness but, despite himself, could not help laughing at the thought of the Chief Constable's face, criss-crossed with scratches. Cruel as it might be, and undoubtedly was, it was good to have something to laugh about, with the Market Place looking as if Genghis Khan had dropped in for tea, and Charlie Appleyard dead.

10

Charlie Appleyard dead.

In the event, Arthur Appleyard, the dead man's father, had taken the news without flinching. His actual words were: 'I was just fixing myself a cup of tea. Would you two gentlemen care for a cup?'

Jurnet did not hold it against him. The detective had played the messenger of bad news too often not to be aware of how varied could be the reaction to hearing that violent death had fastened its talons on a member of the family, wrenching its fabric apart, never to be the same again. In his experience, whatever the circumstances, people were never prepared. Sometimes, Jurnet thought, they ought to teach it in school, bereavement and how to make the most of it.

'We'll need you to come and make a formal identification,' he said gently.

'Can I have my tea first? It's important, in this heat, to guard against dehydration.'

'Take all the time you need. Detective Sergeant Ellers here will be glad to make it for you, if you feel like sitting down.'

'No, thank you.' The man examined Jurnet's sidekick with a frowning distrust before addressing him directly. 'I don't suppose for a moment that you understand about Lapsang Suchong.'

'Not a clue.' The little Welshman, taking no offence, had a go at lightening the atmosphere. 'But you wouldn't believe what I can do with a tea-bag.'

Arthur Appleyard's frown deepened further.

'This is no time for frivolity.'

'No, sir,' agreed Ellers, looking as crestfallen as he must once have looked in the classroom. 'Sorry, sir.'

Silver hair falling over a high forehead, in his baggy grey flannels and fawn cardigan the man, thought Jurnet, looked exactly what he was, a typical retired schoolmaster of the old school, one readier to reprimand than praise. It would take a doling out of fifty lines to bring a smile to that frosty face, and half a dozen of the best across the buttocks to make his day. Tall and thin – even with bent shoulders he was taller than his son. The two seemed cut from a different pattern.

As if to confirm the other's thought, Arthur Appleyard said: 'Like his mother. Always going off at half-cock.' He added: 'I don't think I'll have the tea after all. I'll wait until I get back.'

'Whatever you say, sir.' After a moment's pause: 'You mentioned Mrs Appleyard . . .'

'I'll get my jacket.' Half-way to the stairs which led directly up from the small living-room: 'Dead,' the man said angrily, with a look worth a hundred lines at the very least. 'Died when Charles was eleven. Marching, demonstrating – if it wasn't one cause it was another . . .'

A typical retired schoolmaster of the old school, thought Jurnet, not believing a word of it; any more than he, Ben Jurnet, was your typical Detective Inspector, bright as a button and well on his way up the ladder of promotion instead of a broken man, an empty vessel destroyed by the death of Miriam. Masks. Bloody masks the lot of us, he reflected without surprise or even disappointment, watching as Arthur Appleyard returned down the stairs, tricked out by Props, despite the heat, in an ancient tweed jacket with leather patches at the elbows.

The world was a masquerade.

Except that retired schoolmasters did not ordinarily own property in Bergate.

'Yes. That is my son Charles.'

Astonishingly, Appleyard identified the corpse on the morgue table without an instant's hesitation. Astonishingly because – broken-nosed, the tongue stuffed back into the mouth without art – the corpse could have been almost any young man come to a bad end. Even Jurnet, who had been among the first to be introduced to Charlie Appleyard freshly dead, might well have hesitated to name him first go off, just like that.

Second go off was another matter.

At second go off, Charlie Appleyard, laid out on the slab ready for the post-mortem, remained unchanged in any important particular from the man Jurnet remembered on the Moot and on the telly. By some alchemy, despite the facial injuries, the blazing honesty was there inviolate, the humour of the face unimpaired by death, the ultimate punch line. Only it took a little while to recognize this, to sift the truth from the inconsequential, and Arthur Appleyard had done it right away.

Maybe it was something to do with being a father.

The detective looked at the retired schoolmaster with more warmth than he had previously felt for the man; a warmth that persisted even when the latter, in a rebuking, classroom voice, complained: 'He looks awful.' The sheet leaving nothing but the head visible: 'Strangled, was he?'

Jurnet nodded. 'The killer tightened that chain he wore round his neck. The one with the cross.'

'Foolish affectation. I said to him, "What are you wearing that for? You haven't believed in God since you were out of nappies." ' Leaning forward so that his shadow came between his son and the mortuary light, he said again: 'He looks awful.'

Colton, always given to cherishing his cadavers with a tender ferocity, sprang to the defence.

'Not to worry about the face. All done after death. He didn't feel a thing. Whoever did it must have tipped him over the railings and he somersaulted down the steps.'

'What steps? What railings?'

'We'll talk about it later.' Jurnet ushered the man from the room, the white tiles, the smell of formaldehyde, taking him by the arm and feeling its boniness through the Harris tweed. Compassion once again getting the upper hand: 'Over that Lapsang Suchong, if you still feel like making a cup. If you'd just wait outside a minute with Sergeant Ellers . . .'

After he had gone, safely out of earshot and stiff and dry as ever, Jurnet turned to the police surgeon.

'Anything special I ought to know?'

'Give me a chance, man! I've hardly begun.' Colton, a man who always hated to commit himself except in writing – top and three copies each on differently coloured paper – closed up like a hedgehog, only the prickles showing. 'You'll be getting my report, all in good time.'

'And well worth waiting for.' Awarding himself a bad mark for calling it to his aid, Jurnet deployed some of the charm which he knew from experience often brought results, from men as well as women. 'All I need to know at the moment is whether there's likely to be anything turning up in addition to the obvious.'

'Isn't the obvious enough for you, for God's sake? My guess', Colton admitted, responding as Jurnet had hoped he would, 'is it'll all turn out straight and above board. That chain – that cross against the carotid – what on earth impels people to go around advertising their religion as if it were the logo of a football team is beyond me.'

Jurnet persisted: 'You're sure there's nothing else you can tell me to be going on with?'

'Wait for my report! How many times do I have to say it?'

The tea tasted like cat's piss – high class cat's piss, from a Persian cat or a Siamese, but still piss.

Jurnet put down his cup and said gratefully: 'That's what I call a cup of tea.'

'I always say, once you've tasted the real thing, it spoils you for any other.'

Mr Appleyard looked almost cheerful. Some of the grey had gone out of his face. 'There's still some in the pot if you'd care for another.'

Jurnet put a hasty hand over his cup, guarding its hard-won emptiness.

'One's fine for me, thanks. Though – ' with a nod to where the little Welshman sat, manfully miming enjoyment – 'I'm sure Sergeant Ellers would appreciate a second.' Relenting: 'Later perhaps. We ought to get on. You'll be wanting to hear the details relating to your son's death. There'll be questions we'll have to ask you, and questions you'll be wanting to ask us . . .'

'I don't think I want to ask anything, thank you,' the retired schoolteacher returned with a fretful air. 'As you say, Charles is dead. Murdered, I suppose you mean.' The other nodded. 'Well, then. Nothing I can do about it, so what's the use of mulling it over and over and getting all upset?' Nobody, thought Jurnet, scanning the dried-up visage for signs of emotion, could have looked less upset than Arthur Appleyard. 'I'm sure I can safely leave it for the police to deal with.'

'Not as simple as that, sir, I'm afraid. The police, as I'm sure you'll understand if you think about it, can't operate in a vacuum. If we're to have any chance of nailing the person, or persons, who killed your son, we need all the help we can get from any quarter – all the information we can gather from any and everyone who knew him.'

Making an abrupt noise that might just be construed as a laugh: 'Then you can count me out for a start,' Arthur Appleyard interrupted. 'I'm the last one to ask. Never saw him more than once a year, if that, unless he wanted a favour, or had run short of money.' Appearing for the first time racked with a depth of feeling, the rounded shoulders braced, the narrow chest heaving, the man said: 'I've never been a hypocrite, Mr Jannet – '

'Jurnet.'

'Mr Jurnet. And I don't intend to start now. Naturally, as a law-abiding citizen I'm against anything that breaks the Queen's peace, but if you want to know the truth, I never much cared for the boy, even as a child. Oh, I always did my duty, but we were never on the same wavelength – one of those things, nothing to be done about it. Mother's boy, always running to his mummy. She'd been engaged, broke it off just before we met, and Charles was born seven months after we married, two months premature, so they said, but naturally I've always wondered . . .'

'The past,' said Jurnet unforgivingly. 'I'm sure we're all haunted by the past, what might or might not have been. To get back to the present – I have to tell you that your son was found on the steps leading down to a basement flat in Bergate – number 37 actually. Although we have reason to believe that Charlie was actually killed elsewhere and his body transported to where it was eventually found, I was hoping you could tell me something about number 37 Bergate.'

'Queer kind of street, that.' Arthur Appleyard appeared only mildly concerned by the turn the conversation had taken. 'All those car showrooms, and those run-down houses which were once rather grand. Interesting historically. Used to be quite an aristocratic neighbourhood two hundred years ago.'

'It's certainly come down in the world since then. Now it's the nearest Angleby has to a red light district.'

'I suppose, as a policeman, you'd know all about that. Not my scene, as they say now: though once, I remember, when I was still teaching, I arranged to take a school party there – history was my subject and we were doing a project on local architecture – only the Head made me call it off, the old fool. A mathematician, what could you expect? No feeling for the real world. Even when I pointed out that the children were far likelier to be corrupted by the sight of those gleaming Mercedes than by running into a prostitute or two, who'd all be asleep in daytime anyway, and I'd make sure we were safely back before dark, he still said no.'

'Mr Appleyard,' said Jurnet, beginning to lose patience, 'do you know a young woman called Jenny Nunn?'

The man, unfussed, pondered a moment.

71

'Not to say "know". She was at college with Charles. He brought her round here a couple of times. Last time it happened I was out and I came back to find them coming down the stairs from his bedroom. That's how it is with the young nowadays – no regard for the fitness of things. Naturally I told them both that if they chose to behave like rutting farm animals that was their business, so long as they didn't do it under my roof.'

'Is that why you let Jenny her flat at 37 Bergate?'

'A purely commercial transaction. She was looking for accommodation at the time and, as it happened, I had a flat for which I was seeking a tenant.'

'In Bergate?'

'Since when is it a crime to put your money in property? When I retired I had my pension, I had my savings. I wanted to invest them against my old age.'

'In Bergate?' Jurnet persisted.

'Why not in Bergate? Is it plague-stricken, abandon hope all ye who enter there? The house was for sale. It was going cheap. It was in poor condition but I could see that, put into repair and converted into flatlets, it had possibilities.'

'I'm sure you did, and that it had – distinct possibilities. You do know, Mr Appleyard, that it is an offence to use a house for purposes of prostitution?'

'Just because it's Bergate!' The retired schoolmaster's face darkened with annoyance. 'You might just as well go for all those car salesmen. Who knows, seeing it's Bergate, they aren't including a prostitute along with the air bags and all the other optional extras? All I can say is that the young women who are currently occupying the flats at number 37 supplied me with impeccable references.'

'Including Jenny Nunn who is a self-confessed nymphomaniac?'

Arthur Appleyard said stiffly: 'Miss Nunn's sexual proclivities – any more than those of any other tenant in the house – are no business of mine. She has certainly never imparted them to me. In these days especially, what they do with their spare time is their own affair. And anyway, what has this to do with the death of Charles?'

'I'm trying to find out why they chose to dump his body at number 37 Bergate rather than in any other basement in the city.'

'There we go again – they! Why not come out with it outright and ask if I did it?'

'If you had, 37 Bergate would surely have been the last place you'd have chosen to dispose of the body.'

The retired schoolmaster looked at the detective, eyes narrowed. 'Unless I was very, very clever.'

'Oh, you're that all right,' returned Jurnet in all sincerity, and was about to say more when brought up abruptly by what was happening to Arthur Appleyard's face.

It fell in, imploded, its severe framework collapsed, the lips ruched as if, behind that ruined façade, the teeth had suddenly disappeared into the gums. Two teardrops, produced with effort, squeezed themselves out of the corners of the tightly shut eyes. Into Jurnet's mind came a remembrance from childhood Sunday School: '*O my son Absalom! O Absalom, my son, my son!*'

'He shut me out,' the man wailed in an agony of loss. 'He and his mother, the two of them – they shut me out!'

11

Back at Headquarters the Superintendent had taken up his favourite position, back to his waiting underlings, looking out of his office window.

For once, it wasn't difficult to break the code of that unmoving head, expensively barbered, the strong neck, the shoulders tense under impeccable worsted. Despair, emptiness. Jurnet, entering into its unusual silence, crossed the room to stand beside the man he loved and hated with equal fervour. The least he could do was not insult him with his pity.

His gaze unshifting, the Superintendent said in a voice as brittle as glass: 'The night Warwick waited for Loy Tanner to invade the city he had his men keep darkness at bay with huge bonfires, so as not to be surprised by a sudden attack. How they must have roasted through the hot summer night!' Turning to face his subordinate for the first time, he demanded: 'And where do you suppose they got the wood to keep the fires going?'

Jurnet thought for a moment, then ventured: 'It was a market then, wasn't it, sir, the same as today? I suppose they broke up the stalls, just like now.'

'Just like now.' Bleak-eyed, the Superintendent turned back to the ruin spread out below him. Vanished the happy commerce of the Market Place, of whose noise he habitually complained with the affectionate exasperation of a parent shouting to his children to turn it down, for Christ's sake. The sound track of voices and laughter, cassettes and CDs; twitter of budgerigars, yelp of puppies, the music-hall patter of stallholders extolling their wares to a sceptical audience – all wiped out, no rewind. Not a stall was left standing, the striped awnings lying in tatters among a mess of vegetables, smashed china and saris.

No one as yet, it seemed, had had the heart to begin cleaning up. Pages ripped from soft-porn magazines flapped in a flick of breeze that moved the hot air at ground level only. Only, among the debris, the city pigeons moved with superb nonchalance, as if the banquet spread out beneath their strutting feet was no more than an overdue repeat of that earlier blow-out. 'Four hundred and fifty years, and we're back where we started!'

Back in his chair at his desk, his own importation, none of your police issue, its superb antique acreage separating him from the hewers of wood and drawers of water, the Superintendent's mood lightened, if only a little. He barely frowned when the phone rang; waited with tolerable patience as DI Batterby – ambitious bastard, thought Jurnet; always the first to plump himself in the picture whenever opportunity offered – dived for the receiver before anyone else could get there.

'DI Melton,' he reported back, holding the receiver a little away from him, ready to pass it over if requested. 'Says he's filtered out somebody interesting downstairs he thinks you ought to see.'

'*Ought* to?' The Superintendent's frown, to Jurnet's secret satisfaction, was now unmistakable. Things, thank God, were back to normal. 'Melton? Isn't he from Palmersgate?'

'That's right, sir.' Batterby, as fly as anyone, saw no need to add the obvious, that the place was crawling with buggers bused in from every outpost of empire to help deal with the rabble overflowing the cells on the ground floor. 'Do you wish to have a word?'

'Tell him to bring him up, whoever it is. They've taken their time,' the Superintendent commented acidly. 'Time somebody managed to pin-point who organized this shambles, set the ball rolling. Gave you a name, did he?' he demanded, as Batterby restored the receiver to its cradle. 'Not a chap called Buck, was it, or Joe?'

'He just said a boy.'

74

The boy, red-eyed and trembling, had got beyond crying. Blood from a graze on his forehead had dried down the left side of his face, stiffening the young flesh and petering out beneath a chin downy with a sprinkling of golden hair. Jurnet, who had seen the boy before and been unmoved by the sight, was, at second encounter, shaken by his beauty. Not intending it, he found himself looking away from the boy towards Batterby whom he and the Superintendent, if nobody else at Police HQ, knew as near as dammit to be gay.

The DI met his eyes and looked away quickly, not quick enough. OK, thought Jurnet, unjudgemental; only why the hell doesn't he come out of his fucking closet?

DI Melton, accompanying the boy, had, it was obvious, no hang-ups as to his own sexual orientation. No delusions of grandeur, either, about his own place in the police pecking order. A large man with a watchful face, he ushered the boy to the desk as to the bar of the court.

'DI Melton, sir, from Palmersgate.'

The Superintendent's nod of acknowledgement, if non-committal, was perfectly appropriate.

'As you can imagine, we're grateful today for all the help we can get.' Turning his attention to the boy: 'You're the one who was involved in that travesty of a trial up on the Moot. Something about damage to a pub . . .'

'Danny – ' the boy began convulsively, and stopped, hand to his throat as if the act of articulation were beyond him. The detective from Palmersgate put one of his large hands on the boy's shoulder in a way that was not unfriendly; turned him to face the Superintendent more directly. 'His name, sir, is Peter Gilbert.'

'Pete,' the boy corrected faintly. 'Nobody ever calls me anything but Pete.'

The Superintendent stated rather than asked: 'Including Danny? Did he call you that too?'

Suddenly the boy was talking – fast, too fast, the words tumbling over each other, as if the name, in another's mouth, had released a spring in his own.

'One minute he wasn't there – how could he be there, they'd put him on the train for London, hadn't they, the night before, the train or the bus, I don't know which – an' the next, as we were coming through the Close, with all those clergymen watching an' the flowers an' the cloisters and all that, there he was, running by the side of me, taking my hand. I didn't see where he come from, it was like magic. One minute he wasn't there, the nex' he was running, running like the rest of us, only holding my hand. I wouldn't 'a known he was there at all if he hadn't took hold of my hand.'

'What did he say?'

The boy's bright eyes dulled and went blank.

'I didn't hear what he said, not at first. We was running, all you could hear was the beating of your heart an' the feet beating the ground. All you knew was you had to keep going or the guys behind would be running all over you, leaving you behind squashed like a beetle. An' you couldn't be lef' behind, not for anything.'

Into a moment's silence the Superintendent interjected: 'But you must have been glad to see him.'

'I tole you,' the boy persisted, looking at the Superintendent with something of the impatience the man himself so often directed at others, 'we wasn't thinking, none of us. We was running, there weren't nothing else. Only him – I looked at him sideways and he was laughing – laughing, can you believe it, when Charlie was dead an' the rest of us was running our bloody hearts out! Danny or no Danny, I couldn't stand it an' I pulled my hand away. He didn't want to let it go, I can tell you, but I pulled hard an' he let it go finally, still all merry and bright.

'It wasn't noisy if you mean shouting and like that, but the air was full of noises just the same. You couldn't hear yourself think, let alone what anyone was saying. But then he put his face close so I couldn't help hearing what he said, over an' over.'

'Which was . . .?'

'He said, "It had to be done, Pete. It bloody had to be done. I wrung his neck." Only sometimes he didn't say, "It had to be done, Pete." Instead he just said, "I had to do it." '

The boy looked about him, seemingly puzzled by the still faces of his listeners, the lack of any startled response.

'Tha's what he said,' he insisted. 'Only, like I say, I didn't take it all in at first. I was running, not thinking. I couldn't even rightly say I heard him at the time he said it – the actual words, you understand – with my ears, I mean. But I heard him. I heard him inside myself. I stored it up. Don't tell me Danny didn't say it because I heard him!'

Batterby said softly: 'Of course you did, laddie. Nobody's saying different.'

'In Shire Street,' said Pete Gilbert, 'jest as we were coming up to the Market Place, he got hold of me by the shoulder, sudden like, I didn' know what it was, an' pushed me out of the running, into the door of one of the shops, a shoe shop full of posh shoes, Fowler's, I think it's called. I called out to let me go, but all he did was push me against the glass an' all those shoes and kiss me on the lips. I didn't want him to kiss me no more, I was done with that, but I couldn't help it, I had to let him. When he'd finished kissing, he said he'd got things to do first but after that, he said, he'd go back up to the Moot and get my bag for me. He said, "You don't want to lose yer bag, do you?"

'I hadn't thought it about till then,' the boy interrupted himself to explain earnestly, 'but when he put it like that, well, it did seem a shame to let it go. It was a lovely bag – real leather straps and Elvis on the front in glitter. When you moved it according to the light it looked like he was dancing. Danny give it me for my birthday, he knew I wouldn't want to lose it.

' "I'll pick up your bag an' your things," he said, "an' you meet me up there by the Oak at three o'clock. By then I'll have done all I got to do. Three o'clock. Don't keep me waiting." He was holding my arm, the one with the wrist-watch on it, and looking down at it smiling, as much to remind me he'd given me that too – digital, goes on a battery, you don't have to wind it, *and* it tells you the date and the day of the week – '

'Very nice,' the Superintendent commented. Then: 'Did he give you any idea of what it was he had to do first?'

The boy shook his head. 'He said it was none of my business, an' I didn't think to ask anyway. The truth was, I didn't want to know anyway, because once I'd stopped running I'd started remembering – remembering what he'd said about it having to be done and him having to do it.'

'And what did you understand by those remarks?'

Unmoved by the dignity of the desk, the symbolism of the gold pen, Pete Gilbert shouted: 'Christ, some people are thick! It meant he murdered Charlie, that's what, an' then he has the bloody cheek to kiss me like everything was all right. I couldn't stand it.' The boy looked about him, from one face to the next, entreating understanding. 'I tole him what he could do with his frigging bag. I shouted out I hated his guts, bloody murderer. I could see a line of coppers a little further along, where Shire Street comes out into the Market Place, and I thought, I'll get hold of one o' them an' tell him what Danny's done, an' then he could arrest him. On'y, jes'

77

like when he come, all of a sudden Danny wasn't there any more, only all those shitty shoes the other side of the glass. I couldn't see where he'd gone, either, 'cept that it had to be the Market Place, the way everyone was running. It was like a river, you all had to go the same way, want to or not. But I thought – the Bill will find 'im, they got their special ways.'

At that Sid Hale, a detective inspector who had contributed nothing to the exchanges so far – a narrow bean of a man with a long face that looked perpetually saddened by the world's follies but never surprised by them – actually managed a smile.

'Too right, son. We always get our man.'

'No, you don't,' the boy contradicted. 'I tugged at the copper's sleeve an' all he did was turn an' look down and say, "Go home, sonny." ' Tears of outrage trembling on the curling lashes: 'Jes' because I'm not finished growing, he didn't take no notice. Tha's not right, a policeman.'

The Superintendent, looking serious, agreed. 'Not right at all.'

'I made 'im, though.' Even before the teardrops dried, Pete Gilbert's cupid's-bow curved upward in smiling spite. 'I bit 'im in the arm. That made him take notice all right.'

Sid Hale laughed aloud, something so rare as to make his mates stare at him, discomfited.

'Not that – ' the boy's moment of satisfaction fading – 'it made him go an' catch Danny. He run me in instead, the arsehole.'

12

Up on the Moot it was no cooler than in Angleby below, the Oak a focus of heat instead of the green refuge one might have expected. Overlaid with ground sheets and duffel bags abandoned any which way, their contents spilled out on to the desiccated grass, the place looked slatternly beyond words, a disgrace to a city which prided itself on its wholesomeness. The whole bloody mess, thought Jurnet – feeling slatternly himself after a morning spent in unwilling witness of the unedifying spectacle of the Lord Mayor, the Chief Executive and the Chief Constable manœuvring with locked horns to shift the blame for the day's disaster on to any shoulders other than their own – ought by rights to be rolled up and taken away and dumped lock, stock and barrel: Oak of

Reformation, what was left of it, pasque flowers and all. Assuming there were any pasque flowers left, which was doubtful in the extreme.

In whatever condition Loy Tanner and his men had left the Moot when they made their ill-fated descent on the city, at least they wouldn't have left behind all that plastic tat. Four hundred and fifty years ago everything was biodegradable, even a hero.

From the police car parked on the melting tarmac PCs Blaker and Hinchley, sunk in terminal boredom, kept a token watch over the deserted field, wrappings of Mars Bars and potato crisps advertising how the two had passed the empty hours. All four doors of the car were open, inviting a non-existent breeze.

Just as well for the two of them that Jack Ellers, bringing the Rover to rest directly behind them, had, whether by accident or, more likely, as an act of kindness, sounded the car's horn, otherwise they would never have been aware of its quiet arrival. Even as it was, there was barely time to button their shirts, tighten their belts, get themselves smartly out on to the grass verge by the time their superior officer had himself disembarked and come over.

Jurnet, easily reading their relief that the Superintendent wasn't one of the party, greeted them with a civil request that, whilst they were about it, they might do their flies up as well.

Was it all over, then, down in the city, they wanted to know, childlike and making clear their hope that they were still in time for a piece of the action.

'All over bar the shouting, I'm afraid. What about up here?'

'Dead as a doornail,' Hinchley reported with some bitterness. Blaker, a dedicated bird watcher, was marginally more cheerful. 'A couple of magpies, earlier on. Found some bread that was left lying about. That was all.'

PC Hinchley's grief at having missed the fun was getting the better of his sense of self-preservation: 'All the need there was for us up here, sir, we could'a been down there too, helping out.'

'Not my decision,' Jurnet returned, sharpish: what had happened in Angleby Market Place wasn't a kids' game. 'Nor yours. Let me put you in the picture up here. We're expecting a guy to call, somebody coming back to pick up a piece of gear that was left behind. Somebody we need to have a few words with, quietly and gently. If he shows, it could be any time from – let me see – ' consulting his watch – 'eight minutes on. Jack and I are going to take a look around. If you see him coming up the road meantime, let us know at once. If he comes on to the Moot, don't stop him. In fact, don't show any interest at all – act as vigilantly and on the ball as you were just now when we arrived and you'll be doing fine. Only if, for any reason, he starts to scarper, see he doesn't get far.'

'Sir . . .'

In spite of the heat and the lack of rain there were still leaves on the Oak of Reformation, even if they looked as if all that was keeping them in place was sheer inertia, too much of a fag to drop off.

Treading morosely, making no attempt to skirt the abandoned possessions of Charlie Appleyard's followers, Jurnet grumbled to Jack Ellers beside him: 'Those two bloody comedians! Could have come and gone for all we know. Doubt if they'd have noticed an elephant if one had come by waving his trunk and offered to wash their windscreen.'

The little Welshman wiped his forehead with the back of his hand.

Mending fences, he proffered: 'It's a pig of a day!'

Jurnet said: 'We're wasting our time. I can feel it in my bones.'

All the same, sandwiched between the brazen sky and the hot plastic underfoot, the two advanced further on to the Moot; rounded the Oak to where, bleached against the gnarled trunk, the stair still stood, the staircase and podium where, in imitation of Loy Tanner's sublime gesture all those years ago, Charlie Appleyard had proclaimed that any man, from the highest to the lowest, was to be free to address the assembly – in praise or execration it made no difference, so long as he spoke in the name of justice.

Justice.

Later, Jurnet could not have said whether he actually spoke the word aloud or only felt it, a vibration which strummed through his entire being: could not remember if what he either spoke or felt was spoken or felt in triumph or in mockery.

Detective Sergeant Jack Ellers, troubled by no such uncertainties, shouted: 'Crikey!'

A little above the staircase, from the lowest branch of the tree directly above it, a rope hung down, a rope that looked to be a length left over from the rope which held the staircase in place against the Oak trunk. A rope that ended in a noose.

There was not a breath of air to set the body swaying. Utterly immobile, it looked unreal – or, at any rate, not human. Even in sleep a human being was never quite still. Breasts rose and fell, a sudden twitching of the shoulders, a shaking off of a bad dream – there was always something to reassure an onlooker that there was still life inside the packaging.

On the Oak of Reformation not a leaf moved, not a breath stirred. Unmoving, his head inclined over his left shoulder in a pose of dreadful coquetry, Danny Saunders hung in the sun.

The Market Place was picking itself up. Not back to its former picturesqueness, it had to be said. Instead, it seemed to Jurnet, taking care as he crossed it not to slip on squashed tomatoes or mashed bananas, there was a kind of raffish bravado in the air that reminded him of the way his parents had talked about the Blitz, a sense of self-congratulation at having come through a common disaster together. Even as the city sweepers toiled to clear away the mess putrefying on the cobblestones, and the city handymen to complete the demolition of stalls already reduced to lethal shafts of wood and metal, the market traders were busy bringing in trestles, barrows, anything that might serve as a makeshift counter on which once more to display their wares.

'Ready-chipped china!' shouted the cheeky chappie on the crockery stall. 'Save yerselves the trouble of doing it yourself!'

Taking their cue from him, the fruit sellers were already offering 'Genuine Bruised Apples' and 'Slightly Squeezed Oranges', whilst even Mr Patel, a clever man who had mastered everything about the English except their sense of humour, now displayed a sign on his converted barrow: 'Best Laddered Tights.'

Despite himself, Jurnet had to smile, thereby diluting, in some measure, the mixture of guilt and anger which had possessed him ever since the discovery of Danny Saunders's body hanging, hanging. It wasn't, he recognized, so much the bugger's death as the manner of it that shook him. With murder, at least, you knew where you were. If there was a victim there was also, somewhere, a culprit on whom it was perfectly proper to unload a catharsis of revenge. But who was to blame for a human being's self-destruction if not the world which had failed him, a world which included yours truly?

If it was suicide.

Not that Colton and the scene-of-crime team had done anything to foster his hope that there might conceivably be some other explanation for that ghastly dangling doll. No, they had agreed, one and all, there was nothing to suggest that anyone other than Saunders himself had ended his life.

The Superintendent's pleased reception of this intelligence had made Jurnet want to puke.

'Well, Ben, that just about wraps it up, eh?' The man had settled back in his seat, all smiles. 'Saunders, expelled from the presence, deprived of his pretty paramour, kills Charlie Appleyard but then, rejected afresh by the boy and – we can plausibly take it – overcome by remorse, kills himself.'

Wasting no time in unprofitable argument, Jurnet observed: 'What we need is to lay hands on those two fellows who were Appleyard's assistants, helpers, whatever he called them – the ones called Buck and Joe. We saw them both that first day, if you remember. Nobody we've been questioning seems even to know their surnames. By all accounts they were closer to Charlie than anyone, yet suddenly they seem to have vanished from the face of the earth. Why? Everyone agrees they didn't come down into the city with the rest, which is odd, distinctly odd, considering their position of authority up on the Moot, and nobody can recall seeing either of them since the word that Appleyard was dead first got around.'

'From which you infer – what?'

'Wonder, sir – not infer.' Jurnet ploughed on, only too well aware that, in doing so, he was earning himself no Brownie points. 'Those two could easily have got back to the Moot unseen – anybody could, the surveillance, or lack of it, we maintained up there. Assuming they knew, or thought they knew, that Saunders had done for their leader, their god, they could have passed their own personal sentence on him – strung him up on the Oak and no one the wiser.'

'You read the report.' The Superintendent left his subordinate in no doubt that he was not best pleased with this reconstruction. 'You will have to forgive me if I fail to see the point of this – this Byzantine hypothesizing. Evidence is what we're concerned with, and there isn't a shred of it to connect anyone other than himself with Saunders's death.' With that effortless assumption of authority which always, on cue, made Jurnet positively throb with hatred: 'Simply to reject the obvious for its own sake, Ben, is the sin of pride.'

'Yes, sir.' After that, to confide one's thoughts on suicide was out of the question. Instead Jurnet offered, with malice aforethought: 'There was the knot, of course.'

82

The Superintendent looked up sharply. 'What's this? Something I haven't been told?'

'The knot in the noose, and the bit of rope hanging down from it. I noticed it when we found the body, and I couldn't help wondering. I hadn't seen a knot like that since I was a kid, and only then because I had a great-uncle who worked on the old wherries that used to come up the rivers from Yarmouth. The men who sailed those great old floating bedsteads used to call it a Slippy Jenny because, they said, once you'd tied it – and you had to be taught how, it was fairly tricky – one pull on the end of rope you purposely left hanging and it springs into place like greased lightning and with a kick like a mule. You needed a knot like that, my great-uncle used to say, to stop those ruddy great sails they had in those days getting ideas above their station. What I ask myself is, would Danny Saunders have known even how to tie such a knot, let alone go to all that trouble at such a time, all that weaving in and out of the rope ends, when a simple Granny would have done the trick just as well? We know he came from Angleby, lived on the Stannard estate till he took himself off to London, nothing to do with the sea – '

'Maybe he had a great-uncle like you,' said the Superintendent sardonically. 'Maybe he learned to tie – a Slippy Jenny, was it? – maybe he learned it at the Scouts. Maybe he worked it out for himself.'

'Yes, sir – *maybe*.' Jurnet repeated the final word with relish. 'Except that one of the chaps we pulled in mentioned that the man called Buck was always on about how he had once crewed on a yacht that had competed in the America Cup.'

'Did he indeed?' The Superintendent passed an immaculately manicured hand over his face and sighed. When he took the hand away the patrician features thus revealed looked older, tired, and yet – Jurnet felt his heart leap with a grateful recognition – suddenly imbued with a loving mischief. 'You're at it again, Ben.'

'Sir?'

'You know very well. You do it all the time. Getting involved. Protecting your corpse – in this case, the two of them.'

'Can't do it themselves, that's for sure.'

'True enough. Except that they're past needing anyone's compassion. If you'd said justice, now . . .'

'Comes to the same thing.'

The Superintendent shook his head, his expression deeply sad. 'Not the same thing at all – and we're the ones need *that*, even more than they do. In the meantime, one thing's certain – a fuzzy sentimentality will get us nowhere.'

With the precision which characterized all his movements, the man positioned his hands, palms down, on the desk and sat contemplating them in silence as though they were appendages of whose existence he had only that moment been informed.

Then: 'They say that in 1549, when it was all over bar the shouting, the Earl of Warwick had three hundred of Loy Tanner's followers strung up on the Oak. Three hundred! No trial, they say he wouldn't even let them see a priest, say a prayer . . .'

'Wanted to teach Norfolk a lesson it wouldn't forget.'

'No way you could hang all that many at once. The branches would never have stood the weight. They must have made the poor wretches queue up, like cattle going to slaughter; watching it all happen whilst awaiting their turn.'

Jurnet muttered, barely audible: 'What price history?'

Hearing nevertheless, the other returned: 'Too high, that's certain, *and* no chance of getting a discount! For better or worse we're all prisoners of the past. The most we can claim is that, since Warwick's time and Loy Tanner's, we've come a certain way – not all that far, but still a little.'

The Superintendent looked up from his hands, looked at Jurnet directly.

'Will you be satisfied if I put Hale and Batterby on to your wild-goose chase after the elusive Buck and Joe and leave you, for the moment at any rate, to follow your nose wherever it may lead you?'

Loving the man as much as, only a little before, he had hated him, Jurnet managed: 'Thank you, sir.'

'Strictly for the moment, mind you. The Chief, the Mayor and Corporation are all baying for blood. If we don't turn up at least a bone to throw them, we'll be the ones to find ourselves – metaphorically, thank goodness – dangling from the Oak of Reformation.'

'Have to take that chance, I reckon. They say it took a hundred and fifty years for the last of Tanner's bones to fall down from the castle ramparts.'

'We'll have to do better than that!' The tone had become easy, frivolous even. 'You've seen the boy again, Peter Gilbert?'

Jurnet admitted that he had seen the boy at the children's home where the city's Social Services had temporarily accommodated him.

'Did you tell him Danny Saunders was dead, let him know how he died?' Upon the other's nod: 'How did he take it?'

With some reluctance Jurnet answered. 'He wanted to know if Danny had found his bag before he did for himself, the one with the glitter on it and the picture of Elvis. When I said that, so far as I knew, he hadn't, *then* he cried.'

At that the Superintendent left his chair; went over to the window and his favourite view of the Market Place. Winced as if he had forgotten what was now to be seen there.

Turning his back on that prospect of devastation, he demanded: 'Why on earth, Ben, did we ever join this outrageous profession?'

Jurnet answered: 'I can't remember.'

'Neither can I.'

13

In the small front garden somebody had actually cut the grass. Probably, thought Jurnet, the guy next door, driven to the point of madness by having, day in and day out, to contemplate a slovenliness which not only depreciated the value of his own property but cocked a snook at everything he himself held dear – his mortgage, his DIY, what the neighbours said.

If he *had* been the one to do it, he must have been disappointed with the result. Cropped, or rather, hacked, the yellow stalks looked even more dead than before, if that were possible, the two gnomes who among the waving grasses and the poppies had appeared so optimistic of a catch, listless and defeated, no hope of landing anything in that desert, not so much as a plastic tiddler.

'Awful, isn't it?' Jurnet looked up from the horticultural shambles to see Dr Adamson watching him from her doorstep. 'I can't think what got into Roger.'

'Your nephew did it?'

'I'm not surprised you're surprised.' The woman came towards him, averting her eyes from the disaster area. 'When I got back from town I couldn't believe my eyes. He said he just felt like doing something and this was all he could think of.'

'It'll grow again, soon enough.'

'When the rain comes. If it ever does.' Leading the way into the house she continued on a note of disbelief, 'Usually it takes all one's powers of persuasion to make that boy do anything. And you won't believe what he did it with – my kitchen scissors!'

'I thought it looked a bit uneven.'

'Uneven!' Dr Adamson stopped suddenly, pulled herself together. 'Whatever must you think of me, carrying on like this? As if it matters one iota compared with . . .' Elegant as ever, not a strand of iron-grey hair out of place, she held out a hand to the detective; shook his formally. 'Do come in. I've made some lemonade.'

'I heard it on the television,' Dr Adamson said. 'Heard it and saw.' Her mouth twisted a little as she added: 'It appears I missed all the fun.'

'You've been to the Market Place?'

Jurnet put down his drink, setting it carefully on the floor, for lack of anywhere else to get rid of it. Despite the ice that pushed up the surface it did not seem really cool, served as it was in one of the orange and black mugs which again, as on his prior acquaintance with them, obscurely offended him.

'I've seen it,' the woman answered with a sad composure. 'I came back from London especially to see it before they tidied it up. Wherever possible, I believe – as I imagine you do yourself – in experiencing things at first hand, however painful. Besides, after what happened to Charlie, I guessed you would be wanting to talk to me again.' She regarded the detective, her grey eyes, the youngest things in her face, friendly but challenging. 'When you were here before, you said you needed to know about Charlie. Now that he's dead, murdered, you must be wishing you knew more. You might even be wishing you knew more about me.'

Moving with an unexpected grace, she rose from the outsize floor cushion on which she had been sitting, bent down at Jurnet's side and retrieved his mug, setting it on the refectory table which was pushed against one wall of the sparsely furnished room. Her breasts, glimpsed as she bent over in her low-cut shift, looked firm and desirable.

Coming back from her errand, she finished: 'Just as well, all things considered, that I was up in town when it all happened. At least it means *I* have a cast-iron alibi.'

'Always a useful thing to have,' Jurnet conceded. 'You never know when it will come in handy.'

'But is it?' Dr Adamson persisted. She sank back again on to her cushion, which gave way gracefully. 'I mean – are you sure it doesn't look the teeniest bit contrived to have one's comings and goings during the crucial hours so carefully documented and spoken for? Wouldn't it sound a whole lot more believable to say I was at home alone, nobody phoned, nobody able to vouch for me one way or the other?' The woman tucked her slender legs under her and smiled up at the detective who, to his annoyance, found himself put off balance by her ambiguous charm. 'You'll have to forgive me, Inspector. I'm never more frivolous than when I'm grieving.'

Jurnet said: 'You're right about my needing to know more about Charlie Appleyard. If I'm to find out, not just how he died, but why, I have to learn first what made him tick, what kind of man lived inside his skin.'

'You must have been on the Moot. You must have heard him on television. What you saw was what he was.'

The other shook his head. 'Too easy by half. What I saw was an ordinary guy, no great shakes to look at, no great orator either, who had none the less managed somehow to persuade ten thousand other guys to follow him like the Pied Piper into what, when you came down to it, was a totally absurd situation which hadn't a hope in hell of solving anybody's problems – except maybe Charlie Appleyard's. An outsize ego trip.'

The woman looked up at the detective with something like pity in her disturbingly youthful eyes.

'You realize, of course, you've just described a hero.'

'Shades of Gordon of Khartoum, eh?' Jurnet was at the end of his patience. 'OK, I'll admit, when I first heard him on the telly, I was impressed. Only – you wouldn't know, not being in the business – nothing concentrates the mind like murder, something so out of the normal that you have to stop and ask yourself why – what was so special about your latest corpse that somebody found it necessary to snuff out his life? So if, as in the present case, you've already bumped into the fellow alive and found him nothing to write home about, you can't help wondering whether you got it right at the time. In other words, was it the real man who moved you on the box or only a façade – an actor, a phoney, secretly laughing his head off at the way he's taken everybody in.'

'You've been looking at him with the wrong eyes, Inspector. I know exactly what he was.' Dr Adamson got up from the cushion again, a little stiffly this time, not so young after all. Jurnet, his aggression subsiding, nearly went over to help her, then was glad he hadn't. 'You have absolutely no idea! When he first came to me he had already built up a formidable body of independent research on Loy Tanner. He was more than obsessed with the man – he was possessed, seeing it as his mission to upgrade him from a footnote to local history to the national figure he felt he deserved to be.' The flush in her cheeks subsiding as her habitual good humour resumed its ascendancy: 'He was also, I freely admit, a young man with a degree he didn't know what to do with, he couldn't find a job . . .' Smiling as at a pleasant memory: 'Fruit ripe for the picking by a designing woman, Inspector.'

Jurnet was silent for a moment, digesting this information. Dr Adamson, expecting an immediate reaction, went on a trifle impatiently.

'Don't tell me you haven't already had thoughts that I might have been Charlie's backer, his angel, as they say, don't they, in theatrical circles. I'll be sorry if you hadn't, because the only reason I'm telling you now is that I reckoned you'd be bound to find out once you went through Charlie's things. There must be paying-in slips or something to give the game away, and I'm sure it looks better to tell you first than leave you to find out for yourself.'

Jurnet admitted: 'It naturally occurred to me that you and your nephew were, so far as I knew, the only two people of his acquaintance in a position to fund him. Though, of course, there might have been others. As you say, it's one of the things we have to look into.'

'One person you can cross off your checklist – Roger had nothing whatever to do with it. It was my show exclusively, mine and Charlie's.' With an air of calm satisfaction, Dr Adamson reported: 'To be specific, he'd had about £25,000 to date, knowing that, if needed, there was always more where that came from. With all the dedication in the world it still takes money to get ten thousand people together and on the move.'

'I'm sure.' Jurnet looked at her with conscious effort, concentrating, as if seeing her for the first time: a clever woman, that was obvious, once you left out that fixation on Loy Tanner, one who had come to terms with time, a friendly agreement with give and take on both sides. One too fastidious to resort to the pathetic little tricks some women went in for to hide their age. On the other hand, too sensual to disguise her pleasure in her own body, moving easy and untrammelled in a dress of flowered silk that, in the most understated way possible, hinted at a capacity for passion beneath the genteel surface.

88

Only one thing could have made such a clever woman embark on such a barmy adventure. Knowing there would never be a better occasion, Jurnet asked: 'Did you and Charlie Appleyard have a relationship?'

Dr Adamson laughed aloud.

'A relationship!' she repeated mockingly, eyes sparkling. 'What politically correct gobbledegook we've come down to! Did I go to bed with him, do you mean?' The laughter tailed off, the mockery turned inward to herself. 'No, Inspector, I did not go to bed with him. Not that I wouldn't have enjoyed doing so very much – simply that he was young and I wasn't. I didn't want to push my luck. As I'm sure you've noticed, life is a matter of choices, and – though you might not think so – I am on the cautious side. On the other hand, if I'd known that he was going to be killed I would certainly have yielded to his – I'm bound to say in all honesty – not all that fervent advances.' Still smiling, her head a little to one side, the woman remarked: 'I always say – don't you agree, Inspector? – nothing stays in the memory like coitus interruptus, a love from which, through no fault of one's own, one hasn't yet extracted the last drop of juice.'

By the time Jurnet was himself again, the image of Miriam, legs apart to welcome him, her wonderful hair spread out on the pillow, safely pushed to the back of his mind, Dr Adamson was off at a tangent.

With an unwonted diffidence she inquired: 'That suicide – it was in the *Argus* – that man who hanged himself on the Oak, it didn't give his name, said it hadn't been released yet. That wasn't anything to do with Charlie's death, was it?'

'We're keeping an open mind, as they say. We know who the fellow is, though.' Looking at the woman directly: 'A local lad. I don't suppose you happen to know anyone by the name of Danny Saunders?'

'Danny Saunders!' The other made no attempt to disguise either her surprise or her horror. 'But why on earth . . .'

'At the moment I can't tell you. Suppose you tell me what you know.'

Controlling herself, Dr Adamson said: 'About the boy himself, not much. He worked in the factory for a couple of months, then left saying it wasn't his idea of how he wanted to spend his life. The only reason I know about him at all is because his father, Fred, was our head clicker. No one worked for us longer – '

'Your what?'

'Clicker. A clicker is the worker who lays out the pattern of the shoe on the skin and then cuts it out in the most economical way he can. It's a very skilled job. There are always imperfections in the skins – blow-fly damage perhaps, or something else – and the art is to get the maximum usable area out of every one. Fred was a marvel. He got I don't know how many prizes at the trade fairs. Long after we stopped making shoes that handmade way we kept him on as a PR exercise, a bit of a museum piece, a reminder of how it used to be in the boot and shoe industry. School parties used to come and watch him. He was quite a local character. I know it was the disappointment of his life when his son Danny refused to carry on the family tradition and took off for London. What would he have said now!' Dr Adamson's eyes grew moist. 'Thank goodness he died six months ago.'

'Did you ever run into Danny in London?'

The other sighed, leaned her head on her hands for a moment before looking up at Jurnet with a little smile.

'If only I could decide whether it was wiser to speak to you or stay mum.'

'You want to see Charlie's murderer caught, don't you?'

'I'm beginning to wonder.'

'I don't believe you. You're a woman with standards.' Persisting: 'You did see Danny Saunders in London, didn't you?'

'Once or twice.' The woman moved her head from side to side, unsure of herself. 'I told Charlie he could use my place for meetings. All kinds of people turned up, Danny included. Seems they'd known each other as children.'

'Charlie must have known him as an adult too, to have known his London address.'

'Oh, I don't think so, not necessarily. There was a kind of East Anglian grapevine. It surprised me, I'd had no idea. One brought another along, it was amazing how the numbers grew.' Dr Adamson added, reluctantly: 'I got the impression that, though the two knew each other, they weren't close friends.'

'What gave you that impression?'

With the kind of fastidiousness the detective would have expected of her the woman said: 'I should have said, Danny wanted to be friends. It was Charlie who kept his distance.' After another moment she finished unwillingly: 'Danny wanted to be something more than friends, and Charlie wasn't having any.'

'Danny was gay, you mean? If it makes you feel better, you're not telling me anything I didn't already know.'

'I'm glad of that.'

14

Jurnet was just about to turn the key of the Rover in the ignition when, in his mirror, he saw that another car had drawn up immediately behind him, a snazzy little Lotus in fire-engine red and, with the hood down, enviably more desirable in the prevailing heat than the Rover, hot as a furnace from its long wait at the kerb. When the detective saw, further, that the driver of the car was Julian Grant, he found himself caught between a frisson of pleasure and a tremor of something not far removed from fear. Thank heaven, he reassured himself, at least she had tied back her hair, Miriam's hair, in a pony tail, all but out of sight.

Nothing to worry about.

The girl climbed out of the low-slung car without bothering to open the door and without regard to the expanse of thigh rendered visible by the manœuvre. When she came over to the Rover and peered through the open window Jurnet was able to see that more than the hair was different. The Barbie-doll look was a lot less in evidence, the cupid's-bow lips turned down at the corners, dark shadows under the eyes that had nothing to do with mascara.

Without formal greeting she demanded: 'Are you coming or going?'

'I'm not sure. I was going, only now that you're here, I don't know. I've just been talking to Dr Adamson and, next, I was going to go looking for you, only you've saved me the trouble. I wanted to have a word.'

'Do you have to?' Julian Grant inquired dispiritedly, and, when the other nodded: 'The inevitable grilling of the suspects, eh?'

'Too hot for a grill. Just a cool, low-keyed chat.'

'Well, I certainly don't want to have even that, in front of Addie.' The girl turned away, towards the front garden of Dr Adamson's house. 'Christ!' she exclaimed. 'Roger told me he had cut the grass, but I had no idea. I don't believe it!'

'It'll grow back, once it starts raining.'

The other shook her head, a sudden movement that brought her pony tail swinging disturbingly over one shoulder.

'It's never going to rain any more, hadn't you heard? Noah's flood in reverse. We're all going to dry up and fall apart like desiccated coconut. Those poor little gnomes! I'm going to bring them each back a real live fish from Havenlea. Havenlea,' the girl repeated when Jurnet returned no observation on this last. 'That's where our printers are. They do all the university stuff, so Daddy said I ought to use them. I stopped by to ask Addie if she felt like coming along for the ride.' The corners of that absurdly perfect mouth drooping even further: 'At the moment I'm not feeling all that content with my own company.'

'Understandable. Friends don't grow on trees.'

'Not even on the Oak of Reformation.' The girl must have decided that the sympathy implied in Jurnet's words was genuine because she lifted her head a little and regarded the detective with the first unambiguously friendly look she had ever, to his knowledge, directed at him. 'Why don't *you* come instead, in my car? It'll cool you off a little, if nothing else, and you can ask your bloody questions on the way.'

As they settled themselves in the Lotus, Julian Grant with the bony ease of a jack-in-the-box folding itself back into its accustomed resting place, Jurnet preoccupied with the novel sensation of finding himself in a car sited within inches of the ground, she finished, almost flirtatiously: 'Not that I promise to give you any bloody answers.'

In the event, the two did not exchange a word until they were well out of the medieval maze of Angleby and on the road that ran straight as a die across the marshes towards the sea. Even then, the wind beating at once hot and cool against his face, the landscape swirling past like a world revolving frantically on its axis, Jurnet found it all but impossible to think up, let alone put into words, the questions to which he required an answer from Julian Grant.

That particular countryside, he recognized, had, even when he was seated sedate in the Rover, always spooked him somewhat, less because it was so amazingly flat than that it was not even flatter, caved in beneath the weight of sky pressing down upon it. At Lotus level the two of them – the three of them, Julian Grant, Ben Jurnet, car and all – were no longer separate from the land on either side of the raised causeway but part of it, the thrum of wheels and engine caught up with the rustle of the reed beds that lined the ditches on either side of the road and flung themselves about in a frenzy as they drove by.

In addition to which Julian Grant, blast her, had taken off her headband.

Fixing his eyes determinedly on the occasional windmill, the sole verticals in sight, which poked a defiant finger into the sky, Jurnet finally managed: 'I need to know about Charlie Appleyard at the university.'

'Nothing much to tell. I mean, apart from his thing about Loy Tanner, a perfectly ordinary guy.' Moved by some spirit of mischief, she put her foot down on the accelerator and said demurely: 'I hope you've noticed I haven't gone a mile over seventy.'

Ignoring the diversion, Jurnet asked: 'The four of you – was that always the way it was? You and Roger, Charlie and Jenny Nunn?'

'Two and two, you mean?' Julian Grant frowned. The suggestion seemed to affront her. 'It wasn't like that at all. Just four kids who happened to go around together. Roger wasn't even at the university, anyway.'

'But you and Roger were already an item, surely?'

'Mm.' The other pondered. 'Not really. That was afterwards; after we grew up and one had to decide which box you fitted into. If you want to know – ' the speedometer hand dropped back as she slowed down, concentrating – 'what kept the three of us busy was looking after Jenny.'

Julian Grant raised her foot even further from the accelerator and suddenly it was the same old world again, too bloody hot, too bloody much hair like Miriam's. 'I'm sorry, when you asked, I told you I didn't know what had happened to her. I did, of course. You can't live in a place the size of Angleby and not know when your best friend sets herself up as a street walker. I just wanted to protect her, I suppose – that's what we were doing at university all the time, the three of us, Charlie, Roger and I, looking after Jenny. A habit hard to get out of.' The girl pressed her foot down and set the car racing again. 'I haven't told you anything you didn't already know, have I? I mean, with Charlie found killed on her front steps, you must know how she is with men.'

'I know. She told me herself.'

Julian Grant gave a laugh full of affection.

'She would!' Needing to shout to be heard above the wind, the car noises, no more slowing down: 'She's the craziest person, but clever too. I don't know if it's physical or psychological, she can't help falling for every man she sees – a bit of both, probably. *Really* falling for them, I mean, loving it, every time as special as if it was the first. It's not really fair to call her a prostitute, even if she does do it for money. I'm sure, if she didn't have to pay the rent, buy food and so on, she'd do it without charge for the pure love of it.'

'I know about Jenny. It's the four of you as a group I'm asking about. Charlie in particular.'

'I'm telling you. A society for the protection of Jenny. She hadn't – she still hasn't – any discrimination. Some of the men she used to pick up were not very nice – real screwballs and dirty with it. I suppose she's got a nice pimp to look after her now. I do hope so.' With a giggle that peeled back the years: 'And with it all, would you believe, all those late nights, she was the only one to get a First.'

'As you say, a clever girl.'

'Unless, of course, she slept with the whole Examining Board the day before results came out! Which she was quite capable of doing.'

As they came into the suburb of Havenlea Julian Grant said: 'I thought you were going to ask me what I was doing the night Charlie was killed.'

'OK. What *were* you doing?'

'I thought you were never going to ask. Washing my hair.'

They picked up the wedding invitations from the printers and, at a neighbouring fish stall, two bloaters for the garden gnomes – purchases which, together with the spare wheel and the girl's handbag, all but filled the minuscule car boot.

Whereupon, her shopping completed, Julian Grant declared her intention of going down to the sea.

Jurnet, aware of time wasted and no longer expecting anything much to emerge from an afternoon spent in a resort which advertised itself improbably as the Miami Beach of the Norfolk coast, murmured something about having to get back.

'The sea!' the girl insisted, turning the car in the direction of the promenade: of screaming children and screaming gulls, of ice-cream van jingles, hot dogs dusted with sand and bellies roasting in the sun – all the fun of the fair that Jurnet remembered fondly from childhood days out with his parents.

He smiled, his spirits rising despite himself, savouring on his lips the resurrected taste of peppermint rock with the name Havenlea *printed all the way through!* How on earth did they do it? Even after all those years the wonder of it struck him afresh.

The only thing the matter with Havenlea was the bloody sea.

He intimated as much to Julian Grant when, having parked the Lotus on baking tarmac, they picked their way between the recumbent bodies, seeking a bum's space to call their own. The girl, who had become quiet and remote in direct proportion to the cheerful noise filling the air, had looked at him in some surprise.

'It's got the highest rating for cleanliness of anywhere along the coast.'

'Not Havenlea especially . . .' he began in explanation, and desisted. It was too hot and too personal to let on to Julian Grant what he thought of the sea, any sea, forever heaving up and down as if it was about to throw up: a desert hostile to man. When she found them a place to sit, on damp sand that at least told of the tide's receding, he would have sat down with his back to the water if it hadn't looked peculiar, the politically incorrect thing to do.

The girl clasped her hands round her knees and said: 'I've always loved the sea. We all did. The four of us used to drive out here at night, when there wasn't a soul about, and go bathing without any clothes on.' After a moment she added, with the girlish giggle he had noted earlier: 'We were crazy. It was freezing. We could have got pneumonia. But we kept on coming back just the same. Charlie always said that all life came out of the sea and that one day, finally, it would go back there again.'

Ahead of Jurnet, beyond the holiday-makers splashing in the shallows, the North Sea glittered metallically, sending out signals like an old scrubber got up for a night on the town. The detective shut his eyes on the sight.

'I reckon any life that came out of the sea couldn't get out fast enough.'

'Charlie said . . .' Julian Grant's face closed up. She did not go on with what Charlie Appleyard had said. She stood up and said: 'I'm going for a swim.'

With long, capable fingers she unknotted the beige blouse which, tied at the waist, had revealed a girdle of tanned skin Jurnet found only minimally enticing; discarded the garment to reveal, beneath, an exiguous bikini, white with scribblings of blue. She scuffed off her sandals, unhooked her scrap of a skirt, and threw it down on the sand with the rest. Her G-string matched the bikini top.

Aware that admiring glances from nearby males proclaimed the girl's body eminently worth a lay, Jurnet himself regarded it unmoved. Such boniness, he told himself unforgivingly, could only be a self-indulgence. Only when she stayed for a moment looking out to the line of the horizon, hands on hips, legs apart, and he saw – could not help seeing – curling out from beneath the stitched edges of the G-string, hairs bronze as the bronze hairs on her head, did he remark, in a voice obscurely charged with anger: 'Don't be long. I have to get back.'

'I won't be long.'

He had not intended to spy. So conclusively had the girl shut him out, it had become a matter of honour to reciprocate with a similar indifference; lie back on the hot sand, snatch forty winks, why not, while he had the chance. Yet – half raised, leaning on his elbows – watch her he did as she waded through the fussy little riffling waves, past the last of the paddlers and down the shallowly sloping sea floor.

She did not take her feet off the bottom, he noted, until she was a fair distance out, water up to her armpits; and then, somewhat to his surprise, took to the water in a clumsy, old-fashioned way that was at odds with her streamlined physique: breast stroke, and not very good at that. Somehow he had got it into his head that Julian Grant was good at everything she chose to undertake, from loving to lying like a trooper when it suited her purpose; from swimming to dancing rings round a copper foolish enough to try penetrating her defences.

The sea kept fidgeting as if it had St Vitus's Dance. Amid the glare Jurnet lost sight of the girl's head diminishing into the distance. He sat up, rubbed his elbows and, for a desultory moment or two, toyed with the idea of finding somewhere near at hand where he could hire a pair of bathing trunks. There would be an admittedly childish satisfaction in ploughing out to her across that sticky waste, doing the stylish crawl which had earned him any number of cups in the days when he had been the pride and joy of the Angleby Lads' Brigade. That would put the stuck-up bitch in her place.

If she asked him nicely, he might even offer to give her a swimming lesson.

Jurnet stood up, shaded his eyes, and located the bobbing dot far out. A hell of a way out. A crazy way out for a swimmer who moved in the water as if she had just got her certificate for doing a length of the baths.

Flushed with a sudden, all-embracing anxiety, the detective kicked off his shoes, pulled off his socks, hiked his shirt over his head without waiting to undo the buttons; let fall his trousers and stepped out of them, finding, even in that moment of fear, time to worry shamingly about what people on the beach would think of a guy going down to bathe in his underpants.

The tide had ebbed further, exposing a bedraggled expanse of shingle across which, conscious of his exposure to public ridicule, he sprinted recklessly, eager for the concealment of water. Once past the breakers and caught up in the lovely rhythm of the crawl, his body felt better but his brain was awhirl as he clove the water. Damn, damn, damn. He should have thought. *He should have thought . . .*

The dot was getting nearer, growing larger. So far as he could tell when he raised his head to get his bearings, Julian Grant had stopped swimming. Exhausted? Pausing for breath? Screwing up her courage to bid a last farewell to the world? Jurnet put his head down and redoubled his efforts.

When at last he reached the girl she was lying on her back cushioned by the water, arms and legs moving minimally; enough to keep her afloat, no more. Her hair, wet, could have been of any colour. Her wet face could have been any face, so drained was it of feeling and personality. To Jurnet it looked as if she had already consigned her essential self to the deep, the rest to follow.

She greeted the detective's arrival with neither surprise nor particular interest; merely frowned a little as at some tiresome interruption: but neither, to his relief, did she resist when he took hold of her – somewhat roughly out of fear that she might, at the last minute, take avoiding action – and, wheeling about, set them both on course, back to land.

Christ, it was a long way off. Jurnet, beginning to weaken, found himself thinking with gratitude of Pnina Benvista who, a cripple on land, a mermaid in water, had badgered him into going swimming with her at the Angleby pool at least twice a week. Without that practice, and loaded with the stupid cow stretched out supine against him, he doubted if he could have made it. A right Charlie he would have looked, dragged dead out of the briny in the royal purple boxer shorts the Israeli girl had given him for a Chanukah present.

He would have carried her up the beach if he hadn't feared it would draw even more attention than he sensed the underpants had attracted already. Deploring his vanity even as he yielded to it, he handled Julian Grant with a tenderness which had little to do with the girl herself; guided her faltering footsteps back to the tide mark and the small pile of clothing, setting her down gently, using her skirt as a makeshift towel to catch the drops that fell from her hair on to her shoulders; wiping away the salt encrusted round a mouth whose smallness had somehow become childlike, pathetic, instead of a design fault. Observing that, despite the heat, she was trembling, he would have fetched her hot, sweet tea from the kiosk, bright with streaming bunting, he could see in the distance, but feared to leave her lest, despite all the patent signs of weakness, she might, during his absence, find her way into the sea again and, second time round, oblivion.

His ministrations, such as they were, completed, Julian Grant lay curled up on the sand, for once looking soft, approachable, the intrusive skeleton withdrawn into her body. The sun, not giving up trying, had at last succeeded in striking amber lights in her hair, Miriam's hair.

Jurnet waited a while, then said: 'So what was that in aid of, then?'

'Nothing was in aid of anything. I just went for a swim.'

'So that was it? You could have fooled me. If you don't mind my saying so, you're a lousy swimmer.'

She was obviously on the road to recovery because she obviously did mind. When she spoke it sounded like a defence she had made many times before.

'At Eldon House – ' mentioning the most exclusive private school in Angleby – 'they only taught us breast stroke. They thought overarm wasn't ladylike.' After a moment she added: 'Charlie and Roger never stopped trying to get me to do the crawl, but somehow I've never got the hang of it.'

'To be honest, your breast stroke's not all that hot either.'

'Do shut up!' she said tiredly. 'You sound just like them.'

'Sorry,' Jurnet returned, truly contrite. 'But perhaps you'd care to tell me why, swimming the way you do, Eldon House style, you decided to strike out for China just now.'

'I didn't decide to strike out for anywhere.' Jurnet watched as the girl's eyes clouded over in a denial of remembrance. 'Just to let what would happen, happen.' She sat up, shaking back her hair, which sprang gloriously into its accustomed undulations. 'You're not going to send in one of your official reports?'

'There's no regulation which requires me to make a note of every time one of my contacts decides to take a dip.'

The other lay back, satisfied.

'That's all right, then.'

'What isn't all right', said Jurnet, who had been putting off the moment of truth ever since he had brought the girl ashore, 'is that someone's gone off with my trousers.'

<h1>15</h1>

Not only with his trousers but with the contents of his trouser pockets – his keys and his wallet. Jurnet was thankful that his credit cards at least were safely at home, and his ID card tucked into the breast pocket of his shirt.

It could have been worse, even if not much worse. Already, in his mind's eye, he saw the news spreading like spilt molasses through Police HQ – how Detective Inspector Ben Jurnet, good old Ben, snatching an unauthorized bathe off Havenlea beach, had had his pants lifted and, in full public view, had had to make his way home in fluorescent underpants printed with naked ladies getting up to all manner of interesting things whenever you jiggled your you-know-what. He heard the juvenile sniggers when his back was turned, savoured the elaborate condolences with him in his predicament. Sooner or later, the Superintendent, hearing of it – as hear he must – would let it be known he was not amused at this public loss of dignity on the part of a member of the team of Angleby CID: all the time, back turned to the room, looking out and down at the Market in his favourite posture, except that the immaculately tailored shoulders would be heaving with suppressed laughter.

The girl made a face as Jurnet helped her into the car, on the passenger side.

'The seat's hot,' she complained ill-temperedly, as if it were the detective's fault. 'You should have parked in the shade.'

Jurnet bit his lips, held back the retort that, first, there had been no shade in the tarmacked desert, and, secondly, she was the one who had been driving. Except for the hair, the image of Miriam was fading fast. 'How do I get into the boot? I take it your car keys are in your bag?'

For answer Julian Grant bent forward with what seemed a greater pretence of effort than the movement warranted; pressed some numbers on a pretty little square of some crystalline material set into the walnut dashboard. With a click the boot sprang open.

'It immobilizes everything until you punch out the code. Otherwise, open car, you could never leave it for a minute.'

'Neat.'

Jurnet went round to the rear of the car, pushed the boot fully open to receive on his face a full charge of the perfume of stinking fish. He picked up the Gucci handbag, which smelled terrible, and, with a certain mischievous satisfaction, brought it back to its owner.

The smell seemed to bring her round better than sal volatile.

'What on earth have you done with it?'

'I haven't done anything. It's that fish you bought for those gnomes. I ought to dump it.'

'You can't do that!' The girl was demonstrably barmy. 'I promised them!' Jurnet shrugged. 'Have it your own way. Have you got the keys?'

She handed them over without demur, seemingly content to leave him in charge, and only frowning once or twice when, unfamiliar with the car, he made a faulty selection of gear, or brought his foot down on the brake with less than the delicacy its exquisite innards called for. Jurnet, for his part, despite all that had happened could not but feel his spirits rise as, little by little, he and the lovely car fell into sync.

By the time they were out of the town and on to the marsh again, Angleby bound, it hardly mattered that his underpants had shrunk two sizes, or that, when he shifted in his seat, you could glimpse his bloody balls sticking out. Safe in the car, so long as they weren't overtaken by a double-decker bus, which didn't seem likely, there was only the girl to see, and she, in her present mood, wasn't likely to be turned on by the sight, that was for sure. That he had got damn-all out of her about Charlie Appleyard didn't seem to matter all that much, out on the causeway across the marsh, under the incredible sky.

Tugging his shirt down between his legs as far as it would go, he gave himself up to the present pleasure, sparing scarcely a regret for the fact that he hadn't, when it came to the point, felt able to stop in the town centre outside a menswear shop and ask Julian Grant to take herself and her fishy handbag inside and come out with a pair of jeans size 34. The way she looked – *disconnected* was the word that occurred to him – God knew what she might come out with.

All in all, it came as a surprise – as they neared the one viewing point along the way, an apron of concrete built out over the water meadows – that she asked him to pull off the road, she had something to say to him; even more of a surprise when, he having obeyed instructions, she sat for what seemed to him an unconscionable time looking down at her hands in her lap, saying nothing.

Below them, the reeds rustled unceasingly, on the road the cars went by with a haughty *swish!* At some unimaginable height a lark was singing, so far up as to be not even a dot in the sky – sounds that only served to confirm the silence.

It took only a small noise to fracture it, a small wail without music or dignity.

Julian Grant was crying.

Jurnet let the noise go on for a moment, then, reaching across for the handbag, fished out a tissue and handed it over without speaking: persisting when she turned away her face in watery annoyance.

'Blow your nose.' Having waited until at last she did as he requested, he said: 'You loved Charlie Appleyard, didn't you?'

She did not answer, not immediately.

'Do you know what polyandry is?' she demanded suddenly, turning her face fully towards his.

'The opposite of polygamy, isn't it?'

Julian Grant favoured the detective with a brief smile, for his cleverness.

'In Tibet – in the Himalayas anyway – there are women who have more than one husband – some who live with a whole family of brothers, one woman between the lot of them, all living happily together.'

'I've read about it somewhere.'

The girl had another question to ask.

'Is there any reason why, here in England, anywhere in the West, people have to be limited to loving just one person at a time – why they can't love two equally, or even more?'

'Shouldn't think reason comes into it. Law, local culture, all that. Maybe, in Tibet, it's the healthy mountain air or a shortage of oxygen. Simply that here in Angleby it doesn't happen like that.'

'What do you know?' she challenged. 'It takes imagination to step outside the old clichés, to make yourself open to whatever life has to offer.' Now Julian Grant was looking at the detective with something like pity. 'I bet you've only ever had one girlfriend at a time.'

Julian Grant's hair flamed in the strong light. The woman clothed in the sun. Jurnet agreed levelly: 'Something like that.'

101

'We were four and we were one,' the girl said, as one announcing a triumph. 'We not only belonged to, we were part of each other.' With apparent inconsequentiality she went on: 'I don't know if you've been in Roger's flat, the penthouse he's had built on the roof of the factory – the bedroom, I mean?' She laughed, actually laughed aloud at that and, eyes sparkling, clapped her hands together like a child. 'If you'd seen his bed you'd have been bound to wonder. Talk about the Great Bed of Ware! It's big enough for a regiment. He had it made specially for us. *Our bed . . .*' She quietened, remembering. 'In that bed we learned the secrets of each other's bodies and the secrets of each other's souls.'

The sparkling eyes regarded Jurnet with a child's seriousness.

'I suppose a conventional person like you would call it an orgy, the things we did to each other out of love, but it wasn't at all. It was innocent, it was beautiful. It was all you could possibly want in life.' She finished, low, the laughter subsumed in an aching void: 'I can't believe it's come to an end.'

'What about Jenny? Was it all she wanted?'

'Oh, Jenny!' she repeated indulgently. 'Her and her men, you mean. It's just the way she's made. They don't count, except for the money they pay. Only *we* counted, the four of us.'

Jurnet said: 'What I don't understand, if it's been so perfect, is why you and Roger ever decided to get married. Why not go on as you were? And why Roger especially? Why not Charlie? Why not marry him instead?'

Julian Grant smiled. 'I might well have done. If he'd been rich like Roger they'd probably have tossed a coin and I'd have married whoever won. As it is, Roger's rich and Charlie was poor, and I like having money.' She patted the edge of her seat, expensive leather. 'Roger gave me the Lotus for my birthday. But the principal reason for getting married at all was that the four of us decided it was time we had children, it would be fun – only Jenny has had something done to her, she can't have any, so it was up to me. Not Roger's children, you understand; not Charlie's, not Jenny's, not even mine: but ours, the four of us, because of course, marriage or no marriage, we were going to carry on the same way in that lovely bed, fucking till we got too old, the four of us together.'

'It sounds like a fairy tale.'

'It was.'

'Too good to be true.' Keeping envy out of his voice with difficulty, Jurnet made his meaning clear. 'What a wonderful lot you were, you and your pals! Are you quite sure, though, there was absolutely no jealousy between you? Four for one and one for four? Was it really like that?'

Julian Grant coloured as if she had been found out in a lie. She put a hand up to one cheek, felt its warmth and capitulated.

'Perhaps I should have said five – only I didn't want you to laugh.' She glanced at Jurnet pleadingly before once more transferring her gaze to the marsh and the emptiness of air which encompassed them. 'Do you believe in ghosts?'

To one who, in the dark reaches of every night, conjured his dead lover from the grave, the question presented no problem.

'Yes.'

'Then you'll understand about Loy Tanner.' At the detective's prompt agreement, given without frills or reservations, the girl turned back to him in unexpected friendliness. 'Loy was the fifth in our bed. No wonder it had to be so wide! A hero takes up a lot of room, did you know that, especially a dead one who won't lie down. Every time Charlie was off again about what a great man Loy was – and he meant in every way, in bed as well as out of it – I'd remind him that he was an old man of fifty-seven when it all happened. He'd had his time, he had grandchildren, for Pete's sake, and probably a pot belly from all the ale they drank in those days. If he chose to go out of life with all flags flying, good luck to him, I said – but what did it have to do with us? We were young and Tanner was history.'

'And what did Charlie have to say to that?'

'Charlie?' The girl frowned with the effort of remembering. 'He laughed. We all of us laughed a lot, but Charlie most of all. He laughed and he said that I was talking rubbish. Young or old, we were history too; that the present was a mere punctuation point, gone as soon as it was here, and as to the future, nobody knew if there even was one, let alone what it would contain. Only the past was real, he said, and therefore that's where we were all at, like it or not, along with Loy Tanner, King Solomon, Marilyn Monroe and anybody else you cared to mention. It wasn't true, was it?' she cried with a sudden wildness. 'Charlie's dead and in the past and I'm here marooned in a bloody present which goes on for ever!'

Julian Grant got out of the car abruptly and came round to the driver's side.

'Move over!' she commanded, scarcely waiting for the other to do so before scrambling her way into the driving seat. 'I'm going to drive. Don't worry,' she added, mouth twisting in amused contempt at the look on the detective's face. 'I'm never going swimming out of my depth ever again, I promise, and I'm going to drive very, very carefully, if only to show that shit Charlie Appleyard he didn't know what he was talking about.'

Julian Grant drove Jurnet home, uttering the small noises of surprise more suited to a tourist than a native as, the detective directing, they left behind the lovely city centre and threaded their way through unfashionable streets to reach the delicatessen. Bloody snob, thought Jurnet, full afresh of how much he disliked the girl – almost as much as he disliked himself for being bewitched by her hair.

Almost as much as he disliked himself when – after having her pull up at the side door so that he could slip up to the flat unobserved – it suddenly dawned on him that his door key had been on the same ring as his car keys. Nothing for it but to go through the shop.

'What a marvellously convenient place to live,' the girl, having surveyed Mario's window display, commented with maddening condescension.

'It's OK.'

'I'll wait while you get yourself some trousers and the spare keys and drive you back to your car.'

'No need. I'll need to take a shower.' Back on his home patch he was doubly aware of tensions arising afresh – her hair, so like Miriam's, his guilt, her hair . . . He said: 'No necessity to keep you hanging about.'

'That's all right. I've nothing else on, particularly.' Julian Grant settled herself in her seat as if prepared for a long stay. 'If I feel like it, I might even go inside and treat myself to a salt beef sandwich or something. If I feel I've waited long enough and you still haven't put in an appearance, I'll take off. No problem.'

Lacking any further excuse to postpone the inevitable moment of getting out of the car in his rumpled underwear, of having to run the gauntlet of the shop under the astonished eyes of Mario and of such of his clientele as might at that very moment be sitting at the small white tables drinking coffee and minding their own business until confronted by the horrendous apparition, he launched himself out of the Lotus, ran across the pavement, entered the delicatessen and headed for the stairs deliberately shutting out of his consciousness the reality of the faces turned towards him in incredulous amusement.

An awareness of Julian Grant's laughter, wafting across the space the detective put between them as if the wolves were after him, did not help either.

This time the flat seemed even more than a home, a sanctuary. Even the crucifix over the bed, in Jurnet's fancy, radiated welcome, the drooping head uplifting itself momentarily before its doomful weight took it down again. Gritty with sand and sweat, Jurnet made for the bathroom, stepped into the shower just as he was, let the water soak shirt, shoes and underpants before finding in himself the strength to remove them. Only when clean at last, a residual self emerging from the accretions of the day, did the realization dawn that every bone in his body was aching, every brain cell ready to throw in the sponge; that, to put it bluntly, forays into the North Sea to rescue possibly distressed maidens from hypothetical sea monsters were – if they had ever been – no longer for the likes of him.

Without bothering to dry himself, and taking a piercing pleasure in the small channels that travelled down his flesh, agents of cool refreshment, he came back to the bedroom, flung himself down on the bed and was asleep before – as he had intended – he could check up on what the Man on the crucifix was up to, if anything.

He slept sweetly, untroubled by either dreams or ghosts, whilst the world went on its way and his room fell into shade – a retreat of the light which was probably what, in the fullness of time, awakened him, seeing that Pnina Benvista, the Israeli girl, had taken off her shoes to avoid making a noise, and anyway, she knew the bedroom well enough to be able to steer clear of every creaking floorboard.

Jurnet opened his eyes to find her bending over him, her straight black hair falling over her shoulders, her dark eyes shaded with anxiety.

'Are you all right?'

Wishing to God she hadn't asked, Jurnet nodded: sat up reluctantly, feeling instantly unfresh again in the used-up grunge which was all that was on offer by way of air.

'Touch of the sun, that's all.'

Disguising the effort, he swung his feet round and sat on the edge of the bed, legs dangling. If only, he thought, he did not feel obliged to feel sorry for the crippled girl, unable to tell her to bugger off, for Christ's sake, and leave him alone. *God, how he ached!* Maybe it was true about the sun. More than a touch: a bleeding annihilation.

'The red car is gone,' Pnina Benvista announced. 'The young woman said to tell you she couldn't wait any longer on account of the fish. She said it was smelling to high heaven and if she waited any longer she was afraid the gnomes would refuse to eat it.' A pause; then, as Jurnet made no observation: 'What did she mean, these gnomes? Gnomes are not real, are they?'

His mind taken over by a quick picture of the gnomes, fishing indomitably but in vain the dead grass, Jurnet felt a sudden surge of brotherhood. You and me both, he thought, fishing. Fishing to no purpose. *Who killed Charlie Appleyard?*

To the girl he said, in answer to her query: 'No, not real. Must be some kind of joke.'

'Oh.' The Israeli girl, who had long ago given up trying to understand the English sense of humour, took this well. She came closer to the bed, bestowing on Jurnet's naked body a look of love so unashamedly carnal as to be innocent, immaculate.

The detective could not restrain himself. He groaned aloud.

'You are in pain? Something is wrong?'

'Nothing. I told you.'

'If you are sure . . .' Reassured, she put a hand on his arm, her face alight with the eager stoicism of unrequited love. 'If you are sure, I thought perhaps you might like to go for a swim . . .'

Jurnet heaved his protesting body off the bed, pulled in his stomach, made with the pectorals. Smiled, the biggest effort of all.

'Great.'

16

'I don't know,' grumbled Jurnet, as ever unforgiving of his own shortcomings. 'The guy's too good-looking by half. I know I shouldn't, but I can't find it in myself to trust a bloke who looks like a cross between Adonis and an ad for aftershave.'

Or Valentino, thought Sergeant Ellers with amused affection, studying his superior officer's profile reflected in the mirror at the rear of the lift in which the two were rising to Roger Adamson's flat on top of the shoe factory. Aloud he said: 'You're a touch hard on the bugger. He can't help the way he looks.'

'I said I knew it was wrong.'

The other made no further observation, recognizing that Jurnet was in one of his moods, the way he always was in the first stages of a murder investigation, dissatisfied with every aspect of himself, and especially with his crass inability to reach out and wrench the truth from its hiding place.

With every sign of contentment with the world as it was, the little Welshman conjured up a smile among the chubby rosiness and the freckles which were his own contribution to the merriment of nations.

'Lucky for me I'm only averagely pretty, then.'

The flat was not what, from the little he had seen of Roger Adamson, Jurnet had expected. It was an ambiguous place, all creams and beiges, with no hard edges; no pictures on the walls, everything melting into the next thing so that even its owner, coming forward to meet them across an acreage of floor on whose behalf an entire rain forest must have given up the ghost, seemed himself part of the background, not quite real.

Was Roger Adamson really so modest? The detective, who had expected something much more flamboyant, shook hands with a wariness that the lean strength of the proffered hand only partly dispelled. The fellow had pots of dosh. Could be, Jurnet reminded himself, he had simply turned the place over to a professional interior decorator who happened to be into shades of pale.

Reassured by the panorama of the city, dear and familiar, glimpsed through an expanse of uncurtained window, across an area of roof garden planted with a Japanese austerity, the detective commented: 'Fine view you have up here.'

'Ah, Angleby.' Adamson's tone held affection and exasperation equally. 'Jewel of East Anglia. Too good to be true.' A harsher note ousting the humour: 'I should never have put in those damn windows. Short of letting down the blinds you can't get away from the place, indoors or out.' With an abrupt return to the host, charming and beautiful: 'But you aren't here to discuss the view. Do sit down. Can I get you something to drink?'

The two detectives refused refreshment; perched themselves on the edges of chairs whose upholstery threatened to engulf them. Roger Adamson said: 'I've been looking forward to talking to you. Where do you want me to start?'

'Charlie rang me,' said Roger Adamson. 'He was speaking from a public call box because I could hear the 10p pieces being fed in. He must have fixed himself up with a supply of them. He wanted to know if he could come over for a shower. He said the ones up on the Moot were hopeless, only a dribble came out of them, no pressure to speak of. Of course I said come on over.'

Jurnet pointed out: 'Booking a shower couldn't have taken all that many 10p pieces.'

'No.'

In the unrelenting light that pervaded the flat like some exclusive extra Jurnet was able to see that Adamson hadn't shaved that day, perhaps not the day before either. With one so fair it was difficult to be certain. What *was* certain was that, ordinarily speaking, an unshaven Roger Adamson was a contradiction in terms.

It came into Jurnet's mind that Orthodox Jews, whose stubble seldom gleamed golden in the light, stopped shaving for a month as part of the ritual of bereavement. Not Roger Adamson's scene, of course, but a permissible analogy. The man had lost a friend.

Gently but persistently the detective inquired: 'Why did the call take so long? Was there something else besides the shower?'

The other hesitated, gnawing his lip. Then: 'He seemed down in the dumps, which wasn't like Charlie at all. He said he had to talk to somebody and, I suppose, he just picked on me.'

'Very natural, from what Miss Grant's been telling me about what pals you all were.' Taking the red that rose in Adamson's cheeks as confirmation that the girl had been talking possibly out of turn, Jurnet did not press home his advantage. Merely asked, in quiet tones: 'Did he let on the cause of his depression?'

Despite the smooth tan which spoke of luxury and leisure and everything gained without effort, the young man's eyes filled with tears.

'In a way, in a roundabout way. He started on about how much easier it was in Loy Tanner's time, as compared with today, to capture and retain the attention of the public to what one was trying to do . . .'

'You sure you got it right?' Jurnet was genuinely surprised. 'I mean, with all the media we have around today – telly, radio, newspapers, Lord knows what – how could he possibly have thought that?'

'That was my own first reaction. But you know, once Charlie pointed it out, I could see that, crazy as it seems, he was right. Back then, in 1549, within a matter of days and through word of mouth only, twenty thousand men had arrived on Monkenheath, and, no time at all after that, heralds were galloping post-haste from London to try and negotiate a settlement, armies were moving up to Norfolk to flush the rebels out. Some of the biggest bugs in the land travelled out to the Oak of Reformation to give their opinion on what was going on.

'And even after it was all over and Tanner's body dangling from the castle ramparts, people didn't forget, the flame was kept burning somehow. Because, when the time came, and even though they didn't like Catholics, people flocked to Mary Tudor's standard and soon put a stop to all that nonsense of Warwick trying to make his daughter-in-law, Lady Jane Grey, Queen of England.' Excited by what he had to say, Roger Adamson's voice grew younger, vulnerable. 'Without so much as a sniff of media, Charlie said, they changed the history of England whereas, today, where had they got – he and the rest of them up on the Moot? Bloody nowhere – a nine days' wonder, headlines only till a new story comes along and that's it – yesterday's news, who wants to know?'

'How did you answer Charlie once he'd got that off his chest?'

The other shrugged despondently. 'I did my best, for what it was worth. I pointed out he'd already announced that they were going to stay on the Moot until December, and he could hardly expect the media to hang around for months on end on the chance of something sensational happening in the meantime. I said – oh hell, I don't remember what I said except cheer up, he'd feel better once he'd had that shower, only he ran out of 10p pieces before I'd finished.' Gloomily: 'I should have told him to reverse the charges, only it never occurred to me.'

'It didn't matter. The rest could wait until he arrived.'

'That's just it.' Now the tears were falling unashamedly. 'He didn't. He never showed. As soon as he rang off I got on to Julian to let her know Charlie was on his way, only she said – just as well, as it turned out – that, much as she'd love to come over, she couldn't: she was washing her hair. I knew it was no good phoning Jenny. She'd be working.'

Jurnet observed: 'Washing her hair wouldn't have taken Miss Grant all that long. I wouldn't have thought she'd let a little thing like that keep her from hurrying over.'

Roger Adamson passed a hand over his eyes, eyed the resultant wet on his palm with a rueful wonder.

'Sorry about that. I'll be giving you the wrong idea.' Pulling himself together he looked the detective full in the face. 'Let me spare you your discreet and delicate inquiries, Inspector. I loved Charlie as a friend. I'm not gay. We all loved one another.'

'So I understand from your fiancée. That's why I'm surprised she cried off on the grounds she was otherwise engaged.'

'You don't know Julian. Washing her hair's her own personal way of celebrating Holy Communion. At least two different shampoos and a conditioner, and when she's finished no electric dryer, it has to dry naturally and God help you if you go out before it's absolutely dry, otherwise the ends will split and you'll end up in the lowest circle of hell along with Judas Iscariot.' He finished, lovingly: 'You have to admit she has beautiful hair.'

'Indeed.' Jurnet nodded, remembering Miriam's habit of grabbing whatever came to hand, from soap powder to washing-up liquid, and still her hair looked wonderful. Miriam rushing off to work with water still trickling down her back, drops of it trapped in the downy hairs at the back of her neck. He hugged to his heart momentarily his satisfaction that Miriam had never needed to work at being beautiful.

'Were you worried when Charlie didn't turn up?'

'Not worried. Disappointed. Annoyed with myself for not reversing the charges and continuing the conversation to its end. I just thought, probably there was some difficulty on the Moot that unexpectedly needed straightening out. It crossed my mind he might have gone to see his father – presumably the old man's got a shower in the house and he could have killed two birds with one stone. Or he could have gone over to Jenny's even though there'd be no one there. He had a key – we all have one – and Jenny, as you might expect, has, in the way of her business, got a state of the art shower that'll all but atomize you if you turn it on full, to say nothing of a bidet and several other little gadgets to make you feel good.' A small frown creased the beautiful brow as he added: 'When Julian rang me back – which she did while her hair was drying – and I told her Charlie hadn't turned up after all, I got the impression, from the way she spoke, she wasn't sorry, not really. I understood. She liked us all to be together, not separate. That was the way we all felt.'

Jurnet said forthrightly: 'I gather you shared her with Charlie, and Jenny as well. A *ménage à quatre*, would that be? An arrangement you intended to continue after your marriage.'

'Not share. We all belonged to each other. That's why, without Charlie, we're so bloody incomplete.'

Refusing Sergeant Ellers's invitation to go back to his place – Rosie, his wife, dimpled as a button-backed chair and probably the best cook in the Eastern Counties, had made a vichyssoise guaranteed to cool off Shadrack, Meshak and Abednego, let alone two over-heated Angleby coppers – Jurnet dropped off the little Welshman at his front door and made his way to the quiet suburban street where a modest building housed under one roof with no sense of incongruity a champion-class table-tennis table and the Scrolls of the Law.

Once, in a moment of irritation – the Rabbi, fat, his legs too short for his body, his arms flabby and varicose, having nevertheless just beaten him 21 – 13 – Jurnet had questioned the aptness of the juxtaposition.

Rabbi Schnellman had smiled, adjusting the glasses whose thick lenses magnified eyes that were childlike but not simple, straightening the tiny *yarmulke* that clung to his bald head like a desperate limpet. 'You think we should change it for snooker?'

'I didn't mean that . . .' Already the detective, straining every nerve to become a Jew because Miriam would not marry him until he did, was regretting his words. Not for a guest in the house to question his host's domestic arrangements. Especially as, so far as he was concerned, he would happily have made it tiddly-winks if it shortened the time until he could stand in the synagogue under the *chupa*, the marriage canopy, his beloved at his side. 'I only meant . . .'

'Yes?' Encouragingly.

'I don't know what I meant.'

'Bravo!' Rabbi Schnellman had clapped his plump hands softly. 'We progress. Now that we know the limits of your ignorance, all that remains is to discover the extent of your knowledge. But first – ' with an affectionate clasp of his pupil's arm – 'we will fortify ourselves with a cup of tea.'

Now, in the flat above the synagogue hall, perched uncomfortably on one of the absurd Louis Seize style chairs which had been the pride and joy of the Rabbi's dead wife, sipping tea that brought out a sweat which seemed an insult to her floral and gilt china, Jurnet said: 'I really dropped by to let you know I won't be able to get over for lessons for a while. This Appleyard business – can't say how long it'll take. Besides which – ' the cup seemed to rattle on its saucer of its own accord, the Rabbi looked anxious – 'it isn't as if there's any particular hurry, now.'

'There never is.' The Rabbi reached across the table, took the imperilled china and put it down on the lace-edged cloth spread cater-cornerwise as his dead Rachel had long ago instructed him.

Looking happier: 'Come back when you're ready. *Now* is a movable feast, moving along, now fast, now slow, according to how we choose to hurry along or to loiter by the way.' With a smile: 'Even if we cannot settle man's place in the universe we can always play ping-pong, which I sometimes think comes to much the same thing. Anyway, it is a good release of tension.'

Charmed by the other's reduction of the mayhem at the table-tennis table to an infantile pastime, Jurnet asked, after only a small hesitation: 'What did you mean by "*now* is a movable feast"? Charlie Appleyard used to say there was no such thing as "now" – that only the past was real.'

Rabbi Schnellman shook his head, benign, indulgent.

'Did he say that, when *now* is all there is! He must have got it mixed up with time, which is only an academic convenience, a game clever people have made up and play, like chess, or Monopoly. I'm sorry I did not meet that poor fellow. I should have enjoyed a conversation with him on the subject. A good man, from what I saw of him on the television.'

'Was he? I don't know. We're still in the process of getting acquainted. You could have met him, if you'd wanted to. People like you, people of influence, had an open invitation to speak from the Oak of Reformation, just the way it was with Loy Tanner.'

'People of influence – me?' Rabbi Schnellman chuckled, and then stopped chuckling. Pushing a laden plate towards his visitor, he said: 'Have a biscuit. Mrs Levine, Pnina's landlady, made them for me. A good woman who is very anxious about that child.' After a pause: 'I too am anxious.'

Jurnet said: 'I don't want a biscuit, thanks. And she is not a child.'

Rabbi Schnellman conceded the point, in part.

'You are right. A very capable woman with her head, as they say, screwed on the right way, and her feet firmly on the ground. What she has done to Miriam's business, how she has picked up the threads, is remarkable – remarkable! But in other ways – perhaps it is her disability, perhaps the answer lies in her history – she is very young and vulnerable.' The Rabbi made a minute adjustment to his *yarmulke*, which – it suddenly came to Jurnet – filled much the same function as the Superintendent's gold pen, a talisman, a source of strength and reassurance. 'Sometimes, Ben, I tremble for her.'

Jurnet said: 'I didn't seduce her, if that's what you're getting at.'

'Did I say so? You have only to look into her face to know that she is in love with you.' A moment passed before the Rabbi added: 'And into yours to know it is not reciprocated.'

'She's a grand girl. I'm very fond of her.'

'Yes,' said the Rabbi sadly. 'That's what I'm afraid of.'

Jurnet came into the delicatessen to find Mario making up an order of two salt beef sandwiches for a customer, in Jurnet's opinion, fat enough to know better. Thirsty and out of temper with either himself or Rabbi Schnellman, he wasn't sure which, the detective had half a mind to go to the fridge himself, get out the *citron pressé* which Pnina Benvista had surely put there for him.

Only half a mind because, over the months of his tenancy of the flat upstairs, a habit had evolved, a custom of the country; the Italian bringing the drink over to one of the small white tables and setting it down with conscious ceremony, to watch smiling as Jurnet sipped and pronounced it good.

Usually, if there were customers at the counter when he arrived, the delicatessen owner would serve them rapidly, the sharp knife going snicker-snack through the finished artefact. Today – perhaps it was the heat, though inside the delicatessen it was blessedly cool, that made the man so slow to make change, so intent on small talk that kept the sandwich-buyer from leaving. Ten to one, Jurnet, in a mood to think the worst, told himself, there was no life-restoring lemon to pour down his dehydrated gullet and he'd be back, willy-nilly, to that damned Coke.

But no. At last the bugger departed with his fodder, and Mario brought the drink over to the table, waiting as usual, and yet not as usual. For once, the Italian was not smiling.

Jurnet took a deep draught, leaned back in his chair and said: 'That's good.'

'Is always good.' The other nodded, more vigorously than the occasion called for. 'Pnina knows exactly how much sugar, how much fizz. Pnina – ' The man stopped suddenly, his face screwed up with anxiety.

Not you too! Jurnet thought, finding additional cause for annoyance in the way the man called the Israeli girl by her first name affectionately unadorned, whereas with him it was always Mr Ben. 'What about Pnina? She's come in, hasn't she?'

'She is here, upstairs. Dusting, I think she said. Or maybe hoovering. I think, a little time ago, I hear the vacuum cleaner.'

'In this heat? The girl's crazy!'

'No.' The Italian, having made up his mind, spoke without further hesitation. 'Crazy, no. In love, yes.'

'Not you too!' This time Jurnet came out with the words aloud. 'First the Rabbi, now you! What is this – Be Kind to Pnina Day? Be Beastly to Ben?' He stood up, leaving the glass half full. 'I'm going to get a shower.'

He turned towards the door which closed off the upper flat.

Mario said again: 'Pnina – ' and there she was, a little out of breath as she always was after tackling stairs, whether up or down: wearing a yellow dress which did nothing for her sallow skin and the purple shadows under her eyes even when, as now, her cheeks were flushed scarlet. Head bowed, she stood framed in the doorway, waiting, as waves of shame engulfed the detective, turning his face as red as hers.

Then: 'You bloody fool!'

At that, the girl's head came up in defiant despair.

'I do not care what names you use, so long as you do not have pity.'

'Not you, for Christ's sake – me! Have I really managed to give you the idea that all I cared for about Miriam was her hair?'

'I know it was not all. I know what she was, what you were to each other. I could never try to be another Miriam, I know that. But the girl in the red car, the one with the gnomes – one look and I could see she was not another Miriam either, only a girl with hair like hers. And I thought, if it is only the hair . . .' Pnina Benvista broke off, then in a voice harsh with effort began again. 'The picture on the packet showed the exact colour and how easy it was to do it yourself. Only it is a lie, or I did not do it right, but I don't think so.' Low, at breaking point: 'I am well punished.'

'I tell her,' Mario interposed eagerly, love and concern brightening his dark, Mediterranean features, 'I tell her Sally, two doors down the street, is a fine hairdresser, she could win prizes. Every Saturday morning my Maria goes there, she comes out beautiful. I already tell her Sally will put it right, no problem.'

Not Sally's problem, not Pnina's. Aloud Jurnet said, eyeing with something like affection the absurd patchwork of ginger and orange which had taken over the shining black like some plague of tropical fungi: 'Come back upstairs with me and I'll wash it out.'

The Israeli girl moved further away, rejecting his compassion.

'Not possible.' Tears held fiercely at bay welled up in the dark eyes regardless. 'They say in the instructions it is permanent.'

114

'We can try. If they were wrong about the colour they can be wrong about that. And anyway, permanent can only mean until it grows out. It's not the end of the world.'

Mario put in: 'Sally will find you a wig, I promise you won't know the difference.'

'I am twenty-seven,' Pnina Benvista said, tears and voice under control. 'Too old to behave like a lovesick schoolgirl.' Turning to the Italian: 'I will go to this Sally tomorrow. She can cut my hair short, so there is less of it to see, nothing more. No wigs, nothing to cover up. It is my own fault. As they say, I needed to be taught a lesson, and I have been taught. Now I am going back to Mrs Levine's. I have a scarf in the car I will tie on. I do not want to frighten her, nor the girls at work tomorrow.'

Guilty as hell, Jurnet pleaded: 'Honestly, Pnina, it's not that important . . .'

On her way out of the delicatessen the girl turned back to him, unrelenting.

'Now you are being sorry for me again. I will not have it!'

17

The first of them arrived before it was light, padding through the narrow streets of the little town in small groups, twos and threes, so quietly that those of the locals who were still abed slept on, whilst, of the few that were out and about, hardly any so much as looked out of their windows to see what was up, outside. By breakfast time, however, the inhabitants of Windham, especially those who lived in the vicinity of St Simeon's, could have needed no reminding.

Four hundred and fifty years after Loy Tanner, swinging from the castle battlements, was denied a resting place in the church-yard of his home town, Charlie Appleyard was coming to stand in – or rather, lie in – for him.

Not all the young men pressing towards the church in the cool of the morning had been in on the demonstration up on the Moot, though most of them had. The rest were pleased to claim the connection, no harm in that. A new myth was already in the process of evolving and they wanted to be part of it.

They were, on the whole, a well-behaved bunch, knowing their place, which was not inside the church, with its soaring nave and angels spread-eagled against the roof. Instead, mindful of tombstones, they spread out over the churchyard, keeping a respectful distance from the blue ribbon which fenced off the waiting grave; finding seats on the low encircling wall when there was no more room on the ground, and lining either side of Church Lane once every other available space was taken.

The building, prior to the dissolution of the monasteries in 1538, had been part of an abbey, hence its unexpected grandeur, out of all proportion to its present function as the parish church of a small town. At its rear stood the remains of the chapter house and what was left of a tower whose ring of bells had once called the monks to prayer; and here too, despite its distance from the action, a swarming of young men had gathered, ignoring notices that warned of the danger of falling masonry.

The police, who had been taken by surprise by their early arrival, were relieved to find how trouble-free was their task of keeping order; how easy it was to keep open a passage along Church Lane for the hearse and its attendant vehicles, and for the coffin borne over the ancient flagstones which led from the lych gate to the church porch.

Not fair, thought Jurnet, to keep out of the church itself the only people who seemed actually to want to be at Charlie Appleyard's funeral. The small invited congregation, with their careful, closed faces, looked lost and uneasy in the length, the loftiness, of the nave.

Arthur Appleyard, in a black suit that had to have been hired, and looking like one of the undertaker's assistants, except that their clothes fitted them, sat in the front pew among a cluster of presumed relations from whom he had icily dissociated himself, staring angrily at the coffin waiting in the centre aisle to be properly churched before being taken away and hygienically disposed of. Jurnet wondered who had ordered the single spray of lilies that lay on the box a little askew, as if someone had placed it there absent-mindedly. It did not look like Arthur Appleyard's style.

The only other person equally intent on the coffin was, to the detective's astonishment, none other than Dr Colton, someone he could not remember ever before seeing at the funeral of one of his clients. Normally speaking, once the man had forwarded his report to the coroner, that was that: on to the next mucked-up cadaver, to be further mucked up by the post-mortem before being in turn stuffed mercifully out of sight, enabling the family and friends of the deceased to sit down to the funeral baked meats without throwing up.

'He was so clean,' he had complained to Jurnet at a meeting convened in the Superintendent's room. 'Altogether too much of a good thing. No semen, no recoverable DNA – a wonder he had any genitalia left, the way he'd gone at them. I can't even say how long before death there was any sexual activity, if there was any. I can't even be sure of that. Any more than I can say for certain if he washed himself before death or if somebody else did it for him immediately after.'

'Loose ends,' the Superintendent had murmured soothingly, only to receive in return a look of mixed fury and self-loathing. The police surgeon did not ask much of his corpses in return for services rendered with dedication and the most delicate sympathy: only that they did not take their tawdry secrets to the grave with them. Now, possessed possibly by the overwhelming self-confidence of the place, the trumpeting angels, the massive piers marching towards the altar, no questions to be asked or answered, Colton's expression, unlike that of Charlie Appleyard's father, was not of anger but forgiveness.

It came to Jurnet that the man had come to honour the one that got away.

Dr Adamson was there, as was to be expected, elegant in black and intent on the Order of Service which had been distributed to the mourners on entering; lifting her head to nod briefly to Jurnet and returning to her scrutiny before he had time to face her squarely, discern what might be there to be read in her grey, tale-telling eyes.

Jenny Nunn, demure as a convent girl in a grey suit that came well over her knees, sat swollen-eyed, twisting between hands whose fingernails were devoid of polish a handkerchief of a startling whiteness, a special handkerchief, new for the event. Next to her Julian Grant sat with her arm through Roger Adamson's, their hands interlaced, their expressions sad and preoccupied, bronze hair and gold hair touching. It was, Jurnet suddenly realized, the first time he had seen the two together, obviously lovers, absorbed in each other to the exclusion of everything else, death included.

Biting his lips with annoyance at the effect that, despite everything, the bronze hair was still having on his physical reactions, the detective called up a mental picture of Pnina, her hair cropped

117

by Sally down the street and looking like the mottled pelt of some small dog, not one with a pedigree. It helped, a little, and to his surprise he found himself smiling: whereupon, embarrassed, copying Dr Adamson, he gave his attention to the Order of Service; but his heart was not in it. It was a relief to find Sergeant Ellers at his side.

It was a relief, too, to learn from the little Welshman that outside, in the churchyard and in the town itself, all was decorum, the uniformed branch having next to nothing to do, Batterby and Sid Hale and their helpers circulating unnoticed on the look-out for the elusive Buck and Joe. As for the crew lazily promenading the brilliant sky in the police helicopter, it was a doddle: down below, grief and goodwill abounding.

Even the media were showing circumspection, not their customary ploy. The Sergeant himself, never at ease with a God so different in kind from the one to be found in his native chapels, was the unlucky one. About to retreat thankfully back to the Low Church open air, notes of solemnity issuing from the organ froze him to the spot. Clergy entered stage right, the congregation rose and he was trapped.

They buried Charlie Appleyard without extraneous comment. No eulogy from the pulpit, no one come forward to fill the echoing church with praises of heroic failure and promises of a crown waiting in the hereafter. Maybe the chaos of Angleby Market Place was still too raw for any such kindness. More likely it was that Arthur Appleyard, taking a bleak revenge for his own shortcomings as a father, the dead man's shortcomings as a son, had put his foot down: no.

'As for man, his days are as grass: as a flower of the field so he flourisheth. For the wind passeth over it and it is gone, and the place thereof shall know it no more –'

Not the best moment for Jack Ellers's Mobile phone to put its electronic oar in. Red-faced, the Sergeant withdrew a distance from his superior officer's side, hauled the unfeeling gadget out of his pocket and listened: spoke briefly in acknowledgement. Came back and tugged at Jurnet's sleeve without thought that it was the guy's Sunday best.

By then, as it happened, Jurnet scarcely needed to be told. From somewhere behind the church, distorted by the bulk between but not insulated by it, from somewhere among the monastic ruins a sound had enlarged itself into a shout of terrified disbelief that scattered the attendant crowd like the roar of an approaching tornado, police efforts to stem the onrush as futile as if it were indeed against the elements that they strove.

It was the helicopter crew which had been the first to notice the glimmer on top of the ruined bell tower and the two figures that had somehow – for the stairs and intervening floors had long since crumbled into dust – managed to install themselves there, and which, approaching for a closer look, had been forced to back off as, all of a sudden, the glimmer had blossomed into a tongue of flame, reaching for the sky. The two men appeared to have set fire to a banner attached to a pole, white bunting sewn with what looked to be a representation of an oak leaf, many times life-size, and to be flourishing the unwieldy object, describing figures of eight in the air, to and fro, to and fro.

Chuffed to have something worthy of their attention after the prolonged boredom of going round and round the mulberry bush, the helicopter men's initial approval had quickly changed to incredulous horror. The banner – pole and all – reduced to ashes, the flag wavers – so they radioed down to ground level – had produced two jerry cans, the contents of which they were pouring over themselves, flinging the stuff around like kids – could you believe it? – making a joke of it.

Petrol!

Jack Ellers panted: 'They've called up the Forestry Commission 'copter from Telford Centre – the one they use for dousing forest fires.'

'For all the good that'll do.'

By the time the two detectives had forced their way round to the rear of the church, the two men on top of the tower were well alight. No sound came from them, no screams of agony, no clang of ghostly bells, at least nothing that could be heard above the lamentation, the exultation, of the crowd below. The young men who had entered God's Acre so mannerly, so respectful, were jumping up and down like maniacs, punching the air, pushing the police aside with an arrogance of contempt of which they could never have dreamed themselves capable.

A few, riled out of mind by the fuzz's attempted intervention, pried bits and pieces from the medieval masonry strewn all about and, to an accompaniment of uncouth cries, threw them at the coppers: but they were not many. For all the uproar, the attention of everyone – of the young men and the police alike –

was concentrated on the two figures on top of the tower – two figures who, wrapped in flame, did not appear to move, other than to shrink into themselves, concentrating what had once been human into a tarry essence which continued to burn until the Forestry Commission helicopter arrived and hosed it down, no nonsense, as if they were any old trees that had suddenly got ideas above their station.

With the dying down of the fire the spirit of the crowd gathered beneath the tower flickered, flared up in harmony, then went out. The young men watched in silence as two gloved and helmeted robots were let down on to the tower roof to gift-wrap the burnt-out carrion in silver foil that glittered in the sunlight. Only a sigh, a communal indrawn breath, followed the packages as they swung upward, to disappear into the body of the helicopter.

The show over, the police were scarcely needed to shepherd the throng through the side gate which led directly from the monastery ruins back to the twentieth-century world where barbecues were something that happened to bangers and mash, not your fellow men.

Just as well, thought Jurnet: anything that gets them out of Windham without any hassle. Only when evening came, only when home again and slumped in domestic familiarity in front of the telly, would what had happened that afternoon become real: by which time the crisis would be over, the police stood down, and the Chief Constable and the Superintendent congratulating themselves on their cleverness, blast them.

In front of St Simeon's, in the churchyard, the obsequies for Charlie Appleyard were drawing to a close.

'We have entrusted our brother Charles to God's merciful keeping and we commit his body to the ground in sure and certain hope of the resurrection to eternal life . . .'

One by one, the mourners at the graveside threw earth down on to the coffin, the ladies, allowed in politeness to go first, levering genteel helpings from the pile waiting to fill in the hole once the ritual was completed. Arthur Appleyard, sweating in his tight suit, watched with rising impatience as the rite was performed over and over again; until, unable to control himself longer, he seized the long-handled shovel from the next in line and dug into the pile with it as if he would move it in its entirety in one go.

It was an enormous shovelful and he was, all said and done, an old man wearing a suit that was too small; so that it was not all that surprising that, as he brought the spade round, getting into position to let fly, the jacket, lining and all, with an astonishingly metallic screech, split up his back from collar to hem, allowing a white shirt, dark with patches of sweat, to poke as if thankfully into the outer air.

For a moment the man glanced sharply over his shoulder, as if to catch in the act the perpetrator of the insult to his dignity. No one met his eyes, no one said anything as he flung the spade into the grave with a disgusted 'Shit!' Only suddenly – it was impossible to say whence the sound originated – an imperfectly strangled giggle broke the silence like a mirror cracking across; and then another and another. Even the crimped mouth of the officiating vicar twitched at the corners.

Within moments a collective paroxysm held the party at the graveside in thrall. Trapped between shame and hysteria, Dr and Roger Adamson, Julian Grant and Jenny Nunn and a glossary of relatives were coughing up gobbets of mirth like phlegm until even Arthur Appleyard, swept along by the current, was compelled, willy-nilly, to join in. One could almost fancy a responding chuckle from within the coffin, its brass handles shining through the spattering of soil.

The paparazzi, hovering like hyenas just beyond the dividing ribbon, could hardly believe their luck.

In the next day's papers it all made a weird and wonderful juxtaposition – burning bodies on the ruined tower and, by the open grave, mourners falling about laughing. As Jack Ellers commented, once he had got his own breath back: 'That's show business!'

18

'Well?'

Taken literally, the Superintendent's frosty inquiry seemed unnecessary. Mr Seb Conway, legal adviser to the *Daily Clarion*, often renamed by its critics the *Daily Carrion*, looked the very picture of health. He was one of those artful fat men who are able to deploy their girth politically, as it were, presenting it, according to context, now as a sign of moral gravitas, now as evidence of an all-embracing good humour, a chap you could trust when all about were losing their cool, not to mention their money – or, more likely, yours. Only the eyes, pin-points in the cushioning flesh, added a note of troubling ambiguity which their owner covered up by sporting a serious pair of shades that must have cost a packet.

Jurnet, aware of how much his superior officer detested the wearing of sun-glasses within doors, felt almost sorry for the man. Batterby, who, together with Sid Hale and himself, formed the rest of the reception committee convened to hear what the bugger had to say, had once put in an appearance in that sanctum of sanctums kitted out in just those very things, only to have to listen whilst, in tones of exaggerated compassion, the Superintendent had got on to Social Services to request the immediate delivery of a white stick for the use of one of his staff struck down with blindness, like Samson in Gaza.

'Well?' the Superintendent repeated, picking up and, after the briefest inspection, dropping some photographs which, with a jolly smile, the legal adviser had placed in front of him. 'Perhaps you would be so good as to explain why these have only just reached my desk? You had, after all, more than a week ago, published our photofits of the men we wished to interview in connection with the Appleyard murder, photofits which these photographs confirm to have been remarkably accurate.'

'They do, don't they?' agreed Mr Conway, all smiles, as if the recipient of a pat on the head for being a good boy. 'We guessed you'd be wanting to have them. Our photographers are the tops. We've had several shots done of each bloke. I've merely picked out the best, but we'd be happy to send over copies of the rest if that's what's required.'

'What *is* required, Mr Conway – ' the Superintendent's barked courtesy concealed razor blades, cutting edge at the ready – 'is an explanation of why it is only now, after the events of yesterday, that the *Clarion* has seen fit to get in touch with the police.'

'Exactly what I told the editor!' Mr Conway returned, nodding for all he was worth. 'The first thing I said to him was, "He'll want to know why we didn't go to the police first off, without waiting." '

'Very perceptive of you. And what did your editor reply?'

'He knew you'd understand his position, just as he understands yours, completely. You have a job to do, and so has he.'

'He has a job – ' the Superintendent's voice dropped several degrees below zero – 'which includes an obligation common to every citizen of the realm, to co-operate with the forces of law and order in every way he can. Instead of which – ' switching to a corrosive staccato: 'How much did you pay the two men?'

'Not a brass farthing!' The legal adviser's voice held a note of hushed wonderment. 'We made an offer, of course, the way we always do, based on our assessment of what the story was worth as an exclusive, but they actually – can you believe it? – said no: we'd misunderstood them. All they wanted was to be sure that, in return for our keeping everything under wraps until the funeral and, afterwards, printing word for word what they wanted to say, they promised not to go elsewhere. No details except that they planned to put on what they called a heck of a show which would include some sensational visual material, completely non-violent, we stipulated that.'

The man sat back, so far as he could, uncomfortable in the narrow chair the Superintendent provided for visitors. He clasped his hands round his belly, finding consolation in its familiar bulk.

'They weren't having us on, were they, Superintendent? They delivered, you have to give them that. Not, of course, that we had the foggiest what they had up their sleeves, the pair of them. If we had, you may be sure we'd have alerted the police, the fire brigade, the ambulance service and anyone else we could think of that could have prevented that terrible episode.'

Ignoring the crocodile tears, the Superintendent announced briefly: 'We shall, of course, be sending particulars to the Press Complaints Commission.'

'You must do as you think fit,' returned the *Clarion* man, appearing – understandably in view of the Commission's record – in no way put out by this information. 'I can only bring to your attention that there was no warrant out for the two men – we were careful to make sure of that.' Shaking his head in kindly regret: 'A warrant, of course, would have been a very different kettle of fish. It would have had us on the blower to you before you could say Jack Robinson.'

With a smile that caused his plump cheeks to levitate until they pushed the sun-glasses a little askew: 'Still, not for me to tell you your business, eh, Superintendent? As for us, our prime consideration, as always, had to be the public good, something which at the *Clarion* – as I'm sure on consideration you'll confirm – we take very seriously indeed. What our readers have the right to expect from us, and we the responsibility to provide, is news hot off the press, the truth, the whole truth and nothing but the truth, if humanly possible twenty-four hours ahead of our competitors in the field.'

Mr Conway levered his bulk upright and held out a liberally beringed hand which the Superintendent was suddenly too busy with his papers to take. The other took no offence; instead, swept his audience of detectives with what might, with charity, pass for a kindly glance from those ambushed eyes.

'Take a bit of friendly advice, lads, from an old hand at the game. Anything you want to know, read the *Clarion* first. You won't regret it!'

The Superintendent crumpled up the newspaper and threw it into his waste-paper basket.

'A sentimental caterwaul! Nothing we didn't know already – except that now we can let the Registrar know what names to put on the death certificates. Assuming, even in that, that they were telling the truth.' After a moment's reflection: 'I think we can safely assume they were doing that. Nobody would plan to go out with that kind of bang without making sure his name was on the programme.'

The Superintendent retrieved the page of the *Clarion*, smoothing out the creases he had made in it with small, irritated gestures. 'John Buckingham and Joseph Atwell. Buck and Joe.' Angry, as always, at the fact of violent death, the God-awful waste: 'The poor, deluded fools! What on earth could they think was the possible sense of it?'

Jurnet said: 'Wasn't there something about atonement?'

'Something like that.' The Superintendent discarded the paper and retreated into his chair, pressing his back against its maroon leather. 'Read it for yourself.' After a moment, during which Jurnet applied himself to the text, the others in the room watching silently, the man leaned forward over his desk, touched his gold pen, his talisman, and demanded: '*What* about atonement?'

'That plaque outside the castle – ' Jurnet had found what he was looking for – 'the one they put up on Loy Tanner's four hundredth anniversary. It says it was put there by the citizens of Angleby "in reparation and honour" for what was done to him. Reparation – that's atonement in a way, isn't it, sir? And here's these two saying that what they're going to do – they don't specify what – is in atonement for Charlie Appleyard.'

'So?'

124

'So,' Jurnet plodded on, determined to make his point, 'it *could* be a general statement of their guilt at having failed to protect him. On the other hand, it could mean that they were the ones who killed Charlie Appleyard and this was how they intended to atone for it. They must have felt it was only a matter of time before we caught up with them, and they go out of their way to say they had nothing to do with Danny Saunders's death. But when it comes to Charlie, they don't say anything like that. They talk about atonement.'

'They also praise the man to the skies. They even call him a saint. So why in the world would they want to do him in? As some sick publicity stunt, on a par with their own fry-up?' The Superintendent held up a hand, something derisory about the long fingers, the manicured nails. 'Aware as I am that a violent end in the name of faith is still the done thing for saints, it doesn't, so far as I know, commonly happen as a squalid tipping of a body down the steps to a street walker's front door.'

'No, sir.'

Suddenly, for no reason Jurnet could put his finger on except the innate perversity of the man, the Superintendent was all smiles. Unless, when you came to think about it, there was something irresistibly risible about the image of Saint Charlie Appleyard, sprawled on those Bergate steps choked with Jenny Nunn's cross, eyes popping out on sticks and his halo a little askew with the fall.

Maybe it wasn't as funny as all that.

Maybe what was putting the Superintendent in such good humour was the prospect of at last drawing a line under the case, a bookkeeping line, a line of convenience that would look lovely in police records: Charlie, his halo back in place, in heaven in all his glory, whilst, back on earth, two parcels of charred flesh and bone, duly labelled, were conveniently to hand in the mortuary to be charged with the doing of it.

As so often, just when Jurnet felt those familiar premonitions, that upwelling of heat at what manner of stitch-up the bugger in command was set to perpetrate this time, the said bugger got up from his chair and said quietly, without making a performance of it: 'So, Ben – what about it? Where do we go from here?'

Jurnet found Dr Adamson sitting at her desk, like, yet not like, the Superintendent. The desk, whilst equally large as that which defined the latter's kingdom, had a battered, general-issue look, no patina either of age or power, only of years of careless usage. Certainly no gold pen graced its pitted top; instead, a mess of pencils and biros, rubber bands and paperclips and sticks of adhesive, over which a small desktop computer presided with the detachment of a visitor from an alien planet. Her chair, too, was one to which the Superintendent would never have given house room, differing from the other nondescript chairs dotted about the place only in that it could swivel with an arthritic self-assertion – indeed, by the look and sound of it, insist on swivelling, whether its occupant would or no.

The room itself, to which the detective had eventually found his way by corridors dingy and uninviting, was large enough but notably lacking in charm, looking out on to a courtyard of which the best that could be said was that it provided some insulation from the unceasing traffic of Gower Street. There was more noise from the constant tramp of student footsteps past the door.

Jurnet said: 'I thought, it being the hols, the place'd be as quiet as the grave.'

'It is, compared with the way it is when we're actually open for business.' Dr Adamson smiled, moved aside some papers on which she had been working, and shook hands in the friendliest way. Jurnet thought the woman looked older, tired, less elegant than was her wont, but that could have been the heat which hung about the room as if it had settled in for a long stay. 'I never can decide if they're here in a frantic attempt to make up for time wasted during term, or whether, having achieved the haven of university, they can no longer – even if it's only for a couple of months or so – face the prospect of being chucked into the maelstrom of the real world.' She finished: 'Don't be deceived by the decor, Inspector. This is Fairyland, the country of self-delusion. If you will forgive me for saying so, no place for a policeman.'

'Sorry about that,' said Jurnet. 'Thing is, I've just been over to Camden Town to take another look at Charlie's flat.'

Dr Adamson frowned. 'I thought you gave me back the keys.'

'That's right. I arranged it with the agents. They sent over a fellow to let me in. I didn't think you'd mind. They told me you were still paying the rent.'

'I've been meaning to see to it. I've just been too busy. I thought your people had been over the place already with a fine-tooth comb.'

'Oh, they had. Complete waste of time – not a sausage. Only,

126

after what happened at the funeral, I thought I ought to take another look. Never know what you might turn up.'

Dr Adamson looked at the detective steadily. 'And did you – turn up anything?'

'As a matter of fact, it was quite interesting. There was half a loaf of sliced bread, just going green. A carrier bag with some rubbish to go out – some empty baked bean cans, the boxes from some Chinese takeaways. The bed had been slept in and the sink was full of washing up. Very inconsiderate, I thought, to go off and leave the place in that state, but then, I suppose, understandable: they had other things on their minds. Dr Adamson – ' Jurnet's voice had assumed the careful impersonality of a copper asking questions – 'did you know that John Buckingham and Joseph Atwell – Buck and Joe – were hiding out in Charlie's old pad?'

The effect on Dr Adamson was not what the detective had expected. Her grey eyes brightened, shoulders squared, the suspicion of slovenliness disappeared. She replied calmly: 'I did not know they were there, though I have to say that I considered the possibility that they might be. There were, after all, not all that many bolt holes where they could have gone to earth.'

'In which case, a call to the police wouldn't have come amiss.'

'Look at it from my point of view.' The woman shook her head smilingly, inviting understanding. 'I made up my mind I'd done quite enough interfering. After all, without my money none of this would ever have happened. I'd had quite enough of playing the *deus ex machina*. Of course, if I'd thought for a moment that Buck and Joe had had anything to do with Charlie's death I'd have been in touch with you like a shot, but I knew them, straight as a die. They'd have given their lives for him. It wasn't a situation where I felt myself under any obligation to go out of my way to do the police's work for them.'

'Pity, that.' Jurnet spoke with genuine sorrow for what he was about to do: douse the brightness of those remarkable eyes, slump the youthful posture back to middle age. 'A pity because if we'd been in a position to put our hands on the pair of them they'd have been alive today.'

The silence which followed prolonged itself as Dr Adamson – again, thought Jurnet, just like the Superintendent – rose from her chair, made for the window and stood there, back to the room, deriving what comfort she could from the dispirited laurels and the grey anonymous buildings which were all her view.

At last a murmur, the merest breath.

'Cruel. Cruel . . .'

'True though, isn't it? I'm sorry.'

'Cruel . . .'

'Sorrier than I can say.' Jurnet could not have said why he found an explanation necessary, only that one seemed imperative. 'Because, let me admit it, I'm involved too – me personally: my judgement of people. Call it vanity, if you like, but after the years I've been in my job I pride myself on being able to read character, to recognize who is telling the truth and who's stringing me along. And I'd put you down as someone whose word I could rely on.'

She was a woman full of surprises. She came back to the desk looking her age but in full control of herself, with only a deepening of the fine lines at either side of her mouth as evidence of inner anguish.

She said: 'I'm grateful, Inspector, for the good opinion you once had of me. I'd like to reinstate myself in your good graces. Call it vanity, if you like – ' recycling the detective's own words with a little nod of acknowledgement – 'but I'd like very much to go down in your book as somebody who finds it hard to lie and who, having done it, finds the knowledge of what she has done gnawing at her conscience.' Chin uplifted, challenging, her smile now contained as much mischief as irony. 'Perhaps you'd better get out your notebook after all – because I told you, didn't I, that I was staying up in town the day Charlie was murdered. Well, so I was, but still it's a lie. After all, Angleby is only a little over a hundred miles from London, and now that we have bypasses . . .'

She broke off and began again.

'What I'm trying to tell you is that, on the evening of that day, I drove back there. Charlie telephoned he needed me, and of course I came.

'He phoned. At first I hardly recognized the voice, it sounded so unlike his usual self – depressed, ready to chuck it all in. He wasn't the manic-depressive type, swinging from one extreme to the other. It simply wasn't like him. He said he didn't know what to do.'

'About what, specifically?'

'About the whole thing. He said the media had lost interest and, as a result, not one of the various people prominent in public life he'd invited to come and speak from the Oak of Reformation – the way, in Loy Tanner's time, the most famous and powerful men in the state had practically queued up to make their views known – had shown the slightest interest. He said food supplies were falling off and, worst of all, the men themselves were getting bored and restless and beginning to wonder how on earth they'd ever let themselves be roped in for such a bit of nonsense. If only you had known the calm certainty of the man up to that moment, his faith in himself and in what he was doing . . .' Dr Adamson moved her hands in small gestures of despair which the detective found infinitely touching. 'I couldn't bear it. And I couldn't bear to think what, in that mood, he might do.'

'What were you afraid of? That he might call the whole thing off?'

'That would have been the least of it. It would have been awful, of course, for all those youngsters up on the Moot to have to go away with nothing accomplished, but you know what the newspapers are – a nine days' wonder before they moved on to the next thing, and it would all be forgotten. That was half the trouble, really. Charlie took them up on the Moot intending to stay for three months, like Loy Tanner, but who, today, wants to hang around for three months waiting for a climax? Tanner's men, at least, were kept busy hunting their food instead of having it brought to them by ladies with too much time on their hands – killing the deer or stealing cattle – but the way life is today, it's instant action or else it's an almighty bore. No one has the patience any longer to wait and let time work for you.'

'You said that would have been the least of it.'

Dr Adamson's eyes widened at the memory of that telephone call. She said in a low voice: 'He sounded positively suicidal.' Turning towards the detective: 'You with your talent for summing up other people's characters – would you have put Charlie down for somebody likely to do away with himself?'

'No,' said Jurnet. 'I wouldn't – and I was right, wasn't I?' He looked at the woman, not unkindly. 'You drove down to Angleby to comfort him.'

She met his gaze without embarrassment.

'More to comfort myself, to be honest. I couldn't just sit in town worrying.' She paused, gathering strength for what she had to say. 'I told him to go to the house and wait for me. He knew where the key was, under the right-hand gnome.' Lips quivering: 'I told him where the Bourbons were, in the larder: he loved Bourbons. And then I set out, thanking my stars I'd filled up only that morning and wouldn't have to stop for anything. I drove very carefully. I couldn't take the chance of being caught in a radar trap. All the same, when there was a hold-up just outside Bishop's

Stortford I nearly blew my top. You see, I had heard him speaking. I knew it was terribly important.'

'You loved him, didn't you?'

'Completely. Hopelessly. Though what that has to do with it ...' After a moment the woman finished with a deep intake of breath: 'You're right, of course. It had everything to do with it. Ladies of uncertain age don't leave their cocoa and go dashing off into the night without powerful motivation.'

The face turned to Jurnet was naked, without artifice.

'I was mad with anxiety. I was also transfixed with joy that, in such a dark night of the soul, I was the one he turned to.'

To this last Jurnet, who knew that she was not the only one from whom Charlie Appleyard had sought help, said nothing. Only: 'Tell me what happened when you got to Angleby.'

Dr Adamson turned away; moved towards the window, thought better of it.

'Nothing happened. Complete and absolute anticlimax. Charlie was not at the house when I arrived, he did not come after I arrived. I sat waiting, munching his Bourbons until I never wanted to see another one ever again. When he had not come by three o'clock and I had eaten up the last of the damn things, I drove back to London and my precious alibi. It's funny,' the woman concluded, 'nothing at all had happened, but I knew in my bones that I would need an alibi.'

'And now you've blown it.'

'Yes. It was either very silly of me or very clever.'

Jurnet observed stolidly: 'Doesn't matter which, so long as it's the truth.'

'That's for you to decide.'

'No. Either it is or it isn't.'

At that Dr Adamson's laughter rang out, mocking and surprisingly youthful. 'Now we're getting philosophical!'

Sod you, thought Jurnet, refusing to rise to the bait and taking his leave with the polite obtuseness to be expected of a dumb copper. In the corridor she overtook him, looking flushed but not in the least contrite.

'I forgot to tell you – to warn you. Eleanor – Mrs Grant, Julian's mother – she's on the warpath. You'd better keep out of her way if you know what's good for you.'

As Jurnet stopped, staring uncomprehendingly, she elaborated: 'The wedding invitations!'

'What about them?'

'Julian said you were with her in Havenlea when she picked them up.'

'That's right.'

'Eleanor said that when she opened the box she nearly fainted, the smell was so awful. She said they stank of fish, were quite unusable, and she had to order a fresh set which, apart from the expense, meant they would be sent out much later than they ought to. She's such a stickler for doing the right thing and she was livid. She said you ought to have known better.'

'Known better than what?'

'Known better, in all that heat, than to put them in the car boot next to a pair of bloaters. Julian explained you bought them for your supper and she had no idea you'd put them on top of – '

This time it was Jurnet's turn to laugh. Dr Adamson, smiling herself, contributed nevertheless: 'I can't stand Eleanor Grant either, but I do think you might have been more careful.'

Jurnet said: 'I've never met the lady. If I told you that the bloaters were bought for the gnomes in your front garden to catch on their fishing lines, would you believe I was telling the truth?'

'Of course not,' Dr Adamson returned quite crossly. 'Nobody catches bloaters.'

19

Jurnet had not intended to catch Arthur Appleyard in Jenny Nunn's flat; certainly not to surprise him barefoot and wrapped in a somewhat worn bathrobe which had an air of being comfortably at home there. The journey back from London had taken less time than he had expected, unless it was that, never at ease in foreign parts, he had put his foot down with increasing enthusiasm as the suburbs fell away, and the unpretentious alternatives of heath and arable – no flash-harry mountains or other vulgar excrescences of nature to shut off the heightened sky – advertised that home was near and getting nearer. Even the heat, in that blessedly undemanding landscape, seemed less oppressive, apologetic even. Charlie Appleyard was dead, his murderer still at large, truth was as smelly as a couple of bloaters stinking up the boot of a Lotus, and still he felt happy.

He began to half hum, half sing a silly song that was part of his cultural heritage,

> 'Where do flies go in the wintertime?
> Do they go to gay Paree?'

only to break off when the realization dawned that it was Miriam who had taught it to him.

Going down to the flat in Bergate occasioned the detective some residual unease. He found himself minding where he placed his feet, careful not to tread on the ghost of Charlie Appleyard lying sprawled face up on the steps with a copper cross and chain embedded in the flesh of his neck. The sight of Jenny Nunn, so deliciously cool and youthful in a shift of some gauzy material, did little to restore his sense of reality. How was it possible that a girl who looked like that could be a scrubber – what's more, a scrubber who loved her work? And did that fact make it worse or better?

The girl, smiling at him in unequivocal welcome, made him wonder anew not only what was truth but where in the world he had ever got the idea that he was a good judge of character. Shakespeare knew better when he made – Hamlet, was it? – say that one could smile and smile and be a villain. Good old Shakespeare.

Is this a villain that I see before me?

Jenny Nunn said: 'Nice to see you, Inspector. You know Arthur, don't you? Mr Appleyard, Charlie's father. He came to collect the rent.'

I bet he did, thought Jurnet. Mr Appleyard gathered his bathrobe closer about his elderly body and muttered: 'It's not what you think, Inspector. Miss Nunn and I are going to be married.'

'Isn't it lovely?' Jenny Nunn directed a fond glance across the room at her fiancé. 'He loves me. He truly loves me.'

'Nothing surprising about that,' Jurnet volunteered gallantly.

'Oh, but you're wrong!' The girl laughed happily. 'You know me. I love anybody, absolutely anybody, but somebody loving me, that's a different kettle of fish!'

'Can't be any shortage of those either.'

Jenny Nunn shook her head, conscientiously getting things right.

'Lust,' she corrected. 'Men lust after me – I don't complain, that's the way it is, only it isn't love. Why should it be? You

132

provide a service, they pay for it – *finito!* You have no right to expect anything extra. Even when you give it for free, like I did with Charlie – he was always short of the ready – it has to be truly giving to mean anything, doesn't it? It isn't a gift if you expect something in return.'

She crossed the room to the sofa, nestled herself, head on Arthur Appleyard's shoulder.

'Nobody, not even Charlie, has loved me before. It simply doesn't seem to occur to anyone that a girl on the game wants anything besides money.'

The girl raised her head to kiss Arthur Appleyard on the lips with joyful abandon. Anger, instantly suppressed, rose in Jurnet's breast. She was too young, it was obscene, he told himself; only, at a deeper layer of being, to recognize only too well the source of the envy that consumed him.

With a carefully arranged smile he inquired: 'Fixed the day, have you? That'll make two, won't it? I mean young Roger and Miss Grant. You could make it a double ceremony.'

Jenny giggled and nuzzled Arthur Appleyard again.

'Oh, nothing like that for us. Me in a white gown and veil – imagine! Half the men in the church wouldn't know where to put their faces, let alone their willies. And as for the women, they'll all be saying cattily he's old enough to be my father – '

'Register Office,' Arthur Appleyard put in, briefly and unwillingly.

'Very nice – ' Jurnet, doing his best. 'The office in City Hall is very nice. Vases of real flowers everywhere.' Concentrating on the girl: 'I don't suppose you'll be sorry to be retiring.'

Jenny Nunn sat upright, her eyes round with astonishment.

'What do you mean, retiring? Whatever gave you that idea?'

'I thought, after you're married . . .'

'Where have you been, Inspector?' The girl regarded the detective with humorous pity. 'You *are* behind the times! Arthur's a lot older than you yet he understands that nowadays professional women don't turn it all in once they're married, and stay home to clean the house, cook the meals and do the ironing. *I* certainly shan't. Not that Arthur expects me to – do you, dear?'

Arthur Appleyard disentangled himself from the girl's caresses and stood up, the white robe falling open to disclose his elderly nakedness. *God!* thought Jurnet, without pity.

'I know what Jenny is,' the old man declared, making no attempt to cover himself. 'I haven't any plans to change her nature, even if it were possible, which I know quite well it isn't.' Eyeing the detective with a kind of ferocious complacency: 'And before you start accusing me of planning to live on her immoral earnings let me say that I have my pension as well as a bit put by, more than enough for all my needs – and hers if she's ever in a mind to say enough's enough, as I suppose she may, after the menopause or whatever. You can look at my books if you don't believe me. Neither – whilst we're on the subject – am I marrying Jenny because a wife can't be forced to give evidence against her husband, so don't go getting any false ideas on that account either.'

Something in Jurnet's expression must have touched the man on the raw because he suddenly shouted: 'Don't think I don't know what's in your mind about Charlie! About him and me!'

'What about him and you?' Jurnet asked, in a room which had grown very quiet.

'You don't have to pretend,' said Arthur Appleyard shrugging a bony shoulder. 'I saw the way you pricked up your ears when Jenny told you what we're going to do.'

'Oh for God's sake!' Jurnet returned, but aloud this time. 'Shut up and go and get some clothes on.' To the girl: 'Goodbye, Jenny. I hope you'll be very happy.'

'Thank you very much,' the girl said in her childlike voice, adorable. 'But Mr Jurnet – you haven't said why you came.'

'It's gone out of my mind,' said Jurnet.

The Rabbi, on reflection, was probably the last person to ask.

Nevertheless, hardly had Jurnet found himself in the room over the synagogue, sitting gingerly on one of the Louis Seize chairs, the lace-edged cloth cater-cornerwise on the table, the tea poured into the floral china, than, feeling a right nerd, he found himself, like jesting Pilate, asking: 'What is truth?'

'Feeling metaphysical, are we?' the Rabbi inquired jovially, setting his *yarmulke* straight and sitting back with his hands clasped comfortably over his stomach. 'It must be the heat. Gives rise to mirages. Have one of these scones. Mrs Levine has surpassed herself. Pnina left them off on her way to the swimming pool.'

'Seriously, Rabbi . . .' Jurnet took a scone, bit into it; found it, against his will, delicious. 'I'm serious.'

'And so am I,' Rabbi Schnellman protested, smiling broadly. 'When am I ever anything else? The jam now – that I recommend with only modified rapture. One of the Altman girls – you've seen her, the one with the braces on her teeth – made it at school and she wanted me to have a pot. A lovely child but not, I fear, one of nature's jam makers. Braces or not, to get herself a good husband she will have to do better than that.'

Jurnet took a second scone without being asked, and wolfed it. The Rabbi said: 'I hope I have answered your question.'

'You couldn't have heard me. I asked you what is truth.'

'And I answered you. The answer is "everything".'

Jurnet took a third scone as if there was nothing else left to do.

'Maybe it *is* the heat,' he advanced distractedly. 'I used to think I was a good judge of human nature, that I could tell when somebody was lying or, alternatively, telling the truth. All I can say, if that was ever the case, I've bloody well lost the knack.' He looked at the older man more in sorrow than anger. 'Charlie Appleyard's still as dead as a doornail, I've lost my way, and all you can come up with is "everything"!'

'*All*!' the Rabbi declared, supremely untroubled. 'I should have thought myself that was enough to be going on with.'

'But what does it mean, for Christ's sake?' Recollecting where he was, Jurnet mumbled: 'Sorry. I didn't mean . . .'

'Him too,' returned Rabbi Schnellman, waving away the apology, 'along with the scones, Becky Altman's jam, and anything else you care to mention. Even the lies you complain people are telling you, by the very fact of their existing at all are a kind of truth. Apart from everything else, how can you pretend to know what truth is without lies against which to test it?'

This was not the comfort the detective had come looking for. He drained the remains in his cup, wiped his mouth on the dainty, lace-edged napkin that matched the table-cloth, and got up to go.

'Playing with words,' he pronounced dully. 'It doesn't get you anywhere.'

'Sit down, Ben, and pour yourself another cup.' The Rabbi's voice, whilst not unfriendly, had the unmistakable ring of authority. 'Bats and balls I play with, ping-pong and table tennis, but not words.' Carefully, as one explaining to a child: 'An animal could not know who killed your Charlie Appleyard, or – even assuming it did know – would still not be able to go with you to the police station to make a signed statement telling you who it was. Words. Language – they are not a game, believe me, but the supreme gift of the Master of the Universe.'

135

Jurnet, unappeased: 'In the beginning was the word, is that what you mean?'

'Not precisely the way I should have put it myself,' said the Rabbi, his round face dimpling. 'Let's say, rather, "And God said, let there be light." It comes to much the same thing.' Holding out the fancy dish which matched the rest of the tea set: 'One scone left. Have it, Ben. There're more in the kitchen. It will keep up your strength for the fight.'

Jurnet took the scone: spooned up a runny dollop of the Altman child's jam to go with it.

'Only wish there *was* a fight. At least I'd know who my opponent was.' He finished the scone, licked the stickiness from his fingers. 'Truth . . .' He tried the word on again, for size. 'I suppose, if I could be sure I believed in God, it would be easy.'

Rabbi Schnellman looked at the detective kindly before leaning across the table with a conspiratorial air.

'So long as you promise not to shop me to the Synagogue Board of Management I will tell you a thought that occasionally comes to me in the small hours: that it doesn't matter all that much whether you actually believe there is a God or not, so long as you behave as if there was one.' The bright little eyes twinkled. 'Does that help?'

'It helps.'

'Good!' declared the Rabbi. 'Because now you can go swimming without beating your breast, which is not the best stroke, I'm sure, if you wish to keep afloat. Pnina left your trunks and a towel here for you to pick up. They're in the hall cupboard. She knew you were coming here, and she thought you might care to join her.'

Jurnet stared. 'How could she know that? I didn't know it myself.'

'You'll have to ask her. Will you go? I know it always gives her pleasure for you to see her in the water, no longer crippled.'

'She's a marvellous swimmer all right. There's no one at the baths to touch her. But I don't know . . .' Jurnet hesitated, casting about for an excuse. 'I was planning to go straight back to Headquarters, catch up on the paperwork . . .'

'I think she was hoping especially you would be at the pool tonight. I think there is something she wants to say to you.'

'Oh yes? D'you know what?'

Rabbi Schnellman said again: 'You'll have to ask her.'

At the intersection with the High Road – right to the municipal baths, left to the city centre, the ruined Market Place, Police HQ

136

and life without Miriam – Jurnet took a quick decision: turned left and was almost immediately sorry for it.

So Pnina Benvista wanted to tell him something? What was so important it couldn't wait until they were both back at Mario's at the end of the working day, seated at ease at one of the Italian's white tables, tucking into one of his vegetable lasagnes, specially concocted to comply with the dietary requirements of the Laws of Abraham and Moses?

Or, better still, what more suitable venue for confidences than upstairs in the flat above the delicatessen, in the bed presided over by that crucified God with his veiled downward glance at what was going on a couple of feet downwind of his suffering body?

Come to think of it, too many times of late had the Israeli girl declined such invitations on the grounds that Mrs Levine, her landlady, was expecting friends in for Kalooki and needed another player to make up the numbers; needed help with the cutting out of a new outfit she was planning for her grandson's bar mitzvah; had made a special Israeli meal upon which it was imperative she had an Israeli verdict. The excuses had flown thick and fast.

Who cared?

Caring or not, Jurnet backed the Rover into a side turning and reset his course for the baths, no happier with his second thought than with his first. The girl was a cripple, he was sorry for her and it wasn't fair.

Not fair to her: demeaning, an insult to one who, however crookedly, stood four-square to the world, demanding – and deserving – to be accepted on the same terms as the able-bodied.

Not fair to him, Jurnet, either, to have his feelings for the Israeli girl, whatever they might be, clouded and confused by a sentimental compassion.

Down with pity!

Earlier than they needed to, as if those who timed the city's life couldn't wait for the long hot day to end, the street lights had come on and – prodded by this official notification – the car headlamps similarly, transforming Angleby into a blur of heat and equivocation that did nothing to clarify Jurnet's jumbled thoughts. High up, far above the geodesic dome of the swimming pool and all the shoddy earthbound fluorescence, night spread a calm dark, no comfort to the detective, keeping his eyes on the road.

Unfresh as he was but making a statement about something or other, Jurnet after all deliberately left his bathing trunks and his towel in the Rover. He came to the poolside just in time to see the Israeli girl, lopsided and pathetic, damn her, in her shiny grey bathing suit, her silver cap that concealed her piebald hair, hobbling the length of the uppermost diving board.

At the sight, the detective's eyes shut automatically, reopening just too late to see the crippled girl launch herself upon the air. By then the object of pity had vanished. What met his eyes was a silver bird that, for a precious moment, appeared to answer all questions: a bird that rose in a lovely arc and seemed to hang motionless for an instant before cleaving downward like an arrow into water opening to receive her.

As always, the sight quite erased Jurnet's ill-tempered uncertainties, his thoughts, momentarily, going back to Rabbi Schnellman. Despite everything God, or whoever it was that went by the name, was good, was great. As Pnina Benvista swam several lengths of the pool with effortless ease the whole atmosphere of the place seemed to lighten, as if a rainbow, symbol of hope, spanned the curve of the geodesic dome, red, orange, yellow, green, blue, indigo, violet against the velvet of the night; swimmers and spectators alike enlivened by her surpassing grace.

Even when, changed and showered, she came to him where he sat, at a plastic table beneath a plastic palm tree, her pale blue dress puckered over her deformed hip, something of the magic remained. She sat down opposite him and said: 'But I left your trunks and your towel at the Rabbi's! Didn't he tell you?'

'They're in the back of the car. I didn't feel like swimming.'

'Crazy!'

'Glad you enjoyed it.'

'Gorgeous!' But already she was back in the real world, tugging at her dress in a vain attempt to make the material lie better. Below her navy-blue kerchief, knotted round her head in a complicated, somehow Oriental fashion that made her look like some Ancient Egyptian princess seen in profile on papyrus, her cheekbones stood out even more prominently than usual, her eyes set deeper among purple shadows. She was the only girl he'd met, thought Jurnet, who could look at once ugly and beautiful.

He looked again, concentrating. Beautiful? Wherever did he get that idea from?

To forestall an imminent uprush of the dreaded compassion, he asked: 'Can I get you something to drink? You look fagged.'

'No, thank you, and I *am* fagged. It has been a busy day, a busy few months.' In a gawky movement that cut the detective to the quick despite himself the girl leaned across the table, her pointed breasts explicit. Slightly breathless she said: 'I told the Rabbi. Now I tell you. I am going back to Israel, to Tel Zvaim.'

'Good idea. A couple of weeks' break will do you the world of good.'

'You don't understand.' As she spoke the girl carefully looked away. 'I don't mean a couple of weeks. I mean for good.' Her words quickening: 'Or maybe not for good but for a good while. And after that they want me to go to America, open another branch of the Courland Connection.'

Unable to disguise her pride in her achievement: 'They are very pleased that now the workshop is running as well as in Miriam's time – even better. She taught me so well what I must do. The order book is full for more than a year ahead, we have paid off our debts and sent back to Tel Zvaim more money than ever before, now that there is no one putting his hand in the till.' Pnina Benvista paused, as if expecting Jurnet to make some observation on what she had said. When he said nothing she added with a kind of desperate jollity: 'All the Jews in the US, we should be able to do even better there.'

When there was still no response she sat back and ended quietly: 'I am not trying to blackmail you.'

'I know you aren't.' After a moment Jurnet began inadequately: 'Whatever makes you happy . . .'

'Oh please!' was the bleak return. 'Let us not talk about happiness!' Softening: 'England is a very nice country. Everyone is very kind to the poor cripple. If kindness was all that is needed, I would stay in England for ever. But kindness is not all that is needed. It is a padlock, locking you up inside. Whereas at home –' the Israeli girl smiled, finding cheer in the mere word – 'people who come to visit at Tel Zvaim, they think how terrible, all those cripples together. They can hardly bear to look. What they don't understand is that, when we are all together, there is nothing whatever the matter with us. There, *we* are the norm. Those others, outside the gates, who can walk and run and jump without difficulty, *they* are the freaks. We are so sorry for them, they are so full of problems, their world is so complicated whilst ours is so simple – pain and love, the one more than making up for the other.'

Pnina Benvista looked the detective full in the face. She seemed already to be memorizing it.

Alarmed, Jurnet demanded: 'How soon are you leaving?'

'Don't worry. Not for a few weeks. You do not have to say goodbye just yet. They are sending a new manager from Israel, a very good man, very honest this time, and there is a very clever girl in the workshop here – Lily Mannheim – who will be his assistant. It will not take long but I must stay until they have settled down to work together. Between them, I shall not be missed.'

'I shall miss you.'

'I hope so,' the Israeli girl said lovingly. 'I am selfish. I hope you will miss me very much.'

20

The Market Place was looking its old self again – better than. In place of the faded awnings the new ones shouted their stripes of red and white, white and blue. The uprights of the rebuilt stalls positively dazzled with polyurethane, the name boards along their tops embellished with gilded arabesques that would scarcely have been out of place at Versailles or Fontainebleau.

Mr Peralu (Treasures of the East) had paid extra to have twin plyboard minarets erected at either side of his domain, quite like the Taj Mahal; whilst, at a seemly distance from Islam, the painted pig above Mr Gooch's, the pork butcher, was itself enough to raise the spirits, so plump and rosy it was, the spitting image of Mr Gooch.

'That Loy Tanner bunch', commented Sergeant Jack Ellers to his superior officer, 'did the city a good turn, I reckon, without their knowing it.'

The chubby Welshman paused at a fruit stall to help himself to a peach more than equal to its bright new surroundings; only to find that Angleby essentials had not changed when a voice from behind the counter, chuckling but in deadly earnest, demanded, 'That'll be 30p, Mr Ellers, *if* you don't mind!'

At the chip stall, painted a fresh crimson but broadcasting the same lovely odours as of old, the two detectives found Julian

Grant tucking in with enthusiasm, her bag of chips held at a diplomatic distance from what were clearly party clothes.

'Whatever you do, don't jog me,' she admonished by way of greeting. 'This outfit cost me a bomb, and it's only dry-cleanable, if that, which I doubt.'

The girl, Jurnet had to admit, looked delectable in a two-piece of some faintly glimmering material in a green that looked blessedly cool amid the competing stridency of the refurbished Market. The fact that she wore a wide-brimmed hat which concealed all but a stray wisp of the marvellous hair made it possible for him to make an objective assessment. He followed Ellers in accepting the offer of a chip – 'Vinegar and salt, I hope that's all right?' – bit into it and said: 'Very nice.' It was not his fault that she obviously chose to take the compliment as applying to herself rather than the skill of the cook, as intended.

'I've been to a wedding,' she announced, by way of explanation. 'And what do you think? There wasn't a thing to eat afterwards. One glass of fizz and that was the lot, which is why I was reduced to this if I was to have the strength to get myself home.' With a dazzling smile for the chippie, a young man whose downy cheeks blushed a red even deeper than the hot oil had already made them: 'Nobody makes chips like they do on Angleby Market.' Mouth shining with residual grease in a way that Jurnet found disturbing, Julian Grant bestowed her smile equally on the two detectives. 'Would you care for another? This is my second bag, so you won't be depriving me. I was beginning to slow down, anyway.'

Jurnet said: 'No more, thanks.' And then, perhaps to counter the effect of those shining lips: 'I'm glad we've run into you. I've been wanting to ask you why you lied about the fish.'

'What fish? Oh!' Eyes that were so unlike Miriam's opened wide with a laughter which had the effect of making Jurnet sorry he'd spoken: 'That fish!'

'I fail to understand why you should have let your mother think I was the one responsible for spoiling your invitations.'

'They stank! You could smell them a mile off.' The girl giggled, but her glance was keen. 'Addie must have told you.'

Sorrier than ever that he had opened his big mouth, Jurnet admitted: 'She did mention something . . .'

'Dear Addie! She probably thought you'd find it a good laugh. But really – ' having finished the last chip, Julian Grant turned away to deposit the bag in the mesh basket provided at the side of

141

the stall – 'what a thing to make a song and dance about! Mother does carry on so at the slightest thing, I just wanted to deflect the flak. She's never met you and isn't likely to, so where's the harm? I'd never have thought policemen were so sensitive. Though anyway – ' adjusting her hat and letting – could it possibly be by intent? – a substantial tress of sunlit bronze escape to the outer air – 'it wasn't a lie, Inspector. I'm sure you know I'm not a liar. Just a fib.'

The girl's mouth, Jurnet told himself, was definitely too small; lacking generosity.

'Hard to know where to draw the line,' he observed, inwardly mocking his own pomposity. 'Better to stick to the truth.'

Julian Grant, wide-eyed and teasing: 'What is truth but what it's convenient to believe at any given moment?'

'Do you mind if I hang on to you?' she asked Sergeant Ellers, allowing no time for comment. 'I should never have come on to the cobblestones in these shoes.' The two detectives, their attention thus directed, looked down at Julian Grant's long, narrow feet encased in golden sandals, stiletto-heeled. 'Ridiculous, aren't they? I only wear them for weddings or when I've an enemy I want to put the boot in. But is it all right to take your arm – I mean, is it allowed? No: on second thoughts, I tell you what . . .' She bent over and in a second straightened up, dangling the sandals by their sling backs. 'That's better. I wouldn't want to get you into trouble.'

'No trouble at all, miss,' Jack Ellers assured her, gallant now the danger was past. 'You're going to find it hard going in your stockinged feet.'

'In which case, I'll ask you to give me a piggy back!' The girl set off, grimacing a little but tossing over one cool green shoulder, 'If you keep a little behind me, people won't think we're together!'

There was no reason at all why the two should have stayed behind: but stay they did, moderating their pace to Julian Grant's hesitant progress up the cobblestoned incline of the Market hill. At the top, where a narrow strip had been planted with flowers that were neither real nor artificial but uniquely municipal, flanking the War Memorial, she sank down thankfully on a wooden bench, apparently taking it for granted that the others would join her there, as they, apparently, took it for granted that they would.

Her feet were bleeding, the soles of her tights in tatters.

Jack Ellers, a kind man, said: 'You want to be sure and give yourself a good soak in some antiseptic soon as you get home.'

'I'll do that.' She regarded the little Welshman with something close to affection. 'Would you be a complete angel and go down to the cab rank and nab me a cab?'

'A pleasure.'

When Ellers was gone on his errand, Julian Grant took off her hat, set it on the teak slats between her and Jurnet, a buffer zone. The sun caught her hair, bloody beautiful. She demanded: 'Don't you even want to know whose wedding it was?'

'Not yours, I take it?'

'Of course not! Mine's going to be the super-deluxe model – Wedding March, bridesmaids, pages, the lot. Jenny and Mr Appleyard. He got a special licence. Very romantic, don't you think, to be panting with passion at his age, couldn't wait for the ordinary kind? Roger and I were the witnesses, and Mr Apple-yard – I must get used to calling him Arthur – wore a frock coat, what d'you think of that? Hired, of course. He said he'd hired one for his first wedding and it was only right he didn't do less for Jenny than he'd done for his first wife, whatever her name was.'

'And what did Roger think of it?'

The girl's face clouded, the small mouth compressed.

'To be honest, he thought it was grotesque. We'd planned to treat ourselves to a posh lunch afterwards since we were going to be all dressed up anyway – not that Roger was in a frock coat but he had on one of his trousseau suits, he looked lovely – only the whole thing put him in such a black mood he muttered something about a meeting at the factory and off he went, leaving me to chips or death from starvation. He said the man was old enough to be Jenny's grandfather and Charlie would be turning in his grave.'

'You don't mean he said it to the happy pair?'

'Of course not! Roger's a gentleman. He wouldn't have hurt Jenny's feelings for the world. She was obviously in seventh heaven. Outwardly he did all the correct things. Signed the re-gister, kissed the bride, shook the bridegroom's hand and wished them both happiness – then got away as soon as he could without making it too obvious. Hope he doesn't feel the same at ours!'

'Not long now, is it?'

'Not long.' The girl's face blazed with happiness. 'I know it's old-fashioned,' she said, 'but I can't tell you how much I look forward to being Roger's wife.'

Jurnet offered inadequately: 'Not old-fashioned, so long as it's Mr Right.'

'Oh, it is! It is!'

143

Back at Police Headquarters the Superintendent was looking both satisfied and sad, angry and calm. There had been another murder on his patch, another violent wastage of life which, as ever, had aroused in the man a rage which was itself little short of murderous, whilst at the same time inducing in him a high that, in the boxing ring or the sports stadium, might well have triggered off the darkest suspicions of the guardians of athletic morality.

It was, on the face of it, a pretty straightforward murder, as murders went: a father bumped off, almost certainly, by one or other, or both, of his sons. Since the offspring had already taken off for foreign parts without hanging about for the police, it was going to take a tonnage of paperwork to get them back to Angleby and their just deserts. The widow was under sedation. Everyone who knew the people concerned – the Superintendent passed on the information with a mouth twisted in bitter mirth – agreed that it had been a very loving family, very close.

'Sid and Batterby will be able to cope, I dare say.' The Superintendent greeted Jurnet and Ellers with a smile, the most dangerous in his repertoire, the one that lit up the patrician features but left the deep-set eyes unforgiving. 'No doubt you two have progress to report. Unless, having exhausted every other possibility, you've at last satisfied yourselves that Danny Saunders was telling the truth when he told that boy – what was his name . . .?'

'Pete Gilbert,' Jurnet supplied.

'Pete Gilbert, that's the one – that he did for Charlie Appleyard.'

'I'm going to have another word with the young fellow. I need to go through his statement with him again. There are one or two things –'

'You haven't answered my question.'

'No, sir.' Jurnet added: 'You'll be interested to learn that Jenny Nunn and Appleyard senior were married this morning.'

'Were they indeed!' The device successful, the question not repeated: 'An odd coupling. Any special significance to it, in your opinion? I take it Mr Appleyard has not been removed from your little list?'

'From all I gather, unlikely as it sounds, it's a love match. She's head over heels in love with him.'

'Lucky man!'

The Superintendent turned on his heel, went over to the window and looked down at the Market Place, a prolonged, silent scrutiny. Perhaps it was at the sight of that phoenix risen from the ashes that the face turned back to the two detectives at last was trusting, free of guile.

The Superintendent said: 'I don't need to remind you, Ben, that, whichever way you look at it, Charlie Appleyard was a pretty extraordinary man. We owe it to his memory to make sense of his death – or, if not sense, at least to come to an understanding of the nonsense of it. We can't simply allow him to become a legend, one more of the fairy tales councils put into their tourist brochures and dignify by the name of history.'

Back in his chair, the man leaned back comfortably, admitting Jurnet to an easy intimacy which – for all the other occasions when the younger man could cheerfully have killed the guy – bound the detective to him with hoops of steel: 'How clever they were, those Tudors, to hang Loy Tanner from the castle ramparts. Confronted with that rattling skeleton day after day, you couldn't make up stories. Every time you passed by, going about your business, you only had to look up to be confronted by the brutal truth – the whole truth, nothing but the truth.'

The Superintendent sighed briefly, touched his gold pen, and repeated that final word, lingering over it.

'Truth, Ben. What we spend our lives looking for. But what the hell is it?'

'Just what I was about to ask you,' said Jurnet.

Jurnet came into the delicatessen to find Mario rushed off his feet by an excited party of Italians intent on putting together a take-away Roman orgy. Whilst there was something endearing about the positively sexual passion with which they supervised the selecting of pasta, cold cuts and salads, pizzas piled high as wedding cakes, the men throwing out their arms in commanding gestures, the women's eyes lustrous and inviting, perspiration on their downy lips, it was all too noisy, too tumescent for Jurnet who had been looking forward to his customary *citron pressé* and a bit of hush at the fag-end of the day.

Mario did not have time even to signal his usual smiling greeting to the surrogate son home from his labours. The glance which he might, or might not, have cast in the detective's direction was harassed, uncertain.

Understandable, thought Jurnet, albeit ill-naturedly, with that bloody mafia milling around.

Parched, he went upstairs to the flat and fell over a suitcase parked on the landing.

Alerted by the noise of the fall and the resonant 'Shit!' which accompanied it, Pnina Benvista came hurriedly out of the flat door. 'Are you hurt? I am so sorry.' As Jurnet, sitting on the top stair rubbing his leg, made no answer, she ventured appeasingly: 'Don't worry. It isn't unpacked.'

'Packed or unpacked, bloody stupid place to leave it.'

'Yes. Bloody stupid.' The Israeli girl vanished back into the flat, to return almost immediately with a cool, frosted glass of *citron pressé*. 'Drink this. It is very good for sore legs.'

After his reception – or rather, non-reception – downstairs, the welcome, suitcase and all, was just what the doctor ordered. The girl was a jewel.

Jurnet drank long and deep.

'Ta – ' handing back the empty glass. 'That was a life saver.'

'There is another waiting in the fridge.'

'Later.' Jurnet got to his feet, grimacing a little, for form's sake. He picked up the suitcase. 'What d'you want done with this?'

The girl's smile faded. Like Mario below she looked hesitant, unsure.

'I don't know,' she replied. 'It depends on you.'

He was hungry, sweaty, and now – as if that wasn't enough, blast it! – randy to boot, the remembrance of the morning's encounter at the chip stall surfacing through the rancid smell of his disgusted and disgusting body; pictures of old man Appleyard, back in that basement flat in Bergate, having his way with juicy Jenny Nunn without even waiting to take off his hired frock coat; pictures of Julian Grant, a prize bitch if ever there was one, standing up in church virginal in white veil and orange blossom, next to her jolly Roger. Pictures of the two of them, the knot tied, rolling on the bed, their body smell commingling, none of your cheesy cunt and pongy prick but Armani Aftershave and Chanel Number Five, natch.

And now that suitcase! Even his own crippled consolation prize, the bony bundle standing in front of him like a disjointed doll, couldn't, it seemed, wait to get away. Jurnet's whole being resonated with self-pity and loss. *Oh Miriam!*

There was salad on the table, arranged with a loving care that made him want to spit, and a long-necked bottle of white wine, beaded with coolth. Pnina Benvista caught his glance and seized the opportunity.

'I thought you would find it quieter to eat up here than down in the store. And we could talk.'

Jurnet sat down at the table without washing, took up a fork and messed the salad about, gaining an obscure satisfaction from ruining its television ad perfection.

'So you're off, then, after all, without waiting?'

For a moment the girl looked puzzled, then: 'Oh, the suitcase! No, I am not leaving for Israel, not just yet. Only from Mrs Levine's.' Seeing that there was something in the other's face which told her he was in some measure relieved, she took the plunge: 'I thought, as there is only a little time left and you sometimes seem sorry when we have been making love and then I have to leave and go home, that I would like to move in with you.'

Shaken, Jurnet said, after a moment: 'You're being very kind.'

'No.' The girl shook her head in denial. 'Not at all. You are very good-looking. With very little trouble, I am sure, you can get all the girls you want – girls who are beautiful and not deformed as I am deformed. I am thinking of myself only, to make myself be happy for as long as is possible. If I am lucky I may possibly find – in Israel or in America – another man who, out of pity or because he is temporarily alone, will find it convenient to go to bed with me, but never twice in my life a man I can love as I love you.'

As if it was time to do away with all pretence between them, she pulled off the kerchief which had been covering her hair. 'You see,' she said, bowing her head to give Jurnet a view of the whole length of her parting, 'the black is growing back very quickly. If it is possible, I should like to stay in England until it has all grown out again and I am truly myself, not a bad imitation of somebody else.' A pause. 'And on whether you will let me.'

'What will Mrs Levine, what will the Rabbi say?'

'About Mrs Levine I do not know. She is upset already for the wrong reason. I explained nothing and she thinks she has offended me in some way. If you let me stay I will tell her the truth, otherwise I will make up some excuse, it does not matter what. As to the Rabbi, I have spoken to him already. I did not ask his permission, he is not God. Only told him.'

'How did he react?'

'He wanted to know if I had discussed it with you and I said no. I made it clear that you had not seduced me, that it had been quite the other way round.'

'No more than that?'

147

'Yes and no. He began to talk about his wife Rachel – how, though she had not been beautiful, she had been beautiful in his eyes. How much he had loved her and how much he missed her. He asked me what I would do if you said no. I said one had to go on living, and he nodded his head and said yes, that was the necessary thing.'

Into the silence that followed Jurnet projected: 'And was that all?'

'Not quite.' Pnina Benvista gave an unexpected giggle, momentarily a schoolgirl, young and scatterbrained. 'I had brought him some of Mrs Levine's biscuits, he is so fond of them. He made some tea to go with them, and afterwards we cleared the table, took off the cloth and played a game of Scrabble. I put down the word Jurnet and he said I could not have it because it was a Proper Noun. When it was time to go he said Jurnet was a very Proper Noun and so was Miriam. I said I knew it: I did not need to be told.'

The girl's gaze was tranquil and direct. 'I left my car at the workroom. If your answer is no I will telephone for a cab and take myself and my luggage back to Mrs Levine's.'

21

Jurnet slept, an annihilation so comprehensive that, surfacing, he did not immediately identify either the telephone ring which had awakened him nor the ridge of bone that nestled, not uncomfortably, against his thigh. Back in the real world, he let the phone go on ringing whilst he savoured, in retrospect, the pleasure of being loved as against the ambiguous ecstasy of loving: the odious self-satisfaction consequent upon being the one to dispense favours, the guilt at being able to offer in return only a patronizing gratitude in place of the surrender that, with Miriam, had wracked him with a passion and a pain he would not have forgone for all the world.

At his side, her parti-coloured hair catching orange overtones from the street lamp outside the window, Pnina Benvista opened her eyes and murmured, 'Phone. I love you. Answer the phone.'

Had Miriam ever actually said, 'I love you . . .'?

Jurnet could not remember.

148

He answered the phone; listened, said what was necessary in return, got up and dressed quickly, cheered – once the shrill summons had ceased – to hear in the distance the first experimental cooing of local pigoens testing to see if dawn were really at hand. He loved the quiet of the city night so long as it was not fractured by crime, something which always seemed to him twice as bad when committed in the dark, a sin not just against Angleby law and order but against the vast calm of the slumbering universe.

Beneath its orange street lights Bergate was already bright as day with blue lights flashing on the tops of police cars and an ambulance. Not quite a rerun of an earlier night-time call-out – Jurnet sent up an involuntary thank-you to some indeterminate destination: no body sprawled on the steps leading down to Jenny Nunn's flat, but the same air of dislocation, of a suspension of the natural order of things: lights on in all the upper-floor windows; and the ground-floor tenant, full of self-importance in a baby-doll nightie and time-expired make-up, happily explaining for the umpteenth time how for a minute you could have thought it a bleeding earthquake, the way the walls were positively vibrating from the bangs and the wallops and the crashings, and how she had thought to herself before phoning the police – something, God knew, she wasn't in the habit of doing – one murder on the premises was more than enough, luv, we don't want another.

Judging by the look of Jenny Nunn – pardon, Mrs Arthur Appleyard – on the ambulance trolley, it had been a near thing. Two black eyes, a broken nose and a split upper lip were the least of it. One arm was already strapped, something urgent still being done to both legs. The ambulance men had already fixed up a drip.

The flat itself was beyond their aid, the swagged curtains down on the floor, the upholstery slashed, the carpet a mess of broken glass and decapitated crinoline ladies. Legless, the ceramic giraffe leaned drunkenly against a dainty little table loaded with over-turned bottles whose erstwhile contents contributed a rich odour to the general chaos.

The Regency striped wallpaper looked as though it had been clawed off the wall by some slavering monster with nails a foot long.

Overseen by Hinchley and Blaker, the slavering monster, Arthur Appleyard, out of his wedding finery and back into cardigan and baggy flannels, sat on the ruined sofa looking moderately well pleased with himself. Beside him, enrobed in polythene and, by the look of it, the sole undamaged article in the room, was the hired frock coat, ready to go back to the hire shop immaculate, the customer's deposit against damage safe as – safer than – houses.

The newly-wed Mrs Appleyard opened her eyes at the sound of Jurnet's voice; contrived to raise her head an inch or two and managed painfully: 'I fell down the stairs . . .'

The detective, his heart heavy with pity, smiled down at the small, damaged face.

'Jenny love, there aren't any stairs in the flat.' Better begin as you mean to go on. 'It's all on one floor.'

The eyes closed as the girl mulled this information over, then opened again as she found an explanation.

'Outside. I went out for a breath of air and . . .' The little-girl voice trailed off, exhausted.

'Oh ah.' Jurnet's look round the room inviting her comment. 'And all this? Fell down of its own accord, did it?'

Out of Jenny Appleyard's swollen lips came a travesty of her girlish giggle.

'Arthur and I – we decided – going to redecorate.' Having some difficulty with the word, she tried again. 'Com-pletely re-decorate.' With a panting for breath that modulated into a sigh of pure satisfaction: 'We were – married today, Mr Jurnet.' Her effort to raise her left hand ineffectual: 'You can see my wedding ring. Lovely . . .'

Keeping the irony out of his voice with an effort, Jurnet said: 'Congratulations.'

'I'm so happy.' The head dropping back, the eyes closing: 'Com-pletely re-dec-orated . . .'

Jurnet ordered: 'You go along, Hinchley. Call in for a WPC to meet you at the hospital. Keep me in the picture.'

'Sir.'

When the police constable was gone – when, shortly thereafter, the ambulance could be heard moving off, back down Bergate, its siren splitting the last of the dark – Arthur Appleyard stood up, carefully plucked from his cardigan some feathers which had spilled out of a slashed cushion and said: 'Well, I don't think I need keep you gentlemen any longer.' Looking from one to the other of the clenched faces confronting him, he added with a chuckle: 'You heard what the lady said. Fell down the stairs.'

Jurnet, with difficulty, kept a tight hold on himself.

'Mr Appleyard, you know that is not true – '

'Of course it isn't,' the other agreed promptly. 'But so long as

Jenny keeps on saying so, that's what it was – and she will, no fear of her changing her mind.' Looking about him with undisguised pleasure: 'Nothing to stop a fellow mucking up his own place, is there, if he's a mind to? Completely redecorated, eh?' The man shook with suppressed laughter. 'I should say so!'

Arthur Appleyard was still having trouble with the errant feathers. Two in particular had inserted themselves into the fabric of the cardigan and could not be dislodged without risk of breaking the yarn.

'Knitted, not woven,' the man threw out by way of explanation, ever the schoolmaster, the crusty pedant. 'Unpick one stitch and, before you know it, all you're left with is a ball of used wool.' Desisting from his efforts: 'Like a lot of other things, eh, Inspector? It's the first stitch that counts.' Echoing Jurnet's earlier thought in a way the detective could only classify as spooky: 'Begin as you mean to go on.'

Jurnet observed coldly: 'I hope you're not planning to make a habit of it.'

'Only if it's necessary.'

Somewhere, among the shattered furniture, Appleyard found a chair still with four legs to its name, and sat down at ease, smiling up into the unappeased faces of the detective and his subordinate.

'Tell me,' he asked in an old-fashioned, jolly way, 'what would you say, either one of you, if you were just that morning married, you and your brand-new little wifie back in your flat and having a lovely love-making that goes on all afternoon – lunch and tea and then back to bed again between meals: nothing could be better, you'd say. And then, all of a sudden, your darling girl puts a lovely supper for one out on the table – fresh salmon and cucumber, and strawberries and cream for afters – and says she's sorry, darling, but she won't have time to eat with you, it's time for her to go to work. Whereupon she vanishes into the bedroom and five minutes later out she skips, got up like a tart in a dress with a neckline down to her navel, and says don't wait up for me, dear, I may be late back – what would you say?'

Jurnet said: 'You knew what Jenny was like before you married her. The way she is with men. The way she can't help it.'

'But on her wedding day, for God's sake! And after we'd been at it all day, off and on! An insult, that's what it was, a kick in the teeth. As much as to say, it wasn't enough. I was an old man, I couldn't satisfy her and she was off to someone younger.'

'I'm sure that isn't how she saw it.'

'Oh, she was very sweet and regretful,' the other conceded readily. 'Very lovey-dovey. Said it was one of her regulars, a weekly appointment that had been going on for donkey's years. Said it was a matter of honour with her never to let one of her clients down and she was sure I understood.' Busy with the feathers again: 'Oh, I understood all right!' After a moment of eyeing Jurnet with a calculating stare: 'I suppose she never let you down either.'

Jurnet said stiffly: 'I have never had any kind of relationship with Mrs Appleyard.'

'You must be the only chap in Angleby who hasn't. Damn! There goes another stitch!'

Abandoning the cardigan as a lost cause, Arthur Appleyard continued in hurt tones: 'I wouldn't complain, even on our wedding day, if she was doing it for free. We're going to live in my house and I know beforehand, without being told, that, in between the dusting and the polishing, Jenny'll find time to pop into bed with the postman, the dustman, the window cleaner, anyone in trousers who happens to call by. I'm resigned to that, so long as it isn't done for payment other than the occasional extra pinta, say, or doing the windows inside as well as out at no extra charge.'

'Very laudable, sir, I'm sure.' Jurnet spoke out of the heart of his deep dislike of the man. 'But did you have to make your point quite so savagely?'

'Of course I did. I had to show her how much I loved her.'

22

Even though the drought continued unbroken, the landscape a desert in the making, it was a relief to get out of Angleby into the Norfolk countryside. The ploughs turning in the last of the stubble moved in a haze of dust which lay along the tops of the hedgerows like a blight, their accustomed retinues of gulls contesting with shrill cries the paucity of worms turned up by the questing blades.

'Gone down deep where it's cool,' observed Jurnet, not troubling to explain himself.

'Oh ah,' responded Jack Ellers at the wheel of the Rover, too hot to ask what the hell his mate was on about. 'Somebody's got some sense.'

The villages that showed up periodically alongside the mirage-haunted tarmac, only to recede into nothingness like flats propelled by amazingly efficient scene-shifters, were just that – flats without perspective, only the churches, the sun striking off their ancient flints, having any reality, and that hostile. A rabbit squashed in the middle of the road was the nearest they came to any living thing.

At last the two detectives found the by-road they were seeking, a mere track between hedges. God help them if they met something coming the other way.

'Penston St Swidbert,' read Sergeant Ellers, squinting at the signpost prior to turning left. 'Who's St Swidbert, when he's at home?'

'Only one they could get, I reckon, willing to shack up in a hole like this.'

The place they were looking for showed up as a gap with a sign before they came to the village – if indeed there was a village, which Ellers took leave to doubt: Thatch Cottage Fresh Eggs, a box of raw red brick with a slate roof, the only thatch in sight covering what was in all likelihood a hen house, to judge by some depressed-looking hens engaged in turning over its blanket of mouldy straw. Other sheds and outhouses in varying stages of dilapidation were roofed with rotting felt, save for one, doorless, which was constructed entirely of bright new galvanized iron, a pain to look at in that light.

Out of the glare a dog without breeding emerged barking, to be followed by a young man – boy would be a better description – carrying a bucket filled with something which brought the hens scampering down from their perches revitalized.

The boy threw them the contents of the bucket as if he grudged them every beakful of the mush. 'There y'are, y' buggers!' – before turning, without welcome, to confront his visitors. 'How many you want, then?'

Jurnet got out of the car and said: 'Hello, Pete. Remember me? We don't want any eggs. It's you we've come to see.'

The boy put the bucket down on the scruffy ground as if, empty as it was, it had suddenly become too heavy for him. He looked pale – very pale, Jurnet thought – and taller than when he'd spoken to him last, after the destruction of the Market Place. Maybe the lad had outgrown his strength.

153

The lad said: 'Ma said if anyone come from the police I weren't to say nothin' – I tole you all I had to tell and I was to tell you to piss off.'

'A woman of strong feelings, your ma.' Jurnet smiled. 'Is she home? Perhaps we could have a word and persuade her to change her mind about us.'

'Course she in't home. She's working, what you think?'

'Working where?'

Pete Gilbert shrugged. 'I dunno. Packin' lettuces or cabbages or something. It's all according. They pick her up in a van at the crossroads.'

'I'm sorry about that, Pete, because if she was home I could point out politely that that's no way to talk to police officers, telling them to piss off.' Carefully keeping all threat out of his voice and, in so doing, making the threat all but tangible: 'It's a civic duty to do everything you can to co-operate with the police, I'm sure she understands that. And so do you.'

The boy moved pettishly; passed a thin forearm over his forehead, pushing up the overhanging hair as he wiped away the sweat. After he had done, the golden curls fell back into place. Thinner, taller, Pete Gilbert was even more beautiful than the detective remembered.

The boy said: 'I come to you, remember? I didn' wait for you to come to me, like some might 'a done. I come to you an' tole you all I knew, the lot. So what you here for when I already tole you?'

'Just recapping,' Jurnet responded easily, all reassurance now that the parameters were out in the open, no holds barred. 'Just one of those things we have to do. Boring, but there's bugger-all we can do about it.'

Squinting humorously at the sky, the detective unbuttoned the top of his shirt unhurriedly, taking his time; flapped the open edges to produce the illusion of a breeze. 'Anywhere we can go to get out of this? We're getting our brains frizzled. Aren't you going to ask us inside?'

'No, I'm bloody not!'

'Ah! Ma wouldn't approve, is that it?' And then, sharpish: 'You're a big boy now.'

The other made no reply. Jack Ellers, without being asked, crossed the yard to where a stack of plastic crates teetered against a rusty lawnmower: extracted the topmost three and brought them back into the Rover's shadow, such as it was.

The two detectives sat down, the boy remaining obstinately standing.

Jurnet said: 'What I need to be sure of is we've got the words dead right – the words Danny Saunders said to you when he got you into that shop front, out of the crowd pushing past.'

'I already tole you!' The boy's eyes, blue, the curly gold lashes doubly gilded by the sun, were mirrors of perfect innocence. Jurnet felt suddenly worn out, exhausted by more than the heat. *How could you ever tell where truth lay, in a world so full of disguises?*

'Let's have it again, shall we, slowly and with feeling.'

'I tell you somethin',' said the boy surprisingly. 'What I remember best don't have nothing to do with it. It's what was in that bloody shop window – some riding britches, soft-looking like they was made of suede, on'y it wasn't, wi' leather bits on the insides of the legs so yer don't get yer skin rubbed off when you go riding, an' a cap of black velvet with a small brim, smaller than a baseball one but cool, man, I tell you . . .' He broke off, the red rising in the pale cheeks and as fleetingly subsiding. 'You don't want to hear that stuff.'

'Not at all – ' encouragingly. 'We want to hear the lot, every word. Very good, Pete, very observant. Shows you had your eyes about you. Only what about your ears? Were they pricked up likewise to pick up everything that was said? What I ask myself is, eyeballs on that lovely gear, all the noise going on all round you, could you really swear to every word Danny said?'

'What you mean "swear"? This in't no court of law. I tole you. I heard what I heard. An' as fer noise, there weren't all that much of it. All them feet running, it weren't all that loud. No chanting, no shouting, nothing like that.'

Pete Gilbert's face had become grave, intent, tuned to an inner resonance.

"Cept inside yer head, that was where the noise was, hammering to get out. All the time Danny was talking the hammering went on, but it didn't stop me hearing.' The boy seemed to have forgotten his earlier reticence. 'Danny said, "I had to do it, Pete. I wrung his neck." ' Subsiding: 'Like I already tole you.'

Jurnet let a little time pass before repeating, word for word: ' "I had to do it, Pete. I wrung his neck." ' He pronounced the words as if they were new-minted, an unfamiliar coinage.

Then: ' "I wrung his neck . . ." You quite sure about that, Pete? After all, a bloke isn't a fowl for the pot. You can't wring a bloke's neck like he was a chicken.'

155

'Tell that to Charlie! Danny choked him, didn't he? Put a chain round his neck an' choked him. Jest a figure of speech. Comes to the same thing in the end.'

'I suppose you're right.' The detective let the thought go; hung on to a second one as the boy passed his arm over his brow again, the unbuttoned shirt-sleeve falling away to the elbow. Jurnet reached out and gripped the limb whilst, with his other hand, he pushed back the tumbling curls to reveal an area of raw purple on the young flesh.

'What's this, then?'

The boy jerked away but could not dislodge the restraining hand.

'On'y somethin' I picked up from those sodding chickens. Nothing comes lousier, you'd know if you had to look after them. Ma put on some calamine.'

'Did she now?' With a swift movement Jurnet turned the arm so that the soft underside showed in the sunlight, tender, young, and splotched with another patch of the strange discoloration – larger this time, and more blue than purple. The detective regarded it for a moment, then tugged down the sleeve and let the arm go. 'And did she put calamine on that too?' Head averted, the boy nodded, fumbling with the button on the shirt cuff. 'Doesn't look to have done you a power of good. What does the doctor say?'

'No need to see a doctor for a little thing like that.'

'Come off it, fellow! You hung around with Danny and his sort long enough to know what can happen to guys who let other guys poke their pricks up their rear ends. What you've got on your forehead and on your arm may come from cocks, it sure as hell doesn't come from chickens.'

Pete Gilbert stood blank-faced and unmoving beneath the onslaught. Jurnet, beset by instant shame the moment the words were out of his mouth, said placatingly: 'Look – your ma's out all day. I could get a doctor over here in the morning, after she's gone. She'd know blow-all about it. What do you say?'

The boy said: 'When I were eleven, first year in upper school, my pa went off with a woman used to clean house at the rectory. We ain't seen him since, an' not a penny neither. Ma says tha's enough shame to bear all the years, she don't reckon to give them old ratbags in the village any more excuses to go blacking the family name.' With a certain perverse dignity that pierced Jurnet to the core: 'You can keep your fucking doctor. You can't be forced to see one if you don't want to – tha's right, in't it? Citizens' rights.' Taking the detective's reluctant movement of the shoulders for confirmation, he finished: 'So unless it's eggs you're wanting, what you hanging about for?'

Abashed, Jack Ellers asked for a dozen number 1s; waited whilst the boy went into a shed to get them.

'One pound fifty.'

Jurnet had already got into the Rover.

The way back to Angleby was, if anything, even more depressing than the way out. The dust haze had spread from the hedges to the road where the rabbit lay more squashed, more dead, than ever; with, a quarter-mile further on, a mangled hedgehog for company.

The joys of the countryside! Jurnet found himself panting for the first sight of Angleby suburbs as for an oasis.

'What kind of Ma is it that'll sacrifice her son's life to keep the neighbours from gossiping? Treating *kaposi sarcoma* with calamine!'

'Probably do him as much good as anything the doctor can come up with. You know how it is with Aids.' The Sergeant, usually the joker in the pack, had been unusually quiet, embarrassed even. At last, plainly unsure as to whether he had chosen his moment well, he ventured, concentrating on his driving with an almost comical precision: 'Something I been meaning to tell you. Rosie's expecting.'

Jurnet, who – as the little Welshman knew – had passionately yearned for Miriam to bear his child, contrived a smile whilst his feelings ran the gamut from hatred, malice, envy, to a heartfelt rejoicing at his friend's good fortune.

'That's great! Give her my love and congratulations.'

'She wants you to be godfather.'

'That's very complimentary, but I'm half-way to being a Jew. I don't think I can.'

'Half a godfather's better 'n none! Rosie won't take no for an answer. Speak to your Rabbi and I'll have a word with the vicar. Between the two of them they'll fix up something.'

They came back into Angleby laughing at the absurdity of it. Only when he had parked the Rover back at Police Headquarters and reached into the back for his carton of eggs, did Ellers stop playing the clown.

157

'I hate to hear myself saying it but I'll tell Rosie to give them a bloody good wash.'

23

Rabbi Schnellman was angry, a condition difficult to diagnose in a face set ineradicably in patterns of tolerance and good humour. Even Jurnet, who had thought he understood every aspect of the man, only recognized the anger when it was too late, when the Rabbi proceeded to make mincemeat of him at the Olympic-standard table-tennis table which the latter had imported into the Synagogue Hall as a lure to the Jewish students at the university.

Vanished in a matter of seconds was Jurnet's delusion that, as a table-tennis player, he was – whilst admittedly the Rabbi's inferior – not all that inferior: you won some, you lost some. Now, under the contemptuous eyes of a couple of students awaiting their turn to play, the detective watched with dismayed disbelief as the kindly edifice constructed by the Rabbi over the years to bolster his opponent's self-esteem collapsed with every ball that spun away unplayable, glanced off the table edge or tipped itself over the net, beyond retrieval.

When, with shaming speed, the game was over – Jurnet lucky to have five points to his credit – there were none of the customary emollients and deprecations with which the Rabbi excused his victories. Instead, he handed his bat to one of the students and made for the stairs up to his flat with the one word 'Tea!' flung over his shoulder, more an insult than an invitation.

The tea, when it came, made things a little better; not much, but a little. His dead Rachel's china, the need to handle gently its floral curves and gilded curlicues, to put down the cup and saucer with loving care on her hand-crocheted cloth, worked its familiar magic.

The Rabbi said sorrowfully: 'You shouldn't have done it, Ben.'

Knowing what was coming, Jurnet drained his cup. Demanded nevertheless: 'Shouldn't have done what, Rabbi?'

'You know what I'm referring to. Moved in with Pnina.'

At the risk of sounding unchivalrous – it was hot, the tea only made him feel hotter, downstairs in the Synagogue Hall the Rabbi had just humiliated him in front of witnesses – Jurnet objected: 'For the record, I didn't. She moved in with me.'

158

Rabbi Schnellman sipped a little tea and frowned as if it was not to his taste.

'Downstairs we play games, Ben. Up here, no games, if you please, who moved in with who. You could have said no, sent her back to Mrs Levine. As it is, you have harmed her good name. All the congregation is talking.'

It was too hot. Jurnet lost patience completely.

'Bully for them! Shacking up with an uncircumcised *goy* – makes a change from exchanging recipes for chopped liver or cheesecake! The girl's going back to Israel in a couple of weeks, for God's sake, then to the States and heaven knows where else. I doubt she'll ever come this way again to upset the susceptibilities of your synagogue ladies.'

Jurnet finished: 'Couple of days ago I met a boy with Aids whose loving mum won't call in the doctor in case the neighbours start talking – same thing!'

'Not at all the same thing, quite the opposite. A crippled girl, on her own in the world. They are naturally concerned.'

'But you know Pnina. Don't tell me you let them go around pitying her, without putting them right!'

'They already know the girl, as we all do: admire her independent spirit. Know that to pity her would be a gross condescension . . .'

'Well then . . .' Jurnet calmed down several degrees, asked himself what the hell he was getting so het up about. 'She's twenty-seven, Rabbi, she's not a girl. I gather she told you she's not a virgin.'

'So she told me. And yes – she came to see me, not to ask my advice but to announce what, subject to your agreeing, she intended to do. She said that she had no illusions. She knew you could never love anybody but Miriam, but she said – as if she was telling me something I didn't already know! – that men needed women physically, it was part of their nature, and if she could make you feel a little less unhappy it would be a good memory for her to take away from England with her.'

The Rabbi paused, for the first time in their conversation smiling at Jurnet with the quizzical affection upon which – the detective suddenly realized – he had come to depend. 'She also – and I'd thought she was becoming Orthodox in her old age! – took off that scarf she's been covering up her hair with lately, and told me about the girl who has Miriam's hair.'

With a delicacy that brought a lump to Jurnet's throat, the Rabbi inquired: 'Is it true, there is such a girl?'

'Yes.'

'I should never have thought it possible. But then, Miriam was more than a head of hair.'

'Yes.'

'This girl – is there anything you want to tell me about her?'

'Not a thing.'

When Jurnet came into the delicatessen Mario kept two customers waiting whilst he went to the refrigerator for the lemon drink; took it across to the detective and drew him a little aside.

'Mr Jurnet, is it true what Pnina says – that in two weeks she is going away from you, leaving England?'

Not you as well! Jurnet groaned inwardly. He took a long swig at the drink, finding it less refreshing than he had hoped.

'If Pnina says it, it must be true.'

'But I don't understand!' The Italian pressed on in agitation. 'I thought she was so pleased to be here, living with you all the time now, not just a day here, a day there. When it happened I said to my Maria, "About time" – but now, it seems, she is hardly here but she goes.'

'Better take it up with her.' Jurnet handed over the empty glass, moved towards the stairs. 'Ta for the drink.'

'Mr Jurnet! Is serious!'

'Nothing I can do about it. It wasn't my idea.'

'Mr Jurnet, you must speak to her, to stop this foolishness. For you she will do anything.'

The delicatessen owner put a hand on the detective's arm to detain him, shot a glance of exasperation at the customer who was using a 50p piece to tap the top of the counter in a way suggestive of impatience. 'I understand – ' he returned to the attack – 'you do not, it is only natural, like it that she is crippled. The difference with Miriam is too great. But one must look forward, my friend, not back, to say nothing that one Miriam in a lifetime is more than any man has the right to expect. You know my Maria . . .' The man smiled lovingly. 'Fat. She is fat like a pig. She eats too much pasta, we both do. But would you believe it, when she was a girl she was slender as a wand, a nymph, a princess. Long ago. But I tell you, Mr Jurnet, in that fat woman I still see today that nymph so slim and lovely, and she – ' with a little laugh and a wry shrug of the shoulders – 'she still sees in me, not the belly big as a barrage balloon but the handsome young man she first married.'

160

'Very romantic,' said Jurnet, obstinately uncooperative and pulling his arm away, 'but I don't have any hang-ups over Pnina, thank you, if that's what you're thinking. Her disability, such as it is, doesn't affect me in the least. In fact, I respect her for the way she refuses to let it stop her getting on with life.'

'Is not exactly getting on with life to run away from a lover.'

Succumbing to a weariness of spirit that had been threatening all afternoon, Jurnet sighed.

'Look, Mario – I know you mean well, but mustn't it be clear to you by now that Pnina and I simply don't love each other enough to stay together until, like you and Maria, we both grow fat on your pasta and can only feed ourselves dreams about how it was to be young and beautiful.' With a glance towards the counter where the 50p piece was now tapping out an ill-tempered tattoo: 'And if you don't want to lose two customers for ever, you'd better get back on the job!'

Jurnet came into the flat and looked at Pnina Benvista closely, as, perhaps, he had not looked at her for some time. The sight did nothing to restore his damaged equanimity.

The girl was wearing her kerchief and, with it, a djellabah, or something of the sort, ethnic anyway, with ample folds from the shoulder that completely disguised her deformity, so long as she did not move. With her high cheekbones and olive skin, her eyes deep-set in purple shadow, a face that, given the choice to go either way, disdained to declare itself either ugly or beautiful, she looked remote, the priestess of some ancient cult, to be approached as much with fear as adoration. Only when she moved, her face alight with the pleasure of seeing him, the garment no camouflage, was she again the crippled girl who loved him – selflessly, as Miriam had never loved him; as, if the truth were told, he had never wanted her to.

Masochist – he twisted his thoughts round the word, rejecting its pedantry. Let's face it, if being a doormat was your bag, who wanted to be dusted off and hung on the wall like a bleeding tapestry?

Pnina spoke with a curious lilt to her voice which he did not at first identify.

'The auditor from Israel has been at the workroom all day, going through the books, making sure everything is in order.' She moved her arms in a gesture wholly Oriental. 'I have been speaking Hebrew all day. It is like being thirsty and all of a sudden you hear the spring waters gushing. I cannot think how I have gone so long trying to speak English.'

'Trying! Your Norfolk accent's impeccable.'

The Israeli girl shook her head. 'No. Today I forget everything. To remember has to be in your blood, and English is not in my blood.' She went on, hesitantly. 'A gentleman rung, ring, rang – you see, I cannot remember so many complicated changes.' Carefully, beginning again: 'A gentleman called Mr Adamson telephoned. He says, will you telephone to him, he has something to say about a wedding.'

'OK. I'll do it after I've had a shower.' Half-way along the corridor that led to the bathroom Jurnet paused and called back: 'How about driving over to Havenlea after supper – get a breath of sea air? What do you say?'

'Do they speak Hebrew there?'

The detective laughed. 'Shouldn't think so.'

He came back to the living-room where Pnina Benvista was standing, distance in her eyes.

Jurnet took her gently by the shoulders, sorry for both of them.

'In English we call it homesickness. In Hebrew I don't know what it is.'

'In Hebrew there is no such word.'

'You don't say!' The other was astonished. 'I should have thought, Jews of all people, with that age-old longing for Israel . . .'

The girl shook her head.

'That is a longing for redemption, a dream. Not the same thing at all. To be homesick there has to be a place already known to you, a spot in the universe that is special to you like nowhere else – something Jews are afraid of, so often have they had to move on, or been moved on against their will. In such a world you do not call anywhere home. It is too dangerous.' The girl pivoted on her good leg, letting her gaze roam affectionately round the room. 'When I am gone from here, from this flat on top of Mario's café, wherever I go this will be the place I will always, in English, be homesick for.'

'Mr Adamson?'

'Roger.' The voice at the other end of the line was warm, enthusiastic, far removed from Roger Adamson's customary

162

tones of amused indolence. 'That *is* Inspector Jurnet, isn't it? Thanks for phoning back.'

'What can I do for you, sir?'

'Not sir!' the voice protested. 'Roger.' A boyish laughter came over the wire. 'Behold the bridegroom cometh and all that. I rang up to invite you to my wedding.'

'Very kind of you, I'm sure.' Jurnet thought, The fellow's been drinking. 'I heard it wasn't long to the happy day.'

'Happy day is right, Inspector. Day after tomorrow. Happiest day of my life. And no, Ben – I may call you Ben, mayn't I? – I haven't been celebrating betimes. I'm simply delivering the invitation verbally – too late to put it in the post so's you'll get it in time.'

'I see, sir.'

'Roger!' the voice insisted, a little out of temper at the necessity of repetition. 'And it's for you and your sidekick, or whatever he is officially. Don't think I don't know how it is with you police – how you're bound to have other, more important, things to attend to – murder, rape, somebody's been feeding the meter – but I'd esteem it an honour and a pleasure to have you both present to see me tie the knot.'

'As you say, I can't say for sure . . .'

'Look, Inspector . . .' Roger Adamson had turned seriously cajoling. 'It's going to be a great day, I know you understand that; but sad too, because Charlie, darling Charlie, can only be there in the spirit to share our joy. Julian and me, of course, we'll be there in our glad rags, looking pretty as a picture, and Jenny – never mind two black eyes and her ribs strapped – is going to be matron of honour. But no Charlie. And no one who understands what Charlie meant to us – what he continues to mean, alive or dead.

'And then I thought, since poor old Charlie's caught it, who else is there, apart from the three of us, who understands what Charlie was all about, what his absence means to us?'

'Charlie the hero.'

'Who's made it his business to enter into Charlie's thought processes like they shared a brain, who's never going to sleep at night until he catches up with the bugger who bumped him off, and delivers him safely into the arms of the Law? Why, the Inspector, who else?'

When Jurnet made no response, Roger Adamson went on: 'I know they say – whoever *they* are – that coppers mustn't get themselves involved, that it damages their judgement. But I say bollocks to that, because you are, aren't you, Ben, involved? You can't deny it.'

Jurnet returned briefly: 'I'm involved.'

'What did I tell you!' The voice rose in jubilation before subsiding to a confidential exchange between friends. 'I thought, you'll think me bonkers but at least you'll have a clue what I'm on about. You'll be on the right wavelength. If we can't have Charlie at the wedding, I'd like to think we can have his friends there, rooting for him.'

'I'd hardly say I count as one of those . . .'

'His best friend.' Roger Adamson's happy laugh conveyed over the wires an instant picture of golden curls tumbling; of youthful elegance and beauty. *Behold the bridegroom cometh.*

'St Blaise. Day after tomorrow. Eleven thirty sharp.'

They did not go to Havenlea after all. Instead, they went to bed, sampling its entertainment with a mutual satisfaction, to judge from Jurnet, one arm propped in the small of his neck, glancing down with tenderness and gratitude at the Israeli girl's pied head, resting in smiling slumber against his chest.

Tenderness, gratitude: the detective allowed the words – or rather, the qualities they stood for – to wash lazily over him with scarcely a soaping of introspection. Love, now – that was something else again. Love, like Momma's apple pie, was something that, to be right, you had to make, you yourself, one of the few remaining products you couldn't buy pre-packed and oven-ready.

So, did he love Pnina, or didn't he? *Love her, love her not,* count the cherry stones. He couldn't be fagged.

All the same, Jurnet slid down to sleep a little miffed at the way the girl, on the sole strength of the arrival from Tel Zvaim of one grotty card-carrying auditor, had turned away from his beloved Angleby towards Jerusalem; towards Hebrew and away from the good old English language which, if it wasn't precisely the original handed down from Mount Sinai, was at least that of Shakespeare, Milton and the Marx Brothers, to mention but a few.

'*Ring, rang, rung . . .*' What was the girl thinking of, a girl who, when she put her mind to it, had an English vocabulary the envy of many an Anglo-Saxon, even one from Angleby?

Pnina Benvista lay naked, her skin glowing with sweat, her beautiful pointed breasts a challenge to the deformity below.

What, who, the hell did he want?

Questions unanswered, Jurnet slept; aware, nevertheless, that deep in his inmost being, he knew at last who had killed Charlie Appleyard, even if there wasn't a bloody thing he could do about it.

24

Sergeant Jack Ellers, always the one to put the best face on things, observed consolingly: 'At least we haven't far to go.'

Jurnet, unfresh in his best suit within ten paces of moving out of Police Headquarters' protective shadow, and preoccupied with his conversation, minutes before, with the Superintendent, was in no mood to comment. Or if he had been, the way he was feeling, his contribution would more likely have consisted of a single word, a cosmic philosophy in one syllable: to wit, shit.

Shit. Shit. Shit.

For what else was there to say in the face of the awful incontrovertible rightness of the Superintendent? Of what use to plead: 'I know I'm right!'

Through eyes half closed against the sun, Jurnet called up an instant picture of the way the Superintendent had looked at his subordinate, smiling with the kind of love only the two of them recognized as the thread cementing their web of coexistence: love that combined a genuine sorrow at having to thwart the loved one's deep-laid plans with an impish glee that, for once at least, the bugger wasn't going to have things all his own way.

'Bring me some solid evidence and we'll see what we can do to clothe it further in flesh and blood. But for today, forget it.'

Forget it!

The parish church of St Blaise Ladygate closed in the southern end of the Market Place, one of the few ecclesiastical edifices in the city to which Jurnet, the product of a chapel-going childhood, felt able to extend his qualified approval. Larger than the general run of parish churches, as befitted its central site at the heart of a city living by trade and dying in the confident belief of resurrection into some privatized paradise beyond the blue horizon, it was built in the style known as East Anglian Perpendicular, a style divergent from your run-of-the-mill Perpendicular only in so far as the verticals which gave it its name were programmed to carry the eye down as well as up, as much as to say heaven is not the only option, mate, so don't count your chickens.

Early as it was, knots of women waiting to see the bride were already staking out their territory in the no man's land where the short driveway leading up to the west door debouched on to the public highway. A posse of ushers, groomed to the last bouton-nière, skittered about the area like waterbeetles over the skim of a pond, directing arriving guests to pews on the right or pews on the left according to some arcane code of which they alone appeared to possess the key.

'Bride or bridegroom?' one of these guardians of the gate fired at Jack Ellers, only to be answered with a cherubic leer: 'What do *you* think?'

'Police!' snapped his superior officer, in no mood for jokes, though – if he had been – amply rewarded by the startled glance with which the young man took in the import of two flashed ID cards.

'Complimentary tickets!'

Yet, once inside, for all the nagging anxiety that came from being a player in no way situated to control the moves of the game, Jurnet could not help but feel his spirits rise. Amazing what money could do, he admonished himself, to small avail; turn a paunchy business man into a pillar of the community, full of gravitas in his hired frock coat and his couturier hair-do becom-ingly touched at the temples with strands of purest silver; trans-form his spouse well past her sell-by date into a plausible example of genteel allure.

Under wide-brimmed hats trimmed with flowers and fruits not even to be found on Angleby Market Place, the obligatory gaggle of official virgins, friends of the young couple, glowed like magic mushrooms. A wave of a gloved hand from one of the few hatless women resolved itself into Dr Adamson, partaking of the general atmosphere of slightly hysterical affection.

With it all, nothing could hold a candle to the church itself, the great nave perfumed with swags of roses and lilies, the air filled with light filtered through the craziest east window in Christen-dom. Three hundred years before, Cromwell's men had inadver-tently set off a nearby arsenal, the resultant explosion showering slivers of the most splendid Angleby glass in captivity over a large area of the surrounding parish.

Being Angleby, where nothing of value was ever wasted, the citizenry of the time, without making an undue fuss about it, had set about retrieving leather bucketfuls of fragmented glass out of trees, middens and feather beds – wherever chance had ensconced them – and then turning the salvaged mishmash into a window again.

For of course it wasn't a jigsaw puzzle to be put together in front of the fire on a winter's night. You couldn't have everything. And so, if a seductress out of hell turned up wearing the head of an Old Testament prophet, well, half a floozy was better than none; and if a multitude, napkins tucked in expecting loaves and fishes, had to make do, instead, with wine intended for the marriage at Cana, it was unlikely that anyone complained.

Jurnet's personal favourite was the preacher who, hands raised in blessing, protruded unruffled from the rear end of a somewhat bemused donkey. At last the window, the guests, flowery among the flowers, fell into place, whilst from the organ loft the organist, who had been punctuating the babble below with merry little trills of matrimonial joy, changed his tune without warning and crashed out into the opening chords of Wagner's Wedding March.

On the arm of her father, who was working the Vice-Chancellor thing for all he was worth, Julian Grant advanced up the aisle of St Blaise Ladygate slowly, solemnly, towards the open space in front of the altar, Tom Tiddler's Ground, where Roger Adamson her lover, together with the minister and some Hooray Henry of a best man, awaited her coming. She moved towards her bridegroom almost hypnotically and as one transfixed by joy – 'truly a marriage made in heaven', as one emotional matron overcome with envy whispered to a daughter only too distressingly falling behind in the matrimonial stakes.

Jurnet, at the end of a pew and half turned to watch the girl's progress towards her official surrender of a maidenhead reassumed for the day along with her wedding dress, found himself shaken anew by her beauty – not only the wonderful hair this time, muted beneath a simple veil, but the Barbie-doll face transformed for once into a virginal humility piercing to the eye. Absorbed in the imperative of redefining her sense of self for the rest of her life, she moved in subtle white silk, at once compelling her friends' witness and rejecting it.

'*Dearly beloved, we are gathered together here in the sight of God . . .*'

As the strains of the Wedding March died away the minister came forward, took over: got the show on the road.

What a little liar the girl was, thought Jurnet, almost admiringly, taking in the bowed head, the air of innocent confusion. Jenny Appleyard, née Nunn, the recent bride and present matron of honour, trailing behind with her black eyes and slashes stitched across the cheekbones, possessed more integrity than that quintessential English rose. Yet, noting the delicate triumph with which Julian Grant put one satin-slippered foot in front of the other, it was all but impossible not to believe in love, undamaged chastity, and all the other outmoded clichés. A trembling bride, God bless her, entering marriage which was – hip, hip, hooray – an honourable estate.

Wilt thou have this woman – wilt thou have this man – I, Roger, take thee, Julian, to my wedded wife – I, Julian, take thee, Roger, to my wedded husband, to have and to hold, from this day forward, for better for worse, for richer for poorer, in sickness and in health, to love, cherish and to obey, till death us do part, according to God's holy ordinance: and thereto I give thee my troth . . .

The ring. There seemed to be a bit of trouble with the ring. What in the world had happened to it? Had the best man mislaid it, something he looked only too fitted by nature to do? Had the priest lost it among the pages of his book? A ripple of affectionate laughter ran through the congregation. Such little things gave zest to the best arranged of weddings.

Ah! The bridegroom had it all the time. How handsome he looked, all rosy with embarrassment, as he jumbled in the unfamiliar pockets of his wedding outfit, a cherub out of Raphael or Botticelli. Not in the breast pocket; trousers pockets, no. The minister, a man who prided himself above all on his managerial skills, levered his eyes upward, indicating he was not best pleased. Somebody – who, not for him to say – had goofed. Then hooray! That which was lost was found.

Or was it?

Out of the droll little cubby-hole that tailors hide in the tail of morning coats Roger Adamson produced, not the missing ring, but a bottle. A small bottle, hexagonal in shape and made of glass in a shade of deep Bristol blue, its glass stopper half-frosted, half-transparent. With a quizzical glance about, as if to beseech toleration of his childish gaucherie, Roger Adamson briskly removed the stopper from the bottle, letting it fall carelessly to the stone floor, which it met with a pretty tinkle before reducing itself to a crystalline powder. Whilst his bride waited, finger at the ready to receive the ring which should plight their troth, Roger Adamson, with a lithe movement which was part of the grace which informed every part of his body, raised his arm and, with infinite care, poured the contents of the hexagonal blue bottle over his true love's hair.

A small sibilant noise, less than a crackling, heralded the dissolution of the veil: that was all. Odd beyond belief that such a small noise should carry so loudly in a church gone suddenly dead quiet. As the vitriol, moving without haste, fed itself downward through bronze hair to the scalp beneath, over the white forehead and into the left eye socket before spilling over towards the chin, the silence grew deeper. Waiting.

Waiting for Julian Grant to scream.

25

For the sake of a nail the kingdom was lost. 'For the sake of a bleeding "w",' Jurnet said aloud, aware of the Superintendent's inevitable reaction to bad language, and bleeding glad of it.

Frowning, the Superintendent responded as per expected.

'Too much to expect the English language, Ben, to reorganize itself to suit your particular predilections.'

'Not just mine,' the other returned, unrepentant. 'What with all that racket going on in Shire Street at the time, it was no wonder young Pete Gilbert, having heard what he thought was "wrung" with a "w", should have thought he heard "neck" as the natural follow-on: "wringing his neck", a phrase we're all familiar with. Once you'd settled for "wrung" you could say "neck" followed automatically.'

'Hm.' The Superintendent carefully proffered no opinion of his own. 'And if, following your line of reasoning, it wasn't "neck" that followed that mistaken "wrung" with a "w", perhaps you could share your thoughts with us as to what the following word actually was?'

'I've been milling it over and over,' said Jurnet unashamedly; 'and, given the noise, I reckon Danny Saunders could have said almost anything. It could equally have been "I rung his bird", or,

"I rung Julian Grant." As things are, though, the one I plump for is "I rung his bec". '

'Beck?' the Superintendent inquired frostily. 'As in a small stream, I presume, a rivulet?'

'No, sir. Bec without the "k" – another bit of alphabetic hanky-panky. Unless you saw it in front of you in black and white you wouldn't know the difference. I think that what Danny Saunders actually told young Gilbert was "I rung his bec". ' Noting his superior officer's blank face with undisguised satisfaction, Jurnet relented. 'Jack here will let you into the secret of what a bec is.'

'Good old East Anglian word for a bit of skirt,' the little Welsh-man supplied promptly. 'One only too ready with the glad eye, the come-on – in other words, the beckoning glance. Hence a bec, without the "k", sweet and simple.'

The Superintendent pondered in discontented silence what he had just heard.

'And were you able to check this extraordinary linguistic assumption with Miss Grant?'

'Oh yes,' said Jurnet, seeing in his mind's eye the girl's ruined beauty, the collapsed eye socket eroded by the acid. 'I've checked. She's made a statement.'

'Good. And Adamson, our almost bridegroom?'

'The difficulty there was to get him to stop talking.' Jurnet spoke with an unaccustomed ferocity. 'That young man is altogether too pleased with himself. Seems to think he's struck a blow for history and deserves the Victoria Cross, if not better.'

'Sounds psychotic. Is that what he actually says?'

'Not in so many words. The bugger says he did it out of love.'

26

'Danny Saunders telephoned. I knew the name vaguely, from Roger, something he must have said about the Saunders family having worked in the factory for generations. I wondered a bit how he'd got our number – we're ex-directory – but I assumed that anyway it was Roger he really wanted, and I asked, have you tried him at the flat?

'What he said was that it was me he wanted to speak to. He sounded very agitated, his voice blurred at the edges, as if he might have been drinking: it wouldn't have surprised me. So, to keep him quiet as much as anything, I asked, what do you want to talk to me about?

'It was incredible. Even now, knowing it's true, part of me still can't believe it.

'He said that Charlie, up on the Moot, on the grounds of something or other, not important, had set up some kind of kangaroo court which had expelled him from being part of the Loy Tanner demonstration, which wouldn't have been so bad if, at the same time, Charlie hadn't deliberately got round a boy called Pete who was his – that is, Danny Saunders's – lover and, so he said, as wet behind the ears as a new-born lamb. He said that the boy who, I could take it from him, was his, body and soul, had been bamboozled into staying on at the Moot with the rest instead of following Saunders into exile, or whatever you called it.

'Well. Not only didn't I know whether to believe him or not, I couldn't see what I had to do with it. To be honest, I was embarrassed.

'Gays make me feel uncomfortable. Not that I've anything against them, nothing like that, but mention of any of the few guys in the city suspected of being queer always sets me off in fits of giggles, I can't think why. As I've already told you about me and Jenny and Roger and Charlie, nothing like that ever occurred with any of us. All the times we were romping naked together I'd never seen the boys so much as touch each other in, you know, that way.

'What happened then was that I let Danny Saunders ramble on a bit and, when I could get a word in edgeways, said I was sorry, but I really didn't see how I could help him, nor Roger either. And then he said, "that's all you know!"

'He said he'd done things separately and together with both Charlie and Roger that would make the hair stand up on my head, and that the only reason the whole thing had blown up on the Moot was that Charlie wanted Pete for himself – and in case I didn't believe him, why didn't I pop over to Roger's flat this very minute, where I might find something going on that would buck up my ideas a bit?

'With that, Danny Saunders rang off, leaving me . . . I don't know how to convey how he left me. Of course the whole thing was preposterous, I told myself; and yet . . . My mind, my body, my very soul, was in a whirl. Even before that day, I had sometimes thought, in the lazy, diffuse way one lets things drift

171

through one's mind, that in every love affair there was an element of hate: in fact, the more intense the one, the stronger the other. There were times when Roger and I, making love, all but tore each other apart, coupling like animals: times when I could feel the hatred pulsing through his veins just as I felt sure he could feel the hatred pulsing through mine. But then, afterwards, how we would smile at each other exhausted and full of a perfect trust. This was the meaning of love!

'Was I wrong? I don't know. You know me, Inspector Jurnet – you must have made up your mind that I'm actually a very shallow person, not given to philosophizing about my place in the world. All I'm sure of is that, moved equally by the purity of love and the dreadful, delectable urge to treachery that was somehow part of it, I did exactly what Danny Saunders had suggested: hurried, without prior announcement, to check up on what my beloved – my two beloveds – were up to.

'I had a key to the lift as well as to the narrow, fireproof stair which wound round it, but used the stairs so that the sound of the lift rising to the penthouse level, would not give notice of my arrival. The stair ended at the roof, at the side of the kitchen door. Turn the corner and there was the wide stretch of the terrace, sliding windows pushed back as far as they would go, looking out over the rooftops of Angleby, an enchanted spot to which the noise of the city rose gently muffled, a place out of time.

'The sight of that view, everything in its place – the castle, the cathedral, the streets winding like serpents between the houses and the shops – brought me up abruptly. What on earth was I doing, paying any attention to the word of some lout with a chip on his shoulder against that of the man – the two men – I loved best in the world?

'To distrust them felt so terribly wrong that I abandoned all pretence of moving softly and secretly; ran through the open windows into the living-room to find the two of them, on the floor and oblivious of my arrival, locked one on top of the other, Charlie uppermost, pumping, pumping.

'I'm sorry, Inspector. I'm a grown woman, I ought to know the right words to describe what I saw, but I don't. As a matter of fact the four of us were like that, none of us brought up to use the four-letter words. Even Jenny, who had had to learn them because some of her clients liked to hear her "talking dirty", as she called it, never used them among ourselves. It wasn't that we were

172

especially puritanical or anything like that, simply it wasn't our way.

'I sometimes think if only I *had* known the words, Charlie might be alive today. I could have screamed at him like a fishwife, shouted at him to get off my darling Roger spread face down beneath him in total surrender, his curls hiding his face; let out my anger in a noise that would have drifted away over the terrace balustrade to evaporate harmlessly in the air above the city. As it was, there they were, shining with sweat on the honey-coloured carpet, naked except for one thing – that awful crude cross Jenny had made at her metal classes, something we'd all giggled over behind her back but said was lovely, so as not to hurt her feelings.

'Again, if Jenny had made the chain as well as the cross I think Charlie would still be alive, treading in the footsteps of Loy Tanner. Any chain Jenny might have made would probably have broken at the first tug. As it was, when I took hold of the chain because it was the only thing to catch hold of, the chain did not break. The pumping went on and on uninterrupted. I might as well not have existed. So I tugged harder.

'I tugged until there was a peculiar little noise, not exactly a cough, more a surprised intake of breath, cut off before completed. Whatever it was, Charlie stopped pumping and flopped on to his side, dead. I can't tell you how glad I was the pumping had stopped once and for all.

'Did I intend to kill him? I don't think so, but I can't be sure. I suppose, quite soon now, a judge and a jury will decide what my intentions were. I really look forward to having them make up my mind for me.

'Roger sat up. His chest was red from being pressed down on the carpet, a strangely attractive pattern a bit like an Aztec or an Etruscan tile. I stretched out my fingertips to touch the pattern and he pulled me down, down under his patterned body, the situation with Charlie completely reversed. From being a creature utterly subservient he was in command, rising and falling, pressing me into the floor.

'Again, I don't have the words. There are no words.

'How Charlie came to be lying on the steps down to Jenny's flat in Bergate – why they chose to leave him there, not somewhere else – I'm not sure. There was a period when I wasn't actually taking things in all that well. The person to ask, to know what really happened, is Addie, a wonderful person who always knows the best thing to do. Roger rang her up to come over to the flat and whilst we were waiting for her to arrive we made love again. I can only say I blazed – was positively incandescent with happiness.

'As for Addie, she was magnificent: calmed us down, organized the whole thing without turning a hair. In fact, if it didn't sound such a ridiculous thing to say, I almost felt she was enjoying herself. Of course she adores Roger and all her thoughts must have been how to protect him, but all the same . . .

'I might as well come out with it. For all I know Addie will tell you herself because, whatever else she is, she is an essentially honest sort of person. Well, then: in a way I think she was glad at what had happened – not that Charlie was dead, you could see she was terribly cut up about that, but because the four of us were broken up for good and all. I think she had been jealous of us all along, eaten up with it because we were young and having a wonderful time together, and she was growing old with no one to love her. Otherwise, why choose Bergate? There were at least three disused quarries on Monkenheath where we could have dumped Charlie and where he wouldn't have been found for months, if ever.

'I hope the judge and the jury will treat Roger gently for what he did to me. He loves me – loves me and hates me as I do him – and I had to be punished, I realize that. They say I shall end up with a face of sorts, to say nothing of a beautiful glass eye that will never be troubled by sights it would rather not see. It will be quite interesting, once the grafts have taken and the bandages come off, to get my first look at my new self.

'Will Roger still love me? I sometimes think love springs most strongly from the seeds of death: but I don't know.

'Do you remember the day I bought fish for the garden gnomes and got you into trouble? When I get my lovely new eye I shall go out and buy two new hooks, and attach them to their fishing lines. Who knows what they may catch, gleaming in the sunlight, catching the blue of the sky?'

27

They set out early, partly to get ahead of the traffic but also because El Al, it was well known, always took twice as long as any other airline to process its customers, to make doubly sure there were no bombs lurking in the luggage. Jurnet was driving Pnina Benvista's red Metro, which belonged to the Courland Connection and was to be left there on the way back from Heathrow, ready for the new manager due in from Israel in the course of the next few days.

They drove without speaking, Mario's emotional farewell having drained them of words to say.

'I will look after him, my dear child,' the delicatessen owner had promised. 'Until you return you need not worry. I will look after him. It is a promise!'

The Israeli girl had said nothing to contradict him; that she was not coming back, ever.

The cars and the lorries rolled mindlessly along the motorway, in exact balance, it always seemed to Jurnet, as many coming as going, whatever the time of day. He could not imagine what would happen if one of them, a single one, decided at the last moment against making the journey, throwing the whole lot out of kilter.

For the moment, at least, all was present and correct, the factories, the patches of pseudo-countryside, sliding astern in the regulation manner. At the side of the road and overhead the dear, familiar road signs bloomed like flowers.

Unexpectedly Pnina observed: 'I suppose, in fifty years' time, another hero will come along to celebrate five hundred years of Loy Tanner.'

'God forbid!'

'Why do you say that?' the Israeli girl insisted. 'There are always heroes . . .'

'Most of them like Samson. Or Napoleon. Or, for that matter, Jesus Christ. All left behind more trouble than when they started.'

Nothing more was said as Jurnet threaded the little red car through the Heathrow tunnel and round the one-way system to Terminal 1. The girl said: 'Don't trouble to go to the car-park. It won't be necessary.'

'Right.'

Jurnet drew into a setting-down bay, went to the rear of the car and lifted Pnina Benvista's suitcase out of the boot.

'I'll see you across the road.'

'Is not necessary.' The girl picked up the suitcase, started off, hip turned out awkwardly, clip-clopping across the pedestrian crossing. She wore her kerchief and a deep blue dress that did nothing to hide her deformity whilst it obscured the lovely line of her breasts. She held her head high.

She had reached the further side of the carriageway, the automatic doors of the terminal already opening invitingly, before Jurnet, dodging the traffic, overtook her.

She said: 'You will get yourself a parking ticket.'

'No, I won't. I'll show them my police card. You haven't said goodbye.'

She rested the suitcase on the pavement and said tonelessly: 'I don't care to say goodbyes.'

'Neither do I. Shalom, then.'

With the merest suggestion of a smile: 'Shalom . . .'

'You've got your tickets et cetera, all the bumph?'

'All the bumph.'

Still they stood there, embarking passengers passing to left and right, not all that courteously. Jurnet took a last look at the face austere with its high cheekbones, the shadows under the eyes purple with melancholy, the beauty and the ugliness.

He picked up the suitcase.

'Don't go.'